DIRTY GAMES

EVIE HUNTER

Boldwood

First published in Great Britain in 2025 by Boldwood Books Ltd.

Copyright © Evie Hunter, 2025

Cover Design by Colin Thomas

Cover Images: Colin Thomas

The moral right of Evie Hunter to be identified as the author of this work has been asserted in accordance with the Copyright, Designs and Patents Act 1988.

All rights reserved. No part of this book may be reproduced in any form or by any electronic or mechanical means, including information storage and retrieval systems, without written permission from the author, except for the use of brief quotations in a book review. This book is a work of fiction and, except in the case of historical fact, any resemblance to actual persons, living or dead, is purely coincidental.

Every effort has been made to obtain the necessary permissions with reference to copyright material, both illustrative and quoted. We apologise for any omissions in this respect and will be pleased to make the appropriate acknowledgements in any future edition.

A CIP catalogue record for this book is available from the British Library.

Paperback ISBN 978-1-83518-111-9

Large Print ISBN 978-1-83518-110-2

Hardback ISBN 978-1-83518-109-6

Ebook ISBN 978-1-83518-112-6

Kindle ISBN 978-1-83518-113-3

Audio CD ISBN 978-1-83518-104-1

MP3 CD ISBN 978-1-83518-105-8

Digital audio download ISBN 978-1-83518-107-2

This book is printed on certified sustainable paper. Boldwood Books is dedicated to putting sustainability at the heart of our business. For more information please visit https://www.boldwoodbooks.com/about-us/sustainability/

Boldwood Books Ltd, 23 Bowerdean Street, London, SW6 3TN

www.boldwoodbooks.com

1

Dawn Frobisher laughed along with everyone else but the gesture felt strained, and a tension headache threatened. Sitting slightly back from her best friends, Callie Renfrew and Angie Dalton, she was glad that they were absorbed with the show, oblivious to her reaction. When the gig ended and the lights came up, she plastered on her game face and joined in with the applause.

'That was just what I needed,' Callie said, reaching for the wine bottle in the cooler in the centre of the table and refilling their glasses. 'A little comedy always hits the spot.'

'What did you make of it, Dawn? You've been very quiet, which is not at all like you,' Angie asked, turning to her friend.

'Things on my mind.'

'The job getting you down?' Callie asked sympathetically.

'Yeah, something like that.'

Callie and Angie both leaned their arms on the table and fixed Dawn with impenetrable looks. *Damn!* Dawn absolutely didn't want to answer their questions. Not now. Not ever. Ordinarily, she was good at maintaining a cheerful façade that gave nothing away about her inner feelings.

But not today.

'Not good enough,' Callie declared, earning herself a supportive nod from Angie. 'Come on, Dawn, how long have we known one another? If you have problems, then we need to know about them so that we can help you get them sorted. Don't hold back or you'll really worry us.'

'We enjoy kicking ass,' Angie added, still buoyed up after recently ending her marriage and discovering there was a whole wide world out there waiting to embrace middle-aged women. Forty-something was now the new thirty, or so Angie would have them all believe. At that precise moment, Dawn felt more like she was ninety.

'Jared still giving you grief?' Callie asked, referring to her producer on the local cable channel where she was a contracted presenter and journalist.

If only it were that simple, Dawn thought. She could so easily lie and say that was true. It would satisfy Callie and Angie because they knew she and Jared were often at loggerheads, but the lies she had lived with for the past thirty years were starting to weigh heavily on her shoulders. Shoulders that definitely felt the strain.

'I'm being sidelined by younger models,' she admitted, which was true, but wasn't the main reason for her depression.

'That is *so* unfair!' Angie cried indignantly. 'You've given your all to that station and they're lucky to have you.'

'It's ageist, is what it is,' Callie said, frowning. 'What can you do about it?'

'I'm going under the knife.'

'What!' Both ladies exclaimed loud enough to draw attention to them, despite the fact that the room was crowded with noisy drinkers.

'You absolutely don't need to,' Callie said alone. 'You're gorgeous.'

'The bloom has faded from this particular rose,' Dawn replied, sighing. 'Facts have to be faced.'

'Why not change direction and go solely into print journalism?' Angie asked. 'You did a first-rate job of exposing that organ-transplant disgrace that my ex not-so-nearest-and-dearest got himself mixed up with.'

Dawn tried not to frown at the memory, aware that frowning exacerbated her wrinkles. Then she remembered her appointment with the plastic surgeon, thought, *What the fuck* and frowned anyway. It was a small rebellion that only she could enjoy.

'Others latched onto it, as well you know, and I got squeezed out by the big boys.' She fiddled with a napkin. 'Whoever said life was fair obviously wasn't a journalist.'

'You were toying with the idea of writing a novel,' Angie reminded her. 'Why not give it a go? You'd be brilliant at it.'

'I might be okay at the writing part, but it's getting recognition in a crowded marketplace that would be the problem. Since self-publishing became so popular, the world and his wife sees an opportunity to take the writing world by storm. It's said that everyone has a novel in them and in most cases, that's where it should probably stay.'

They all laughed.

'What's happening with you guys?' Dawn asked, anxious to change the subject. 'I haven't seen you much since the shit hit the fan with Paul. You okay in the penthouse, Angie? No regrets about giving up the family home?'

'None whatsoever,' Angie replied without hesitation. 'Best move I ever made. I still feel bitter about Paul's betrayal but in many respects, he did me a favour. I could so easily have remained stuck in a marriage where I thought everything was rosy, wasting my life while he had it away with a Croatian prostitute. How stupid was I?'

'You weren't stupid, just trusting,' Callie said. 'I, on the other hand, have always known that Gavin has a roving eye. I suppose I've been carving my own path and turning a blind eye up until now. Well, there's no supposing about it. I was too scared to up sticks and leave when I first caught him out a few years into our marriage.'

'Really?' Angie asked. 'That soon after you tied the knot. What a rat!'

'I realised then that he wouldn't change. So, I had two choices. Either put up with his philandering or give up my comfortable life and go back to a bedsit. Call me selfish, but...'

Dawn tuned out, feeling a fresh wave of guilt. Gavin had strayed way sooner than a few years into his marriage and she had a first-hand reason to know.

'How are the kids coping with Paul's new family?' she asked, steering the conversation onto slightly safer ground.

'Henry refuses to see them. He's still working at the car showroom and sees his father there occasionally. Paul's trying to win him round apparently, but Henry has a lot of anger issues and is having none of it. Their relationship is fraught, and Melody and the child don't exist for him.'

'Well, Henry did harbour romantic aspirations about Melody himself,' Callie pointed out, 'so probably feels like an idiot now.'

'Yeah, but I can see that he's hurting.' Angie sighed. 'I just want to draw a line under my marriage and start anew.'

'With Tom?' Callie asked, her eyes sparkling as she shared a glance with Dawn.

'Tom and I are friends, nothing more. No, really!' She laughed as she held up a hand in protest. 'Besides, he still works for Paul, and it would be like... well, I don't want to think what it would be like. It's too soon and anyway, he's way younger than me. It would be like child exploitation.'

'He's hardly a child, darling.' Dawn flashed a mischievous smile. 'I wouldn't kick him out of bed.'

'Not happening,' Angie insisted.

Callie grinned. 'Keep telling yourself that.'

'No news from Gavin yet, Callie?' Dawn asked. 'He's been gone nearly four months now. Someone must have seen something or at least know why he scarpered. Ours is a small world.'

Gavin Renfrew had always flirted with the letter of the law and broke it with complacency when the need arose. But he was clever, let others take the risks and hadn't had his collar felt. That was partly due to the fact that he had several high-ranking policemen on the payroll. He did, however, often get on the wrong side of his partners in crime and did disappearing acts until the latest situation righted itself, leaving Callie alone to hold the fort. Not being involved in his criminal activities herself, she could honestly claim that she didn't know where he'd gone or why.

'I know what you're both thinking. He must be dead.' Callie waved the hand holding her glass in an expansive arc, somehow managing not to slop its contents over herself. 'Perhaps he is,' she conceded. 'But... well, I know this will sound stupid, but I think I'd know if he was no longer breathing, and I just don't feel it. It's more probable that he's got himself into something that's too big for him, can't find a way out and so has done what he always does when things get hot and gone to ground.'

'For this long, though?' Angie asked gently.

'I know. But now that O'Keefe has disappeared, and Stafford is keeping his distance, I no longer have entitled thugs thinking they can pressure me into doing stuff I don't want to.' Callie sat back and let out a protracted sigh. Only she knew that O'Keefe, Gavin's main local rival, was dead. She knew because she herself had killed him in self-defence, and her loyal PA, Darren Bishop, had disposed of his body. 'It means I can sell the spa for a handsome profit after a year or so, if I want to, once the books are straight. But it also gives me the freedom to start looking for Gavin without a line of people breathing down my neck.'

'Do you *want* to find him?' Dawn asked.

'Not because I want him back but because I can't move on, not properly, until I know where he's got to and why.'

'Isn't it better to leave well alone?' Dawn asked, sharing a look with Angie. 'You're trying to distance yourself from his criminal activities and associates. Don't poke the bear, would be my advice.'

'Talking of his associates, George Markham showed his face yesterday.'

Dawn felt warm all over. George was one of Gavin's business partners. He'd known Dawn for years and possessed the ability to expose her youthful indiscretions if he felt the need and Dawn had never been comfortable in his company. She was even less comfortable when he approached Callie for any reason at all.

'What did he want?' Angie asked. 'Fishing for news of Gavin, is my guess.'

'Not precisely. He wants to hire my meeting rooms at the club.'

'Whatever for?' Dawn's journalistic antenna twitched. 'There are tons of pubs and hotels that hire out private rooms in Brighton. I know your spa is currently *the* trendy hot spot and rightly so, but what has that to do with George?'

'Perhaps the restaurant is what he's after,' Angie suggested, referring to Spartacus, the Michelin-starred eatery attached to the spa that was booked up for months in advance. 'He wants to jump the queue.'

'I don't think it's that. He would have said if it was the case, and I'd have found him a booking so that he could wow whoever he wants to impress.' Callie frowned as she tapped her fingers on the arm of her chair. 'Anyway, whatever he wants to do, it won't be legal, and I don't want any part of it.'

'It has to involve Gavin in some way,' Angie said. 'Not directly, but I'd guess George wants to convince people that he's taken over from him.'

'Taken over what?' Callie asked.

'Whatever Gavin was into before he did a runner.' Angie shrugged. 'It seems like the most logical explanation.'

'Yeah well, if he thinks to impress people by using my premises and implying that he has my approval, then he's onto a loser. We had quite the argument about it yesterday,' Callie chuckled. 'I think he expected me to be a pushover.'

'That's men for you,' Angie replied. 'They constantly underestimate us.'

'You really are worried about your job, aren't you, babe,' Callie turned a concerned look upon Dawn. 'You've hardly said a word all night and ordinarily, we can't shut you up.'

'Sorry, I know I'm not good company right now.' Callie's compassion only served to increase Dawn's feelings of guilt.

'You don't have to apologise to us,' Angie replied, squeezing Dawn's hand. 'We understand your frustration and we're here for you.'

'Why don't you write it down?' Callie suggested.

Dawn blinked at her. 'Write what down?'

'The whole ageist thing. You've worked hard to get where you are, you do your research and present balanced arguments, and yet because of your age, they want to shift you over and let someone younger take your place. That is *so* not fair and will resonate with a lot of women.'

'Ha!'

'She's right!' Angie insisted. 'Don't listen to your detractors. They're jealous of your success. Anyway, don't get mad, get even.'

'We see it all the time,' Callie added. 'Young, pretty things who can't string a sentence together without the aid of an autocue. Airheads, the lot of them.'

Angie nodded. 'As with everything, it's different for the men. I don't see male presenters getting booted out because their hair's turned grey. It would make a brilliant piece. Enough to get noticed by the nationals.'

'You know what they say about revenge,' Callie said, winking at her friend. 'I'd like to see your channel closing you down if you get that discussion started.'

'It's an idea.' Dawn nodded slowly. 'But they probably wouldn't run it if it criticises their management style and I am contracted to work only for them.' Besides, Dawn absolutely did not want her rivals in the industry to turn the tables on her and dig into her own past. 'Anyway, Callie, what are you going to do about George's need for your meeting room?'

'Absolutely nothing.' Callie set her chin in the stubborn line of determination that Dawn recognised so well. Once Callie made her mind up then it would take an earthquake to change it. Whatever George wanted her approval for, he'd have to find another way. 'I've told him no and that's an end to the matter. There's nothing he can do as far as I'm aware to force me.'

Dawn briefly closed her eyes. 'At least you have Darren to protect your back. Not that you need him,' Dawn added hastily when Callie frowned. 'I know you're well able to fight your own battles, but a little muscular support never hurt anyone.'

Callie's PA, a guy fifteen years her junior, had worked for her at Gavin's behest since the opening of Frenchurch Spa five years previously. The business had been intended as an instrument through which Gavin could launder dirty money, and a means to keep Callie occupied. He had not expected her to have a flair for the business and make such a success of it.

'Well, girlfriends.' Dawn drained her glass and stood. 'I must love you and leave you. Whilst I still have a job, I need to be up at silly o'clock to cover some protest or other in central Brighton tomorrow.'

'Eric is picking me up and dropping Angie home,' Callie said, referring to her chauffeur. 'He can take you too.'

'It's out of your way.' She kissed them both. 'Don't worry about me. I'll grab a cab. Laters.'

She fluttered her fingers and left them to finish the wine.

* * *

Callie and Dawn left the central Brighton comedy club fifteen minutes after Dawn. Callie had never seen her friend so subdued before and was convinced that her depression ran deeper than her potential axe from a relatively small, local cable TV channel. She desperately wanted to help her in much the same way that Dawn had been there for her and Angie in Angie's hour of need. Dawn had gone above and beyond, placing herself in danger in order to expose O'Keefe's human organ trafficking scam.

'Dawn needs our help,' Angie said, voicing Callie's own thoughts, 'but hell will freeze over before she asks for it.'

'I know. It's the journalist in her. She's grown accustomed to keeping things close to her chest.'

'But we're her friends. She knows us better than anyone and must realise that she can trust us.'

'I've never known her to be so quiet,' Callie said. 'It just isn't like her but there's not much we can do to help her if she refuses to open up to us. And she insists she's striking a blow for feminism by making it in what's still looked upon as a male occupation.'

Angie nodded. 'She's married to her career but look where that has gotten her. She should have taken time out to have kids. She'd have made a great mum.'

'We don't all have maternal instincts, Angie.'

'You say that, but if you'd had a baby yourself, you'd understand.'

'Well, that ship has well and truly sailed, and I can't say that I'm sorry.' Callie grinned as she trotted out the well-rehearsed lie. 'You never stop either worrying or complaining about your four.'

'True. But that's all part and parcel of being a mum.'

'I'll have to take your word for it.'

Fortunately, the car arrived at Angie's marina apartment at that point, which brought an end to the conversation and prevented Angie from noticing Callie's distress. It was a conversation that they'd had in various forms many times over the years and Callie had become adept at hiding her feelings, but today, her friend's casual remarks had struck a nerve.

She hugged Angie goodbye and spent the rest of the journey back to Frenchurch village mulling over her childless state. Despite her protests to the contrary, it had deeply bothered her when she'd been unable to conceive. Gavin had refused to be tested, insisting that there was nothing wrong with him in that department and wouldn't even consider the possibility that he might be firing blanks. Men could be *so* sensitive about that particular subject. Callie had herself been tested, without telling Gavin, and there was absolutely no reason why she couldn't conceive. Ergo, the blame had to lie with Gavin.

But she hadn't dared raise that possibility and had instead

kept her feelings to herself for all these years. But sometimes, when she least expected them to, regrets crept up on her and she wondered what it would have been like to have a proper family life. You can't miss what you've never had, had always been her mantra, but even so.

She thanked Eric when he pulled the car onto her drive, got out and opened her door. The house looked dark and felt unloved, Callie thought, glancing up at the edifice and wondering how long she ought to hang on to the monolith. It had been Gavin's idea to move to such a barn of a place, in which they'd rattled around for more than two decades. Gavin had always been one to try and impress by flaunting his wealth, accumulated thanks to his criminal enterprises, but Callie had had enough of the ostentation. Not that she could do anything about it. The property was in her sole name –a precaution insisted upon by Gavin when they made the purchase. If his collar was felt, the house couldn't be seized. Gavin *would* deign to reappear at some point and all hell would break lose if she'd gotten rid of the property.

So, until that time or until his body was found, she was stuck in limbo.

2

Dawn reached her central Brighton apartment and closed the door behind herself with an unmitigated sigh of relief.

'God, will the guilt never go away!'

She threw back her head and shouted the words at the ceiling. Her Persian cat, Saffron, uncurled herself from a cushion and peered up at Dawn through piercing, blue eyes, no doubt wondering what the latest drama was all about.

'It's all right for you,' Dawn told the feline, stroking her sleek, ivory coat and stirring up a storm of purring by way of reward. 'All you have to do is eat and sleep and protect the balcony from infiltrating birds. Life for humans is a little more complicated than that.'

Although, Dawn supposed, it didn't have to be. The premise was the same for all forms of animal life. Or should be. Humans were generally considered to be the superior species – although Dawn often wondered about that – and had made their lives unnecessarily complex with their constant battles for superiority.

Dawn kicked off her shoes, poured herself a large glass of water to counter the effects of the alcohol she'd consumed and resisted looking in the mirror. The wrinkles wouldn't disappear because she willed them to, she repeatedly told herself. Her career in television, such as it was, was in danger of stagnating before it had even taken off, and all because she'd passed the age of forty. It was so fucking unfair! She wanted to kick something but restrained herself, aware that it would achieve nothing other than a sore foot.

It didn't seem to matter that she was a diligent reporter who checked her facts a dozen times before presenting a story. The younger, prettier things were shallow imitations of the professional she prided herself upon being, but the camera loved them so who cared.

She actually preferred written journalism, but the stubborn part of her character made her cling tenaciously to her career with an admittedly small cable channel, dreaming of the big time. She was damned if she was going to be forced out simply because of the way she looked. Or because she sometimes ruffled feathers in her quest for the truth behind a story that would bring the break to secure her future. Jealousies were rife in such a competitive industry, and she suspected that someone with the producer's ear had been bad-mouthing her. She thought she'd found that elusive break when she was the first to expose the human organ trafficking scam that Angie's husband had involved himself with, but she hadn't covered her back properly and others had swarmed in to snatch the scoop from beneath her nose.

'It won't happen again,' she told a disinterested Saffron.

Dawn picked up the forms she'd printed out from the local private hospital and tried not to wince when she looked at the cost of a total face and neck lift. Seventeen thousand plus! But, she reasoned, it would be money well spent. She was overdue some leave which she could take while she hid herself away after surgery and waited for the bruises to fade. Whilst she was recovering, perhaps she'd start putting together the book she'd been planning that would expose the cut-throat nature of the business that went by the name of local news.

Callie and Angie were both convinced that the resulting book would be a bestseller that blew the lid off the industry, but they were loyal friends and therefore biased. Would Joe Public really give a shit about the behind-the-scenes backstabbing on such a small channel, Dawn wondered, tamping down the guilt she felt whenever she dwelt upon her own betrayal of Callie's friendship.

She was no nearer to reaching a conclusion and thinking about taking herself off to bed even though she wasn't especially tired when the doorbell rang. She glanced at her watch.

'It's nearly midnight,' she said, frowning. She was a private person and had few visitors. Especially not at that time of night. 'Are you expecting anyone, Saffron?'

Her cat opened one imperious eye, then closed it again and returned to her slumbers with, Dawn was convinced, an indifferent shrug.

The journalist in Dawn made it impossible for her not to want to know who'd come calling at such an unsocial hour. She walked to her video entry phone and glared at the figure standing on the outside step, stamping his feet impatiently. He bowed his head, and she noticed a bald spot appearing on his crown. He was a vain man, and she wondered if he knew that his crowning glory was losing the fight against the ageing process.

'George Elliott.' Dawn mouthed his name, totally flummoxed, wondering how he even knew where she lived. He was Gavin's understudy, or whatever the correct term was, in his criminal enterprise. All well and good, but what the hell did he want with her? Should she let him in? Dawn pressed the button to release the front door, even as the questions tumbled through her head.

There had never been any real possibility of her leaving him standing. She had to know what he wanted, and how he'd found her.

Dawn stood at the open door to her apartment as George emerged from the lift and headed towards her, his handsome face wreathed in smiles that only served to increase Dawn's suspicions.

'Sorry to call so late,' he said, grabbing her hand and kissing the back of it in an old-fashioned, courtly gesture.

'What do you want, George?' she asked, opening her door wider and ushering him into her hallway. Whatever he did want, she decided that it wasn't a conversation she intended to have in a semi-public place. Anyone could emerge from another apartment at any time, and she didn't want her neighbours to know her business.

'How have you been?'

Dawn stood in the hallway, arms akimbo, and glared at him. 'You came here at midnight to ask me that?'

'No need to be so hostile,' he replied in the persuasive tone that reminded her of Gavin, causing an acute pain to rip through her insides. How was it possible that even the thought of her best friend's husband still held the power to cripple her emotionally and physically all these years later? 'Just needed to see you in private. The witching hour's always best for private meetings, I find, and I happen to know that you're a night owl.'

How does he know that?

'You'd better come in then.'

She opened the door to her lounge, aware that she'd never get rid of him until he'd said whatever he'd come to say. Saffron continued to occupy the most comfortable chair in the room and didn't move a muscle. A peel of laughter echoed through the walls, implying that someone was having a party close by.

'Nice,' George said, glancing round the room. 'I like what you've done to the place. No chance of a whisky, I suppose.'

'You suppose right.' Dawn folded her arms and leaned against the nearest wall. 'Okay, you're here and you have my attention, so out with it. What do you want? Did Gavin send you?'

She regretted the last words as soon as they left her lips.

'Still carrying a torch for him, I see.' There was glee in George's expression.

'Grow up, George, and tell me what you want.'

'Poor Callie's in quite a state. I saw her the other day.'

'I know. She told me. And despite what you think, she's doing just fine on her own, thanks very much.'

'There are rumours circulating that she knows something about O'Keefe's disappearance,' George said, a calculating look in his eye.

'Yeah, right!' Dawn waved the suggestion aside. 'Get real, George! If you came here wanting to know if there's any truth in such an outlandish rumour, then you've obviously lost your marbles. Besides, if you want to know that badly, why didn't you ask her yourself when you saw her?'

'Hardly the sort of question you'd throw into casual conversation.' George pranced around the room like a caged animal, setting Dawn's teeth on edge. Whatever he'd come here to ask her, she knew damned well that it didn't have anything directly to do with O'Keefe's disappearance – a disappearance that had left the whole of the Brighton criminal fraternity guessing. And jockeying for position now that O'Keefe's return seemed more unlikely with every passing day. 'No, what I need from you is a favour.'

'What sort of favour?' Dawn asked, narrowing her eyes in suspicion.

'Nothing heavy. I just need you to persuade Callie to let me use her private rooms for a few off-the-grid meetings.' He shrugged a little too casually, as though it was no big deal, but the gesture gave him away and Dawn understood then that for some reason, it was a very big deal indeed.

'You already asked her, and she said no. I don't know what you expect me to do about it, and anyway, why would I?'

'As a favour, like I said.'

'There are dozens of places in Brighton where you can hire private meeting rooms.' Dawn glowered at him, feeling the antagonism rising from him. He clearly didn't like anyone, but especially women, telling him to do one. 'Why are you so set upon using the spa?'

'My reasons don't matter.' His expression hardened and she was suddenly afraid of him. The large room seemed a lot smaller with such a big man prowling around it. She glanced at Saffron, who continued to snooze through the drama. No chance of her turning into a guard cat any time soon, obviously. 'But I do need access to Callie's private rooms; that's all you need to know.'

'Sorry, George, but you've had a wasted journey.'

'I heard your career is on the skids,' he remarked, his expression set in stone.

'What!' Dawn was furious when her spontaneous response only served to confirm his statement.

'Look, I'm not without contacts and if you do this small thing for me then I can help you out. Phil Carson and I go way back.'

He was referring to the cable company's main backer. One word from him and Dawn's career would be secure, and yet she balked at the idea of having George fight her corner. Even if her desperation overcame her pride, everyone at the station would assume that George was promoting her interests in return for sexual favours. George was an attractive older man, she conceded, but his looks, charm and personality paled into insignificance when compared to Gavin's charisma. Dawn had always been able to understand why Gavin was a natural-born leader – Paul, George and others his lieutenants.

'Thanks, but I don't need your help.' She walked towards the door. 'I think you'd best leave.'

George remained rooted to the spot. 'I know,' he said, fixing her with an unwavering death glare.

She blinked at him. 'Know what?' But Dawn had a terrible feeling that she knew the answer to her own question.

'Don't make me spell it out.'

'Sorry, George, but it's late, I'm tired and I have an early start tomorrow. I'd like you to leave now, please.'

'I know you had an affair with your "best friend's" husband,' he said, appearing to enjoy her reaction when she felt the colour drain from her face and she abruptly fell into the nearest chair before her legs gave out on her. So much for fronting it out! *Way to go, Dawn.* 'I know it started not long after he married Callie, that it lasted for two years and, I'm guessing here, that you still carry a torch for the bastard. It would explain why you've never married or had a serious relationship since then.'

'Gavin has affairs all the time.' Dawn could hear the quiver in her own voice. It was obvious that George knew her guilty secret and since Dawn herself had never told anyone, Gavin must have confided – boasted even – to his partner in crime. She had plenty to feel bad about but she straightened her shoulders defiantly, damned if she'd crumble in the face of George's crude threats. 'And as for my own love life, which is none of your business, you have absolutely no idea who I've seen over the years. Just because I don't need a big, strong man in my life to fight my corner, doesn't mean that I'm hung up on ancient history.'

Except that it does.

'Keep telling yourself that, darlin'.'

Dawn fought the urge to wipe the smirk from George's face. He was ten times stronger than her and any physical attack would not only be easily countered but would also play straight into his hands, revealing that he'd hit upon her Achilles heel.

'I am not your darling.' Dawn lost all patience, all professionalism, any attempt at pretence, and shouted the words at him. 'Get out, George! We have nothing more to say to one another. If you want Callie's co-operation then talk to her, not me. I can't help you.'

'Now don't be difficult.' George's expression turned dark, dangerous. 'You can get Callie to do anything you like. She owes you after the way you helped her and Angie out recently and got certain parties off her back.' George snorted. 'Paul's a damned fool, I always said as much, but Gavin had a blind spot where he was concerned and thought the sun shone out of his backside. But anyway, we digress. Do this small thing for me, Dawn, and Callie will never find out about you and Gavin.'

'There's nothing to find out.'

George let out a long-suffering sigh. 'We both know that's not true.'

'Gavin is a womaniser. Anyway, Callie's through with him. She thinks he's dead and is getting on with her life. She isn't interested in ancient history.'

George waggled a finger in her face. 'We both know that isn't true as well,' he repeated. 'So don't play me for a fool. She might have turned a blind eye to his womanising in the past, but if she found out about a two-year affair with her best friend then...'

'She'd get over it.'

Dawn realised how lame that sounded when George merely grinned at her. She watched Saffron as she lazily stretched and then settled back down again, wishing for the second time that night that her own life could be equally uncomplicated.

'How's Jago?' George asked casually into the ensuring silence.

Dawn's entire body went rigid. 'Who?'

But she knew that her reaction had given her away. How the hell did George know about Jago? she wondered. She hadn't told a living soul.

Not even Gavin.

'Do you know just how badly Callie wanted a child when she married Gavin?' George asked, his voice annoyingly conversational. 'Gavin said she never gave up banging on about it for years. How would she feel if she knew that you gave birth to Gavin's son twenty-eight years ago?'

3

George watched Dawn's stunned reaction with a combination of satisfaction and sympathy. She was a feisty piece at the best of times –opinionated and self-assured – but right now, she looked vulnerable and... well, devastated to be exposed for a cheat who practised double standards, using her looks and femininity to get ahead. George's fleeting sympathy was replaced by the more common blazing anger he felt whenever he recalled just how easily Gavin bent women of all ages to his will – including Dawn. He'd been a married man at the time and still was, for fuck's sake, but tying the knot had barely caused a hiatus in his seduction routine.

Paul Dalton had been just the same, except for the fact that he was more circumspect about his conquests. Angie hadn't had a clue that he put it about until he was daft enough to get stuck on a tart who worked out of his brothel. George somehow resisted the urge to roll his eyes. The fool seemed to think that Melody had returned his affections, which was nothing short of ludicrous. She'd only stuck with Paul because he'd fathered her child and because it got her off the game and out of the clutches of the hard bastards who'd smuggled her into England and expected their pound of flesh in return.

George, on the other hand, had never been married. He'd tried to date Dawn back in the day, if only to protect her from Gavin's predatory tentacles. George knew he would use her and then cast her aside when he got bored, just as he always did. Dawn had deserved better than that but clearly didn't recall turning him down all those years ago with the minimum of civility. He had meant that little to her. It had rankled at the time and the insult had continued to fester away, but George was a patient man and now, finally, it was payback time.

Women! He'd never understand what made them tick but he'd seen the way they reacted to Gavin more times than enough. The worse he treated them, the more tightly they clung. Dawn hadn't been much different except... well, except for the not insignificant fact that she'd had Gavin's kid.

Gav had got careless. He'd mentioned it just once when George had been alone with him, vowing never to make the same mistake again. Two weeks later, he'd had the snip and as far as George knew, to this day, Callie wasn't aware.

George had seen the opportunity that had arisen from Gavin's rare moment of confidence and realised that one day, he'd be able to use what he knew to help himself. He just hadn't expected the wait to be such a long one. Gavin had absolutely no idea that he'd become a father. He'd told Dawn to get rid of it, given her the dosh to make it happen and simply assumed that she'd done as she was told.

But Dawn didn't do as she was told. George knew because... well, if he was honest with himself then he'd have to admit that he was a little bit obsessed with the TV reporter. Okay, more than obsessed, but perhaps that was because he didn't take rejection well. The obsession in question irritated the hell out of him but even the passage of time had failed to push Dawn from the forefront of his thoughts. Some would argue that a quarter of a century was a long time to bear a grudge. It wasn't a grudge precisely, George reasoned, but more a case of payback time.

'You gave birth to Gavin's son in St Mary's on 14 May twenty-eight years ago,' he said conversationally, as Dawn's jaw continued to hang open. 'You named him Jago and gave him up for immediate adoption. But I bet a day hasn't gone by without you thinking about him, wondering what he's doing and what sort of fist he's made of his life. Am I right?' George held up a hand. 'No, don't bother to answer that. I can see from your face that I've hit the nail on the proverbial.'

'No one knew,' she muttered, so quietly that George barely caught the words.

She looked so desolate that George was required to fight the urge to take her into his arms and comfort her. 'And no one ever will, especially not Callie,' he said, ruthlessly squelching his desires. God alone knew, when it came to Dawn, he'd had enough practise. 'Provided you do what I ask of you.'

'Callie won't change her mind, if that's what you hope your crude attempt at blackmail will achieve,' Dawn said, recovering her composure with a speed that drew reluctant admiration from George. 'In fact, it will likely harden her resolve and break up our friendship. That must make you very happy.'

'Oh, I think you can persuade her, given how close the two of you are, and what's at stake if you don't.'

'She won't believe you.' Dawn tossed her head defiantly, fire now blazing from her eyes. 'Gavin isn't here and even if he was, he couldn't confirm Jago's his because he doesn't know I went through with the birth.'

'Darling, I was dating one of the maternity nurses at St Mary's at the time of the child's birth. She was very obliging and provided me with all the information I needed.'

'Which wouldn't include the name of the father because I didn't give it,' Dawn shot back at him.

'No, but here's the thing.' He paused, enjoying the fact that he could keep her hanging. 'I've kept tabs on Jago.'

'You know where he is?'

George could see that Dawn regretted showing so much enthusiasm the moment the words left her lips. She turned away from him and made a fuss of the stupid cat curled up on a chair, presumably an excuse to regain her composure.

'Oh yes, I know where he is, and I gather he's keen to find his birth parents.'

'If he was then I would have been told. You're blowing hot air as usual. No wonder Gavin never gave you much responsibility.' She sent him a scathing look and the desire to comfort her was replaced by the burning need to wipe that smirk from her lips with the back of his hand. He resisted. Somehow. Still holding on to the belief that a little charm and coercion would make her see reason. 'You're more of a liability than a help.'

'Don't provoke me, Dawn. You don't know what I'm capable of.'

'I know you see an opportunity, what with Gavin in the wind and O'Keefe on the missing list. The various criminal factions in this town are gathering their forces, ready to fight for control, and you see a chance to move fast and be kingpin.' She sent him a withering smile. 'You're way out of your league. Give it up and be grateful for what little autonomy you still have. If you play nice, I dare say O'Keefe's successor will give you the crumbs from his table. Or hers. I gather his wife is holding the fort and she's as hard as they come. She'll see through your stratagems in a heartbeat.'

George shook his head slowly. 'No, no. You don't get to call the shots, or to divert me. We're here to talk about the son you abandoned. The son who's looking for answers which I am in a position to provide.'

'Only with a DNA test. Even if you somehow got a sample from me and it's a match, you can't prove who his father is, and I sure as hell won't tell.'

'Oh, but I will get my proof *if* you force me to take that route. The decision is yours. Obviously, my first port of call will be Callie. I'm sure she'll be interested in what I have to tell her. I have a few pictures of you and Gavin together at that club you used to go to. I tend to keep souvenirs. I often find that they can come in useful. Anyone looking at them will see that you were more than casual acquaintances. You're all over him like a rash, sweetheart, so you can't deny the affair.' George waggled a hand from side to side. 'Well, I suppose you could try. Gavin always kept you mostly out of sight. Only a few of his most trusted people knew anything about you and they wouldn't have thought much of it anyway. His women never lasted long. You were the exception.'

'Well, there you are then. You have no proof, other than old pictures that don't mean a thing. Gavin always got up close to women when there was a camera around, and Callie knows it.'

'I don't need proof.' He paused, fixing her with a hard look. 'If Callie confronted you, would you be able to convincingly lie?' A slow, satisfied smile disturbed his lips when she folded her arms, lowered her gaze and looked away from him. Things hadn't been going quite the way that George had hoped up until that point. He'd been losing control of the confrontation, but it was now back on track, with him firmly in the driver's seat. 'I thought not. I'm guessing that the guilt has been eating away at you all these years and admitting the truth to your friend would almost be a relief.'

'What is your problem with me?' she asked. 'Why are you attempting to strong-arm me? What have I ever done to you? I barely know you.'

'You know me plenty well enough. You just never bothered to look at me because you were so besotted with bloody Gavin.'

'You're jealous.' This time, it was Dawn who flashed a mocking smile. 'That's what all this is really about. I remember you asking me out once and telling me you could do more for me than Gavin ever could. Well, let me tell you this: regardless of my relationship with Gavin, I would never have taken you up on your offer. You're not my type, so get over yourself and find another way to rule the world. I'm not playing.'

George slowly shook his head. 'Don't imagine I'm bluffing. I need this favour. Get Callie to see things my way and we'll be even.'

'Even if I could do what you ask, I reckon you'll be back again the next time you need something. You're enjoying being let loose in the playground and attempting to be head teacher.' Dawn walked towards the door. 'Get out, George, and don't come back. I mean it. You really don't want to take me on because, trust me, if you ruin my world then I am more than capable of returning the favour.'

'I'll give you a week. No more than that.' George followed her to the door and tweaked her chin between his thumb and forefinger, causing Dawn to recoil. 'I'll be back then and won't take no for an answer. If you come up with the goods before then, call me and let me know.' He placed his card on the hall stand. 'And bear in mind, I can sort out your career hiatus for you as well. One good turn deserves another.' He waggled his fingers at her as he left her flat. 'Take care of yourself, princess.'

*\ *\ *

Dawn resisted the urge to slam the door and instead closed and bolted it with the minimum of noise. Despite George's cataclysmic revelations and demands, she felt inexplicably calm as she walked back to her living room on steady legs. It was a long time since anyone had mentioned Jago's name in her hearing, mainly because no one other than the nurses at St Mary's knew it. But she had thought about him every single day for twenty-eight years, always regretting her decision to give him up. Only Gavin's insistence that he didn't want kids had persuaded her to do so, mainly because she believed him when he told her that he planned to leave Callie so they could be together.

And yet he had dropped her like a ton of bricks just weeks after she'd broken the news of her pregnancy to him.

She perched on the edge of the chair occupied by Saffron, absently stroking the cat as recollections of her naivete caused her to shake her head. How gullible had she been? In hindsight, it was obvious that Gavin had no intention whatsoever of abandoning his marriage, but she had been too young, and too much in love at the time to see the truth that stared her in the face. Worse, Gavin had sworn her to secrecy, so she'd been unable to discuss her situation with a girlfriend for the fear of frightening him off. Even back then, Gavin hadn't been the sort of person to take disloyalty lightly. She realised now that she should have spoken to someone she trusted. Whether or not she would have acted on that person's advice, even if she'd known it was sound, was another matter entirely. Besides, Callie and Angie had been her best friends then and still were. How could she explain to Callie that she'd 'accidentally' fallen into a madly passionate affair with her new husband? Even now, the guilt ate away at her like a cancer, but she had been so head over heels that given her time over, she would almost certainly do the exact same thing again.

What did that say about her morals?

And now what to do about George and his very real threats? That was her most immediate concern and all that she should be thinking about. She sensed that the use of Callie's private rooms was vital to him and that he wouldn't be easily deterred from causing trouble for her if she called his bluff. A part of her had wanted to beg him for more information about Jago but instinct had held her back. Even in the midst of her shock, common sense had prevailed. If George had told the truth and Jago *did* want to get in touch – a situation that she had both dreamed about and dreaded since he'd turned eighteen – then surely she would have heard something from the adoption agency by now.

If George could lie about that then the chances were that everything else he'd said to her had been a fabrication designed to spook her into action. He'd been right about one thing, though. She would find it hard to lie to Callie, even though she'd been doing so if only by omission for twenty-eight years. That being the case, she would find the strength to confront her if necessary, deny everything and continue with the lie. She owed her friend at least that much. And if Jago did somehow magically appear, and if it could be proven that Dawn was his mother, there was still absolutely no way in this world that his paternity could be established. Only two people knew the truth. Dawn would never tell, and Gavin was on the missing list. Much as she wanted Gavin to reappear, if only so that Callie could move forward, she now had a pressing reason of her own for him to remain absent.

Dawn didn't take kindly to being manipulated. Why did George need to use the spa's facilities quite so badly? She'd sensed that his approach had been personal but found it hard to think why. She barely knew the guy other than as someone who worked for Gavin in a supportive capacity. Always a follower, never the boss. She recalled that he used to look at her a lot, and quite intently. He'd attempted to engage her in prolonged conversations too, but Dawn had barely heard a word he'd said. Her attention had been all for Gavin.

'He asked me out,' she told her cat, 'and I didn't turn him down very gently, but even so...'

Her suggestion about his ambition to rule the criminal enterprises in the town had been made flippantly, but she wondered now if there was any truth in it. The various crime families were circling their wagons, waiting to see if O'Keefe and Gavin reappeared before moving in to take control, but George wasn't in their league. Dawn had been doing a little nose-poking regarding the vacancy for a mastermind, hoping to do a feature on the channel. Phil Carson, who had the ultimate say, and rejected the idea out of hand, had warned her not to agitate the situation. Red flag to a bull that, she thought. Any reporter worth her salt who was told to drop a story, tended to do precisely the opposite.

George had given her a week, which was a lot of time to do more digging, she reasoned. There had to be a way to find out what his intention actually was and to nip it in the bud. Gavin had something big in the offing, that much she did know, which made his sudden disappearance that much harder to fathom. If George happened to know what that something was and hoped to take over, then holding meetings at Gavin's spa would give the impression that he had the boss's backing and was standing in for him until he came back.

Would he come back? Dawn was furious with herself because she'd never stopped loving him. Never stopped hoping that he'd come back to her. And, to her shame, she'd have taken him without a backward glance, or a care about what it would do to Callie. Love was very definitely blind and accounted for the fact that Dawn had flitted from relationship to relationship for years, none of them ever lasting for long.

Now all she really cared about was that he was still breathing. Waiting for news was wearing on her nerves every bit as much as it had to be on Callie's. When he came back, Dawn hoped that whatever had caused him to scarper would become clear. Callie would perhaps on this occasion stick to her word and kick him out and then, just perhaps...

Dawn nodded, happy with her own logic, despite the fact that it showed her in such a bad light. Happier still that she could think so coherently at a time when memories of Jago had been stirred up and the possibility of actually seeing him seemed tangible. So real that she had never felt closer to him. But that closeness was forbidden, she reminded herself. He had been adopted and, she hoped, had enjoyed a happy and protected childhood. She had abandoned him and had no part in his life.

It was better that way.

Sighing, Dawn took herself off to bed, mulling the situation over. She was pretty sure that George was foolishly attempting to muscle in on whatever Gavin had planned. And to find out what that something was, she would need to involve Callie, and more specifically, Darren, Callie's PA who kept his ear to the ground and probably knew more than he realised. She would have to tell Callie that George had paid her a visit, of course, but she could say that he'd heard about her career hiatus and offered to help her in return for a favour.

Yep. She slid between the sheets and extinguished the light, aware that she wouldn't sleep as she wondered what Jago was doing at that precise moment.

4

'Everything's starting to look kosher, Darren.' Callie leaned back in her chair, consumed by feelings of satisfaction mixed with underlying concern. All the time she had free rein, she could make her business entirely legitimate. But the prospect of Gavin breezing through the door like he hadn't been on a lengthy sabbatical and messing things up refused to leave her. 'For the past three months, not a pound of dodgy money has gone through our books.'

'You need to be careful, Callie. A sudden drop in expenditure will create alarm bells with the tax office. You know very well that they have you in their sights. Well, not you but Gavin, which amounts to the same thing in their eyes.'

'I know, but there's only so much renovation and stuff that I can legitimately claim for, and I'm most certainly not going to create invoices. That would defeat the object and make me directly responsible for fraud.'

'I realise that, but there are still some things you can do that will enhance the spa and reduce your tax liability.'

'But increase my expenditure.' Callie leaned back in her chair and sighed. 'Yeah, I know it has to be done.'

'And you can afford it. Both the spa and the restaurant have never been more popular. The funds are rolling in.'

Callie flashed a smile, more appreciative of Darren's common sense and sound advice with every day that passed – as sure as she could be of his complete loyalty. 'Okay, so what can't I do without?'

'Well, there's some new gym machines that would be worth a shot. Members seem to think they'll tone faster and lose more weight if they exercise on the latest gismo. If nothing else, it'll give them bragging rights and enhance the reputation of the spa. And a couple of the saunas are showing their age.'

'Okay, get Laurence to report on what's needed,' she replied, referring to her recreations manager – a fancy moniker for the guy who ran the gym. Everyone nowadays seemed to need a title.

'Will do.'

'Is there anything else?' Callie asked, mentally checking her to-do list, which never seemed to get any shorter.

'No, I think that about covers it.'

Darren stood just as the office door opened and Dawn put her head round it.

'Anyone at home?' she asked, her smile looking strained.

'What are you doing here?' Callie asked, standing to hug her friend. 'No stories to chase down?'

'Actually, there's something I need to talk to you about.' Dawn looked unnaturally serious, increasing Callie's nascent concerns. She knew her friend so well that she could tell at a glance something was way off with her.

'I'll leave you to it then, ladies.'

'No, Darren, stay if you wouldn't mind. You might have some bright ideas to help me get out of the hole I've dug for myself.'

Darren glanced at Callie, who nodded.

'Right-ho.' He smiled that enigmatic smile of his and resumed his chair. 'Anything I can do to help, you have but to say the word.'

Callie offered her friend an encouraging smile, wondering if her unscheduled appearance had anything to do with her unnatural reticence the previous evening. Dawn was always the life and soul and never quiet. Clearly, she had something on her mind and Callie would happily do whatever she could to help just as soon as she'd unburdened herself.

'Those people at the TV studio bullying you again?' she asked.

'Not precisely.' Dawn took a deep breath and failed to make eye contact with Callie. 'Look, the thing is,' she eventually said, stumbling over her words, 'I received a visit from George Markham late last night.'

'Blimey!' Callie blinked. 'It must have been late because we were out on the town until some ungodly hour. What on earth did he want from you that couldn't wait until a more civilized time?'

'The same thing that he wanted from you.' Dawn lifted her head, and this time met Callie's gaze head-on.

'Use of my private meeting rooms?' Callie frowned, feeling discomposed and irritated that George had gone behind her back. 'What the hell? I already told him no. Whatever makes him suppose you could change my mind? And come to that, why are you even here telling me about it? I assume you made it clear that there was nothing you could do. End of.'

Dawn threw up her hands, looking very distressed. 'If only it were that easy.'

'What?' Callie half-rose from her chair. 'What is it, Dawn?

Why are you so wound up?' Callie frowned, her suspicions now on high alert. 'What's he got over you?'

'He's found out that my career's on the skids and has offered to put in a word with Phil Carson.'

'The money man behind the cable channel?' Darren asked.

'That would be him. Apparently, George and he are tight.'

Callie began to feel even more annoyed. She knew how hard Dawn had worked to get as far as she had. She also knew that she'd chosen a cut-throat industry in which to try and make her mark, but Dawn was fiercely independent and would never allow a man to fight her battles for her. She had always seemed slightly scathing about Callie's determination to cling to Gavin and made a point of labouring the success she'd had without any help from the opposite sex.

Callie had recently been forced into making her own stand for independence whether she liked it or not. And she had made it work, but she sometimes missed Gavin more than she would ever admit to a living soul. She had survived all these years of being married to him by pretending her feelings for him were ambivalent, aware that he'd have run a mile, long before now, if she'd tried to clip his wings.

She'd known from day one that he was a rogue, which had perhaps been part of the attraction. Late at night, she had often laid in her lonely bed, wondering where he was and why he hadn't let her know that he was okay. She would still fight his corner if asked, even if she was fiercely determined not to take him back. She blamed her oscillating feelings for the man she'd married on an abiding love that would never waiver, despite the fact that he'd had more women than she wanted to know about. They never lasted and he always came back to *her*.

'You're the one, Cal,' he'd told her more times than she could recall. 'The others are window dressing. They don't mean anything.'

But something had obviously changed. Callie's pride wouldn't permit her to think that he'd permanently dumped her. If that's what he'd decided to do, then he'd have told her to her face and would have wanted to do something about their house and the spa, both of which she owned, on paper at least. And so, while Callie waited for him to show his face again, she'd set out to make the business clean. Whatever George Markham needed the private rooms for, it wouldn't be legal, and Callie was through with dancing around the law. Her friends knew it and had encouraged her, which made it that much harder to fathom why Dawn thought she'd change her mind.

Dawn definitely wasn't telling her everything.

She was convinced that George was doing something dodgy that she wanted no part of – not even by association. She had worked hard to get her books clean and had no intention of allowing her business to be dragged into George's murky world.

'So, you expect me to...'

'Hell, no!' Dawn held up a hand and Callie gladly shut up, pleased to see some of Dawn's feistiness returning to her demeanour. 'The thing is, we need to figure out what George is up to and put a stop to it, before he puts a permanent stop to my career. There'll probably be a juicy story in it, too.' She rubbed her hands together, briefly grinning. 'George kindly pointed out, in case I hadn't gotten the message, that he could make or break me with just a few words. Seems Phil Carson owes him a favour or two.' Dawn shared a look between the two of them as her smile faded. 'That's why I came here in person. I reckon that whatever Gavin's latest brainwave happened to be, George fancies stepping into his shoes and taking over, given that Gav's remained on the missing list for so long.'

Darren glanced at Callie. 'That would make sense,' he said slowly. 'And explain the need to use your rooms. Not only are they entirely secure but the use of them would indicate that he's acting with Gavin's approval.'

Dawn nodded decisively. 'The same thought had occurred to me.'

'And just the sort of scheme he'd try.' Callie tapped her fingers restlessly on the surface of her desk, wondering what the hell Gavin had gotten involved with and whether it was his latest scheme that had caused him to scarper. 'It would imply that he had my backing as well. Problem is, I have absolutely no idea what Gavin planned to do next.'

'Why not ask George?' Darren suggested.

Callie blew air through her lips. 'He'd never tell me.'

'We'll have to confront the situation, if only to help Dawn.' Darren spoke with authority.

'Do what's right for you, Cal.' Dawn leaned forward and touched Callie's hand, her expression intense. 'I'm a big girl and I can fight my own battles. I just thought you needed to know what's going on.'

Callie smiled, sensing there was more to it than that. A phone call was all that had been needed. Perhaps it was simply a case of Dawn being worried about her career. Callie would accept that explanation but for the fact that Dawn had been off her game the previous night, before George had tried to strong-arm her. There was definitely something bothering her friend which she had yet to reveal.

'How can we find out what Gavin had planned, Darren?' she asked. 'Have you heard any rumours?'

Darren shook his head. 'Nope, but I can ask around. Someone's bound to have heard something.'

'Use my name,' Callie said. 'Make them think I know more than I do, which is the sum total of sod all.'

'Could that be why he scarpered, do you think?' Dawn asked. 'Something too hot to handle? Gavin's a big man with a bigger reputation for being hard. But there's always someone bigger and tougher. And younger. If he trod on someone's toes, invaded someone else's territory, they'd be out for his blood.'

'It's possible,' Callie conceded. 'The problem is, Gavin was a secretive bastard... Hark at me, talking about him in the past tense.' She sat a little straighter, catching sight of Dawn's distraught expression in the periphery of her vision. *What had she said to upset her? she wondered.* 'Gavin's a secretive sod,' she amended, 'and never allowed the right hand to know what the left was up to. In other words, only Paul and George are likely to know what he had in the offing, and even they wouldn't have known all the details.'

'But if we're right and George knew enough to pick up the reins,' Dawn pointed out, 'then there must be a way of finding out.'

'Why has George left it so long to make his move?' Darren asked.

'He assumed Gavin would come back but now that he hasn't, he like everyone else assumes he's six feet under,' Callie said briskly. 'Much the same with O'Keefe. The various factions have held fire before now trying to muscle in on O'Keefe's territory, but I hear it won't be long before they fight it out. Even Mrs O'Keefe can't rein them in.'

'You don't think George has his eye on the main prize, do you?' Darren gave a theatrical shudder, making Callie and Dawn smile. 'O'Keefe's territory, I mean. That would be suicidal. George isn't the brightest spark but surely even he isn't that stupid either.'

'God, why can't people be satisfied with a law-abiding existence?' Callie asked. 'Anyway, see what you can find out, Darren.'

'Will do.' Darren gave a little salute and left the ladies to it.

'Dawn, I know you're desperate to get George off your back but hold fire,' Callie said, eyeing her friend with compassion. 'Let him stew for a bit. If he contacts you again before we come up with a plan, refer him to me.'

Dawn nodded but remained uncharacteristically subdued. Something was definitely off with her. Ordinarily, a tsunami of suggestions to get the better of George would be tumbling from her lips. No one could accuse her friend of lacking imagination. Callie didn't want to invade Dawn's privacy... Hell, yes she did! They were friends – more like sisters – and had no secrets from one another. If Dawn was getting pressured from another quarter, then Callie needed to be there for her.

'Wanna talk about it?' she asked.

Dawn blinked at her like a rabbit caught in headlights. 'Not sure what you mean.' She folded her hands in her lap and didn't meet Callie's eye.

'Come on, babe, it's me you're talking to. Are you getting harassment at the studio? Say the word and I'll send the boys round to sort them out.'

Dawn cracked a smile that appeared strained as she gathered up her bag and stood to leave. 'Really, I'm good. No need to worry about me. Anyway, I have to dash while I still have a job to get to. Call me if Darren hears anything.'

'Pop round to mine tonight. We'll have a brainstorm. Angie needs to be involved. The three sisters strike again. We're invincible, in case you'd forgotten.'

Dawn hesitated for a beat too long. 'Sure,' she said. 'That will be great.'

She gave Callie a hug and was gone.

Callie leaned back in her chair, more confused now than she had been when Dawn had burst into her office.

'What the fuck is going on with her?' she muttered.

* * *

Dawn rushed off to meet John Shelton, her cameraman. They were covering a local council meeting where objections were anticipated to the plans for a contentious new housing development on the downs above Brighton.

'Quite a turnout,' John remarked as he fiddled with his equipment and simultaneously nodded towards the packed public gallery in the town hall. There was a lot of noise and, it seemed, two factions were gathering. Those in favour of the development and those firmly opposed to it. The latter group was, unsurprisingly, much larger and more vocal. There was a lot of interview fodder present, but Dawn was preoccupied and failed to summon up much enthusiasm. The planning committee would do what it wanted, regardless of the opposition, she knew from experience, idly wondering who on that committee the developers had bribed to see things their way.

'So cynical,' she muttered.

'What?' John glanced at her. 'Did you say something?'

'Nothing worth hearing,' Dawn replied, still fuelled with guilt about ancient history.

She thought she had come to terms with her betrayal of Callie's trust, but George's demands had unsurprisingly stirred it all up again. And Callie's fierce determination to help her had only served to increase Dawn's guilty conscience. As had George's suggestion that he knew of Jago's whereabouts. Given all the stuff she had on her mind, how the hell was she supposed to concentrate on a contentious council meeting that would only see a couple of minutes' airtime *and* make her report interesting?

Sighing, she dragged up a modicum of professionalism from somewhere and tried to pay attention when the meeting got under way.

The gathering became increasingly rowdy as insults flew across the chamber and the weak-seeming leader of the planning committee struggled to keep order. The application was finally granted on a split majority, at which point Dawn seriously thought there might be a riot. Busy outside the town hall, interviewing the leading lights from both campaigns, it quickly became clear to Dawn that the developers had won this particular skirmish but that the war was far from over: a point she would be sure to get across in her report.

As the crowd dispersed, no doubt heading for the local hostelries either to celebrate or plot their next moves, Dawn did her live piece for the camera, being deliberately contentious in line with the channel's policy. There was no such thing as neutral journalism in her particular world.

Job completed, John set about packing up his equipment as a familiar figure caught Dawn's eye. She looked over her shoulder as the man disappeared rapidly from view, collar turned up, hands thrust into the pockets of his coat. Dawn had only caught a brief glimpse of his face but that had been enough for her to recognise him.

'What the hell is his interest in this business?' she muttered, finally fully engaged with the planning application.

She followed George Markham into a nearby alley that led directly to the high street. It was a shortcut that turned into a drugs den after dark, she knew. She hadn't seen George in the chamber, but he must have merged with the crowd and was now close on the tail of Morgan Fraser, the youngest member of the planning committee, who had spoken eloquently about the need for affordable housing in the area. It was his vote that had swung the decision.

And he and George were now having a furtive meeting in a dangerous alleyway.

Dawn held back, not wanting to be seen. Their discussion was heated as both men kept checking to ensure no one was watching them. Morgan waved his hands about as he spoke, then George reached into his pocket, produced an envelope and passed it to Morgan. It disappeared into the younger man's pocket with a sleight of hand that would have made the most proficient of illusionists weep with envy.

'Gotcha!'

Dawn shot off a few snaps with her phone, hoping against hope that she'd captured the exchange. She had thought that fat wads of cash stuffed into envelopes would be old hat but presumably cash was still king, at least insofar as bribing bent councillors was concerned.

Dawn quickly retraced her steps, fearful of being seen and now fully engaged with the planning-application debacle. She filed her piece for the next news bulletin and then made her way home. Some in-depth research was definitely in order. What connection did George Markham have to the building project, for a start, and why had he bribed Morgan Fraser? And how did he know Fraser would be susceptible to a bribe, for that matter? What did he have on him? Presumably, he wouldn't risk approaching an honest man.

Dawn needed to know a lot more about Morgan. She checked the snaps she'd taken on her phone, wishing she could have got closer. But by enlarging the shots, there was no doubting who the two people were. Unfortunately though, she hadn't been quick enough to capture an image of that envelope changing hands.

It didn't matter, she told herself, as she got into her car and headed for home. She now had an angle to delve into that might well give her some bargaining power with Markham.

5

Callie was relieved to see some improvement in Dawn when she arrived at her friend's home that evening. There was a spring in her step and an urgency about her, putting Callie in mind of a tightly coiled spring. Angie, who'd arrived half an hour previously and was already making steady inroads into the wine, jumped to her feet and hugged Dawn.

'I heard you have a spot of bother, and that Charlie's Angels are back in business,' she quipped, flexing her muscles.

'God help Brighton, in that case,' Dawn replied, but it was clear to Callie that her heart wasn't in the banter and that she was making a huge effort to participate. Whatever she had on her mind, it clearly didn't make allowances for trivialities.

Callie handed Dawn a glass of wine, which she accepted with a nod of thanks before sinking onto the sofa.

'I come with news, ladies,' she said.

Callie and Angie listened as Dawn told them about Markham and his presence at the planning meeting.

'That explains why you look so... well, manic. No offence,' Callie added, holding up a hand to prevent Dawn's protest.

'What on earth is George up to?' Angie asked. 'Who are the developers, Dawn? Have you looked into the names of the partners and done some digging?'

'Naturally.' Dawn pretended to be offended by the question. Digging for answers was, they all knew, second nature to Dawn, who never took anything at face value. 'The developers are a London company called Fairclough Investments. They were represented at the planning meeting by Greystocks, their solicitors.'

'Ha!' Callie wrinkled her nose. 'That shower are about as straight as a nine-bob note. Now I *know* something isn't kosher.'

'You and I know they have dodgy connections, but they're clever and know how to play the game,' Dawn reminded them all. 'As far as Joe Public's concerned, they help old ladies to protect their pensions and generally take the side of the underdog pro bono, so they can do no wrong.'

'Yeah, that's true, but the work they do for some of our less upstanding citizens doesn't make the headlines,' Callie said, nodding. 'I know that Gavin put some of his affairs in their hands but don't ask me what because I have absolutely no idea. I remember him grousing about their exorbitant fees, though. Anyway, just the fact that they would take him on as a client when his reputation is less than stellar tells us all we need to know about their ethics.'

'Innocent until proven guilty,' Dawn reminded them. 'Gavin hasn't got a record, remember.'

Callie glanced at her friend, wondering why she was so quick to defend Gavin. 'You obviously feel the same way about Greystocks as I do,' she said. 'Have you covered any of their court appearances where they've defended villains?'

Dawn's face reddened. 'Not personally, but word gets around. I heard Gavin mention that they were the go-to legal firm for those with enough dosh to get them out of the mire. He described them as sharp-witted Rottweilers.'

'When, babe?' Callie raised a mildly curious brow. 'Gavin doesn't talk about that stuff in company.'

'Perhaps it wasn't Gavin.' Dawn flapped her wrist in a dismissive gesture. 'I'm a reporter. I get paid to poke my nose into other people's business.'

'Yeah, that would be it,' Angie said, grinning.

'So,' Callie said, feeling uncomfortable for reasons she couldn't identify about the exchange with Dawn, 'to the matter in hand. We know that Markham bribed a councillor to swing that vote and we know that Greystocks represent the builders. That's two heavy bats swinging in favour of the development. What do we know about the directors of the building firm, Dawn?'

'Nothing.' Dawn twitched her lips as she grudgingly made that admission. 'They are foreign, with offices in Malaysia.'

'Then they must have someone other than Greystocks managing their affairs in this country,' Callie pointed out.

'Yeah, I'm sure they do but I haven't had a chance to look into that side of things yet. I do have a job to do. Well,' Dawn added, 'at the moment, I do. If I neglect it, then it will give the bigwigs all the ammunition they need to kick me out and I refuse to make it that easy for them.'

'They must have an office in the UK though, probably in this area,' Angie said. 'It seems odd that you haven't found anything online, and I know you'll have looked.'

'I'm on it,' Dawn said. 'Leave it to me.'

'Okay, so dodgy planning developments aside, what we need to find out, ladies, is why George has gotten himself involved and, more to the point, why he wants to use my private rooms.' Callie took a sip of her drink. 'If you can find a way to link him to bribery of a council official, Dawn, then it will get him off my back, earn you a scoop and his reasons for wanting to muscle his way in here will no longer be relevant.'

'Yeah, which is why I've been delving into Mr Morgan Fraser's background,' Dawn replied, in professional mode once again. 'He's only thirty-five. Married with two kids and lives in a five-bedroomed house on that fancy upmarket new estate in Roedean.'

'Blimey! That would have set him back a few bob.' Angie raised both brows. 'Those places are high end. How could a thirty-five-year-old afford it? What does he do to earn a crust, Dawn, other than to accept bribes?'

'He's a management consultant with Braverman Enterprises, according to his bio on the council's website, with a background in public relations.'

'Braverman?' Callie tapped her fingers. 'I know him. He's been to ours. One of Gavin's cronies, I do believe.'

'Well then, there's no smoke without fire.' Dawn checked her notes. 'I found out more about his house. He's got a hefty mortgage on it. His kids are at a private school and the fees are astronomical.'

'No wonder he's taking bribes.' Angie grabbed the bottle and topped up their glasses. 'What does the wife do?'

'She's an online influencer, or trying to be. Her family are quite wealthy, from what little research I've had time to do. They have a country pile outside Chichester where Felicity Compton, as she was then, grew up winning gymkhanas and all the other privileged-upbringing stuff.'

'So she's accustomed to the best of the best. Hence the big house.' Callie took a moment to think the matter through. 'Why the local council for Morgan, though? It would be time-consuming and doesn't pay particularly well. Does he have political ambitions?'

'No idea,' Dawn replied, flipping through her notes. 'He works out of Braverman's Chichester office where he's listed as a director.' She pulled up a publicity shot on her phone, which showed the head and shoulders of a handsome young man with thinning, blond hair. In the second photo, an attractive woman dominated. Morgan and the kids almost failed to make any impression when posed beside a vibrant woman with Raphaelite hair and piercing, green eyes.

'That's Felicity?' Callie jabbed a finger at the screen.

'Well, I doubt it's the nanny,' Angie quipped.

'She's a regular at the spa,' Callie said. 'She's obviously unmissable, so I've noticed her, but I didn't know her name.'

'I wonder what a stunner like that who comes from a moneyed background is doing with Morgan,' Angie remarked, wrinkling her nose. 'They don't look like a match made in heaven but then, looks aren't everything, I suppose.'

'Well, ladies.' Dawn leaned back in her chair. 'I think an interview with the chairman of the planning committee is long overdue. People will want to know why such a contentious application was granted. Feelings are running high, that much I know for a fact, and the malcontents will want to know what made him vote in favour of it.'

'He will probably decline to be interviewed,' Callie warned. 'Especially if he has something to hide, which we know that he does.'

Dawn grinned and tapped her phone. 'I have that picture of him and George in that alleyway, don't forget. If I mention that I saw him covertly meeting with George, I'm sure he'll cooperate.'

Callie nodded. 'His life is balanced on the cusp of a maxed-out credit card, it seems to me, so of course he'll do whatever it takes to hold it all together. Be careful though, babe. Even tame animals can turn nasty when backed into a corner.'

'Don't worry, I'll have John and his camera with me, and no one messes with John. Besides, I'll also make it clear to him that I have those pictures and that more copies are safely lodged elsewhere, so it will be in his best interests to play nice and tell me what I need to know about George.'

'I'll look out for Felicity the next time she comes in, and invite her upstairs for a coffee on the basis that she's a valued regular customer and I'd appreciate any suggestions she might have for improvements. Members like to be consulted, it makes them feel important, and I'm sure she'll have a lot to say.'

'Thanks, Callie.'

'No problem. What are friends for?'

Dawn glanced away and didn't answer.

* * *

Dawn left Callie's a little over an hour later, plagued by a guilty conscience that was in danger of consuming her. Her friend had been so unstintingly supportive, totally loyal to their friendship and firmly in Dawn's corner. Not just on this occasion but ever since they'd first met as young students struggling to make the rent but never failing to have a good time. Now that they could afford to party in style, it didn't seem like nearly so much fun.

George's remark about Callie having secretly always wanted children had lodged in Dawn's brain, stripping away her justification for what she'd done: the justification she'd invented in her mind so that she could live with herself. Her secret love child wouldn't have mattered to Callie, she'd managed to convince herself, because Callie had always been fatalistic about her childless state. Dawn now wondered if that had been a show, her way of coping. Had she lain awake at night, lamenting a situation that she'd never have been able to discuss with Gavin?

Gavin didn't do touchy-feely discussions and would likely have told Callie to get over herself.

Sighing, Dawn headed for her apartment, now feeling as anxious as Callie herself did to find Gavin, albeit for different reasons. A part of her hoped he was dead; that way, the truth would never have to come out. But a larger part of her really wanted him still to be alive. Things were held together when Gavin, with his larger-than-life personality, was around. And even if George did spitefully intend to drop her in it, with Gavin back on the scene, he wouldn't dare. Even if he did have a death wish, Gavin would be able to convince Callie that the suggestion was ridiculous.

'What a mess,' she said to Saffron by way of greeting.

Saffron rolled onto her back and exposed her belly, graciously permitting Dawn to give it a rub, making her feel grateful for the privilege in the way of cats the world over.

She knuckled down to more research after that but still got nowhere when it came to identifying the names of anyone in the UK representing Dorchester Consultants other than Greystocks. Dawn excelled at rooting out hidden details – it went with the territory of being a journalist – but this time, she was obliged to admit defeat.

For now.

'Anyone would think they have something to hide,' she told Saffron.

She stretched her arms above her head and yawned. It was now gone midnight, but she knew John, her cameraman, was also a night owl and so had no qualms about calling him. He answered on the first ring.

'Hey, what's up? I didn't think we had anything lined up for tomorrow. It's your day off. And mine.' His voice was now full of suspicion as he let out a resigned groan. 'Okay, out with it. What are you plotting?'

Dawn chuckled; he knew her so well. 'You really didn't think I'd let that dodgy planning consent go uncontested, did you?'

She recalled that he hadn't seen the exchange in the alleyway between Morgan Fraser and George and so updated him.

'Yeah, I can see why that would have gotten your knickers in a knot,' John replied, chortling. She knew his reticence was feigned. He was as anxious as she herself was to see her position with the TV station solidified, not eradicated. 'Okay, I assume you're going to ask Fraser for a statement, and you need me there to record the proceedings for prosperity.' He sighed. 'When and where?'

'How about catching him outside his place of work in the morning?'

'You mean at first light tomorrow morning, as in about six hours' time?'

'Come on, John. Sleep's overrated.'

'Yeah, yeah. Okay, tell me where and I'll meet you there.'

Dawn reeled off Morgan's office address.

'You do know it's impossible to park in that part of town,' John pointed out with another groan.

'That's what I like you about, John. Your positive attitude.'

'Get off the line and go bother someone else. I'll see you in a few hours' time.'

Dawn thanked him, cut the connection and took herself off to bed.

* * *

George Markham was a creature of the night too. He left Phoenix, the brothel in which Gavin had a majority shareholding, his requirements temporarily satisfied. The place wasn't the same without Melody there, though. She'd been a *real* professional, head and shoulders above the others when it came to instinctively knowing what a man needed. But she was now shacked up with Paul, busy playing happy families, and George was left with a raft of second-rate girls to choose from, none of whom made much of an impression on him.

Neither Gavin nor Paul had shown their faces at Phoenix for months and weeks respectively and the cracks were starting to show. Lucy ran a tight ship but there needed to be a man at the helm to ensure that no one took advantage. Gavin's body needed to be found, and found soon. George was convinced that he must be dead. He'd never disappeared for this long before. He knew that others would move in on his operations soon enough, but the problem was, there was absolutely no word on the street as to his fate – well, only rumour, nothing concrete.

Absolutely no one appeared to actually know what had happened to Gavin. If he was shacked up with his latest squeeze, then no one knew who she was. Besides, his women never lasted that long, with the notable exception of Dawn. George knew that the nosy reporter still carried a torch for Gavin and was pretty sure that her feelings were reciprocated. Gavin was simply better at hiding it and only someone as observant as George would have seen the lingering looks Gavin bestowed upon Dawn whenever they were in the same room.

The thing was, with O'Keefe on the run too, the criminal fraternity was getting itchy feet and if George didn't move fast and take firm control, then others would beat him to it. The waiting was over. That was why it was so vital for him to get the use of Callie's meeting rooms at the spa and bring this latest ruse to fruition. Only then would he be taken seriously by the people he needed to impress. It galled him to think that they would only speak with him if he could convince them that he did so with Gavin's prior approval. Even so, he'd swallow his pride and play the game. Let the people who thought they were in control realise only when it was too late to do anything about it just how ill-advised they had been to underestimate him.

He nodded to Pete, the head security guard, as he left the brothel. He didn't trust the man one inch. He'd always been a favourite of Gavin's and if anyone knew where to find his erstwhile partner, it would be him. But George was damned if he'd reveal weakness by asking. Besides, Pete wouldn't tell him. If Gavin wanted him to know where he was, then he would have been in touch before now, issuing instructions that George would be expected to follow to the letter. Instructions that he *was* adhering to – well, more or less. The fact that he hadn't heard a dicky bird since they'd been issued reinforced his belief that Gavin was six feet under.

'Night,' Pete said almost dismissively.

George ignored the man and strode towards his car, more determined than ever to earn the respect of people who currently thought him to be a waste of space. Well, joke or not, it was thanks to him that the planning application for that new development had gone through. He walked a little taller as he thought about the audacious action that he'd taken to bring that situation about. His success had earned him a decent payday, financial freedom to pursue his ambitions.

It had been a shrewd move on his part to contact Barry Harper at Greystocks when he heard the application had come up against a slew of protesters. He'd promised to get it approved, and he'd done it. Unfortunately, he couldn't boast publicly about that particular achievement.

Now for the big time.

He'd give Callie the week he'd promised her to come to her senses while his own attention was focused on Birmingham. If all went to plan, then would be the time to do whatever it took if she dug her heels in. But really, without Gavin to protect her interests, she was fair game and no match for a man of his stature.

He had absolutely nothing to worry about as far as Callie was concerned. She'd toe the line or bear the consequences, he told himself, as he drove through the gates and headed for home, thinking of the improvements he'd make to the brothel when he had it under his control.

Pete, with his disrespectful attitude, would be the first casualty.

6

Dawn beat the sun out of bed the following morning. She dressed quickly in clothes she'd picked out the night before but spent more time applying make-up with care. Being accustomed to facing the camera at ungodly hours, she knew that being well turned out often left more of an impression upon viewers than the content of her report. Joe Public's attention span wasn't at its best at first light. In this case, she hoped to catch one bleary-eyed miscreant of a councillor off guard when he arrived for work.

Despite his protests, John had nabbed a parking space close to Morgan's office, just as Dawn had known that he would. She found a space a bit further up the road and strolled back to join her colleague and friend.

'Nice day for it,' he remarked, turning up his collar to protect himself from the strong sea breeze, accustomed in his line of work to long waits in all sorts of weather. There was rain in the air. Dawn rolled her eyes, aware that it would play merry hell with her hair.

'Morning,' she replied cheerfully, wrapping her scarf a second time around her neck and shivering. 'Any signs of life?' She nodded towards Braverman Enterprises' glass-fronted offices. The lights were on in reception but there were no obvious signs of activity.

'Only just got here myself.' John glanced at his watch. 'It's still only eight o'clock and,' he added, nodding towards a coffee shop along the road, 'since I'm doing you a favour off the books, it's your round.'

Taking the hint, Dawn went along to the café and bought coffee for them both at an exorbitant price served by a sleepy, disinterested barista with acne and attitude.

'Here you go,' she said, handing John his flat white and taking a cautious sip of her own brew. 'Why do they make these things so scalding hot? Is that what they teach them to do at barista school?'

'It's one of life's mysteries.' John yawned expansively behind his hand.

'Late night?'

'Nah. I was well settled in to catch some Zs but some inconsiderate sod called me at midnight.'

'Get over yourself,' Dawn replied, giving him a nudge with her elbow and laughing. 'You know you love me really.'

'Hey-up.' John poured the remnants of his scalding drink down his throat – how did he do that? – and nodded towards a man striding purposely towards Braverman's offices, his eyes glued to his phone. 'Incoming.'

'So I see.' She tipped away the remnants of her coffee, trying not to resent the fact that it had cost a small fortune, and she hadn't even had time to drink it. 'That's Morgan Fraser. Ready?'

John hoisted his camera equipment. 'And willing. This should be fun. I love it when you get a bee in your bonnet and become a crusader.'

Dawn had a reputation for not pulling her punches when it

came to cases such as this. She couldn't tell John that this was personal and for that reason, she had no immediate plans to change her modus operandi.

'Morgan Fraser?' she asked, stepping in front of the man, microphone in hand.

Morgan was so focused on his phone that he almost collided with her. 'Yes. What can I...' He saw the camera and the microphone at the last minute and his expression turned wary. 'Who are you?'

'Dawn Frobisher, *Sussex News*, do you have a moment?'

'Well, I...' He made a show of glancing at his watch.

'You're a rising star on the local council. My viewers will be interested to know what drew you into politics.'

A dawning of suspicion evidenced itself in Morgan's expression. 'If you want a public-interest piece, then make an appointment with my secretary. I'm sorry, but I don't have time to go into all that now.' He returned his attention to his phone, seeming nervous and distracted. 'I have a full schedule today.'

'Complaints are pouring in from viewers regarding the permission you granted for that new housing development.'

'People always complain about decisions of that nature. There would be just as many complaints if we'd turned it down.' His attitude became a mix of pomposity and patronisation. 'It's a balancing act. No one wants new houses spoiling their view, but people do have to live somewhere and as a council, we have government targets regarding new builds that we are required to meet.'

'Then why were so many councillors opposed to the project?' Dawn held the microphone closer to Morgan's lips. One or two people had stopped to watch, curious to see what was going down, but the majority kept their heads down, impervious to their surroundings as they scurried off to work. Even so, there was enough of a crowd now to make Morgan feel even more uncomfortable. Someone recognised him, pointed a finger and called out abuse. Things couldn't have worked out better if Dawn had orchestrated the supporting cast herself and she didn't hesitate to capitalise.

'I dare say their decisions were politically motivated rather than taken with the welfare of the community in mind.' Morgan pushed the hair out of his eyes and looked everywhere except at Dawn. 'That's why the chairman of the planning committee has to be impartial.' He seemed pleased with that argument and stood a little taller. 'But now, if there's nothing else—'

'Those houses will be very expensive. Beyond the reach of most people. How does that help the average person trying to get a foot on the property ladder? There is certainly no social housing included in the scheme. I know because I checked.'

'Look, I'm sorry, but I'm late for my first meeting.' He turned away and stepped towards his office door. Several people were standing in the reception area, Dawn noticed, staring out at Morgan.

'There is just one more thing.' Dawn allowed a lengthy pause. Morgan could have used it as an excuse to escape but something in Dawn's tone held him rooted to the spot, increasing her suspicions about his activities. 'It's about your friendship with George Markham.'

'What?!' All colour drained from Morgan's face. He glanced over his shoulder, as though seeking an escape route, but remained standing where he was, looking terrified. 'Who? I don't know what you're...'

'If that's the way you want to play it.' Dawn sighed, produced her phone and pulled up a picture of Morgan and Markham in that alleyway – the one that clearly showed something changing hands.

'Oh God!' Morgan clutched his head in his hands and then remained deathly silent in the middle of an otherwise noisy, vibrant town. He could have bluffed it out, Dawn knew, because it wasn't obviously an envelope, but thankfully, he hadn't looked closely enough to realise it.

Dawn indicated that John should stop filming. 'That coffee shop along the road.' She pointed, as though Morgan wouldn't know where it was. 'Meet me there in an hour. Just me. No cameras. Nothing on record. Don't contact Markham in the meantime. Just you and me having a little chat.' Dawn smiled and chucked Morgan under the chin, as though he was a child. 'You know you want to.'

'He will ring Markham, of course,' John said as they walked away.

'Oh, I'm sure he will. In fact, I'm counting on it.'

John chuckled. 'No point asking you what you're up to, I suppose. I know you won't tell me.'

'All in due course.' She smiled at her colleague. 'Thanks for coming out, John. I appreciate it.'

'All part of the service, ma'am.' He gave her a mock salute with the hand not holding his gear and sauntered off in the direction of his car.

With time to kill, Dawn wandered back to the coffee shop and invested another small fortune in a beverage and blueberry muffin. The place was only half-full now that the rush-hour crowd had dissipated. She found a quiet table at the back of the room that gave her a clear view of the street, and more especially of Morgan's office. If her quarry scarpered, or if Markham turned up, she would know.

Dawn took a bite of her muffin and sat back to think about Morgan's reaction, wondering what George had on him other than being aware of his tight financial situation. Perhaps that was enough, but her instincts told her it was more than that. None of her online sleuthing the previous night had thrown up any clues, but everyone had secrets, didn't they? Secrets that threatened to bring them to their knees. She knew better than most that it was true and that the passage of time didn't always lighten the load, making past errors of judgement easier to live with.

At first glance, Morgan seemed to be the squeaky-clean family man that he made himself out to be.

A little too squeaky clean.

A local councillor probably thought he was too far down the political food chain for anyone to take much of an interest in him and that his secret was safe. It very likely was since her research had failed to throw anything up. That being the case, she'd just have to persuade Morgan to 'fess up. She had her ways!

Dawn extracted her tablet from her bag and, taking a deep breath, she started delving. If George had been able to find Jago, then Dawn should be able to as well. She had often been tempted to do so but had resisted the urge to look for her son. She had forfeited the right to call herself his mother when she gave him up for adoption. She had salved her conscience by telling herself that if Jago wanted to know her then he should be the one to get in touch. It would have been easy enough for him to do it once he'd turned eighteen. She had waited for months, holding her breath, hoping for a call that didn't come and being forced finally to accept the brutal truth. He didn't want to know her.

What else could she have expected? She'd often wondered since then.

Markham had in some respects done her a favour. He'd forced her to face the issue, and she would now try to find Jago. Had Jago somehow found out who his father was? Had Markham told him, and what, if anything, had Jago done with that knowledge?

Finding her son wouldn't be easy because Dawn had no idea what name he went by. Presumably, he'd taken his adoptive parents' surname. Did he still go by Jago? Needles in haystacks sprang to mind as Dawn hit a brick wall each way she turned. Births, deaths and marriages were little or no help. All she could glean from that source was the number of baby boys born in the area on the same day as Jago.

'The adoption agency it will have to be,' she muttered beneath her breath.

She just wanted to know what name he went by, nothing more. Well, actually a lot more but that didn't necessarily mean that she'd make contact. It would stir up a whole can of worms. Jago probably resented her, which was understandable. Equally understandably, if he didn't already know who his biological father was, it would likely be one of the first questions he'd asked her. She thought of Callie and shook her head decisively. That was one secret she would never reveal.

A squeal of tyres and a car sounding its horn for a protracted moment immediately outside the café drew her attention. The driver was now leaning out the window, berating someone who'd walked across the road, directly in front of him, forcing him to slam on the brakes. That person apologised and scurried towards the café.

It was Morgan.

'I hope you teach your children better road-safety techniques than that,' Dawn said when Morgan came up to her table and loomed over her, resentment oozing from his stance. There was sweat peppering his brow and it wasn't a particularly warm day. Perhaps his near-death experience with the car was the reason for it, but somehow Dawn doubted it. He looked as though his legs wouldn't support his weight so Dawn took pity on him and pulled out a chair, which he almost fell into. His mouth opened and closed with no sound emerging. He then smacked his lips together, crossed his legs as he sat sideways on his chair, giving the impression that he was ready to bolt at any moment, arms folded defensively across his chest.

'What can I get you?' she asked, not unkindly.

Whatever Morgan had gotten himself into, Dawn's experience told her that he was in over his head and close to breaking point. He asked for tea, and she went to the counter to get it for him.

'Now,' she said, returning to the table with tea for him and another coffee for her. 'Why don't you tell me what's going on?'

'I can't.' He shook his head, looking defeated yet defiant. 'You don't have any proof that I've abused my position and if you try to go public with what you think you know then I'll sue.' His threat sounded hollow, and he probably realised it. He was not, Dawn sensed, a strong man but one who'd been manipulated by an ambitious wife and father-in-law.

'Oh, Morgan.' Dawn sighed and shook her head. 'If I had a fiver for every time someone on the take has said that to me… What is it?' she asked, when he puffed out his chest and he looked on the verge of denying it. 'Don't you think we journalists do our homework?'

When he remained stubbornly silent, staring into his tea like the solution to his problems lurked somewhere in its milky depths, Dawn took the initiative.

'Let's save time by me telling you what I know about your situation.' Dawn cleared her throat. 'You have a large house that's mortgaged to the hilt, two kids at private school and the fees are crippling you, especially now that you'll have to pay tax on them. Your wife only plays at having a career. Your own work is commission based, and the economy has caused the commissions to dry up recently…' Dawn had made the last bits up but when he didn't protest, she knew she'd hit the nail on the head. 'Your wife's family mix with the elite and, I'm guessing here, have aspirations to see you rise up in the political world.'

His head jerked up. 'You're good at what you do,' he admitted grudgingly.

'So tell me,' she said quietly.

'You've got most of it right.' He tapped the fingers of one hand on the table's surface, staring off into the distance. 'My wife doesn't understand the meaning of economy. She's never had to. A spoiled childhood doesn't come close to describing her early years. Whatever Felicity wanted, Felicity got.'

'How did you meet?'

'What's someone from her background doing with the likes of me is, I think, the question you really wanted to ask?'

'Perhaps it's the one you want an answer to yourself.'

He shrugged. His momentary defiance evaporating. 'We met at uni. I worked, she partied. She was fun and I was captivated. We had a drunken fumble one night and... well, she fell pregnant. There was never any question of us not marrying. The Comptons do not have children out of wedlock,' he said, mimicking a voice that likely belonged to his father-in-law.

'Blimey. You've found yourself between a rock and a hard place, haven't you?'

Another shrug. 'I love my kids, so something good came out of this mess.'

'You live separate lives?'

'Pretty much. Felicity won't do anything to upset her father, which is why she stays, I often think. All the time she plays her part, she lives the life she wants, except for having me in it. Her parents put down a hefty deposit on our house, but I've had to remortgage twice now to keep our heads above water. I've tried to tell her that, but she still spends money like water.' He threw back his head and closed his eyes. He looked less frightened now and seemed relieved to find a receptive audience as he articulated his woes. '"Go to Daddy" is her response to everything, but how can I? My pride is all I have left.' He snorted. 'Or was.'

Dawn felt almost sorry for him. 'You're don't really want to get into the political life, do you?'

'I thought I did and that I could do some good, but just a taste of local politics has put me right off. All we seem to do is squabble about inconsequential things and stab one another in the back. My kids are better behaved.'

'But you can't tell your father-in-law to take a hike?'

'Hell, no! That would be the end of my marriage. If Felicity had to choose between me and her daddy then she and the kids would be gone and I would be painted as the bad guy. Trying to see the kids would be futile. Felicity's father knows how to bear a grudge. I would be blamed if the marriage failed and would probably find it hard to get gainful employment in this town.'

Dawn wondered if it would be such a bad thing if the marriage did end. As a father, he still had parental rights. Anyway, who was she to judge, given the mess she'd made of her own personal life?

'So,' she said, forcing her sympathy back into its box, 'tell me about Markham. How did you get involved with him?'

'He approached me in my local pub. I dunno why… well, I do now but hindsight is fucking irritating! We got into conversation. He knew a hell of a lot about me which, at the time, I didn't find suspicious, idiot that I am. Felicity always says I'm far too trusting and need to toughen up if I want to get anywhere in the political world. Anyway, we got onto local politics, which is what always seems to happen when people realise that I'm a councillor. I mean, I go to the pub to unwind. Would they start telling a doctor all their ailments when he's off duty?'

He shrugged, not appearing to expect an answer, so Dawn let him run on, not wanting to break his thread.

'We got onto that planning application. I was very careful what I said at that point, even though he'd been plying me with what I now suspect were large gins. I'm a bit of a lightweight when it comes to the booze but that night, I was in no rush to get home. Felicity and I had had a row, and I knew it would continue until she had the last word the moment the kids were in bed. That was a situation I was willing to postpone indefinitely.'

'Go on,' Dawn said, watching his Adam's apple bobbing as he swallowed a mouthful of what now had to be lukewarm tea. He didn't appear to notice.

'What more is there to say?' Morgan shrugged, looking miserable. 'Off the record, you know the truth. The man had compelling reasons for wanting the development to go ahead.'

'What reasons?'

'He didn't say but I got the impression that he worked for the developers. Well, he must do, mustn't he? What other explanation can there be? Anyway, he was willing to pay handsomely to ensure that it was approved.' He appeared to realise just how frank he'd been and backtracked. 'Like I already said though, you have no definitive proof. My meeting with Markham might look suspicious, poor judgement or whatever, but you can't prove I did anything untoward.'

'I'm not interested in destroying your career.'

'Right.' There was heavy emphasis on the one word that implied Morgan didn't believe her.

'It's Markham I'm after,' she said, deciding upon transparency. 'He's got fingers in all sorts of dodgy pies, and I fully intend to bring him down.'

'Ha! Good luck with that one.' Morgan sent her a suspicious

look from beneath hooded eyes. 'Anyway, why would you? What's he done to you?'

'Let's just say that I've been on the receiving end of his toxicity. Someone has to stop him and I'm in a better position than most. The power of the press, and all that.'

'Well, I'm not proud of what I did, but that housing development would have got the go-ahead eventually. I simply sped matters up. Markham had the power to destroy my reputation, my image, my family life. Everything. I've given my all to that council and got fuck all other than grief in return, so why shouldn't I accept the odd reward?'

Dawn didn't want to get into a discussion about ethics. Besides, in her experience, politicians were amongst the sleaziest creatures on God's green earth. Even so, she got the impression that Morgan would ordinarily stick by his principles. It had to have been something more than the prospect of a decent payday that made him accept a bribe. But whatever that something was, Dawn knew he'd never tell.

Then something in the effeminate gesture he made reminded her of a picture she'd seen of Morgan online, posing outside a bar that she knew was a gay hangout. The pieces to fall into place, alleviating the need for him to make embarrassing confessions.

'You're a closet gay,' she said, widening her eyes as realisation dawned. 'And Markham's got evidence.'

7

Callie disliked Felicity Fraser on sight. She was the type of vain, self-assured woman who kept the spa profitable with their constant attempts at bodily perfection, but Callie could see from her expensive attire and the way she lorded it over her group of friends, who appeared to hang on her every word, that she was all style and no substance.

'You look amazing. We must be doing something right.' Callie plastered on a smile for the woman as she intercepted her in the entrance lobby and led her upstairs to her office. 'I'm so glad you could accept my invitation. It's ladies like you, natural leaders, who make this place what it is. Where you go, others will follow.'

'Well, I suppose I do have some influence over my group of friends. Goodness knows why but they all seem to crave my good opinion.'

'Which is why I asked you to brainstorm with me today. I would value your suggestions when it comes to moving forward. In my experience, a business that rests on its laurels tends to stagnate.'

'I'm so glad to have met you at last.' Felicity actually gushed the words, making Callie want to vomit. She hated sycophantic behaviour. 'I have a dozen friends who haven't been able to get membership here. I've told them how exclusive it is. I mean, no one wants to be a member of a club where just anyone can join, do they? I am so glad you've been clever enough to restrict the numbers.' She paused. 'Even so, my friends are exceptions to that rule. I don't suppose there's any chance...'

'If you give me their names, I will ensure they go to the top of the waiting list,' Callie replied, crossing her fingers behind her back.

That did the trick, just as Callie had known would be the case. 'That is so very kind of you. I will tell them. They'll be delighted.'

And you'll take the credit. 'One good turn deserves another.'

Angie, walking just behind Felicity, rolled her eyes at Callie as she joined them and overheard the exchange. Angie stifled a giggle, well aware of Callie's dislike of pretentious, entitled females. Since her spa was half-full of them, she chose to believe that she was cashing in on that dislike rather than encouraging it. Personally, she still hankered after her student days, sitting crosslegged on the floor, drinking cheap plonk and planning the next revolution. The good old days that hadn't seemed quite so good at the time. Everyone had to grow up at some point, Callie reasoned, and join the capitalist economy that every young generation felt duty bound to protest against.

Darren, at Callie's behest, was already in her office, standing beside the bar. He smiled at Felicity Fraser in that suggestive manner of his that never failed to capture its recipient's complete attention. Felicity, at first cooing at the view of the atrium below them, immediately transferred her attention to Darren and fixed him with a speculative look.

'You are acquainted with Darren, Felicity? I can call you Felicity?' Callie might as well have been speaking in Swahili for all the response she got from Felicity, who actually wet her lips with the tip of her tongue as she continued to look at Darren. 'He's my rock. This place would grind to a halt without him.'

'I can well imagine.'

'Can I get you something to drink, Mrs Fraser?' Darren asked, lowering his voice an octave or two. 'A smoothie, perhaps.'

'Oh no, thank you. Just some sparkling water. Raspberry, if you have it. So good for the complexion.' She patted her face self-consciously.

'We'd be a sorry excuse for a spa if we didn't have it. Natural mineral water, obviously, and completely sugar free.' Darren poured a glassful with a flourish. 'And as to your complexion,' he added, handing the glass to Felicity and brushing his fingers against hers, 'you have absolutely no need to worry on that score.'

'Why, thank you, kind sir. Now, Darren, tell me all about this wonderful office,' Felicity said, glancing at the array of screens.

Callie and Angie stood back, completely forgotten by their guest, happy to enjoy the show. And Darren, who's job description definitely didn't stretch to flirting with the clientele, went above and beyond with elan. He turned his head at one point and winked at Callie, clearly enjoying himself.

'She'll drop her knickers for him in a heartbeat,' Angie remarked *sotto voce*. 'So much for being the loyal wife and devoted mother she makes herself out to be whenever she gets her mug in the local press doing good works, which seems to happen with boring regularity.'

Felicity finally ran out of questions to ask Darren and recalled that Callie and Angie were also in the room.

'This is amazing,' she said, plonking herself down at one end of a sofa and glancing up at Darren, clearly expecting him to occupy it with her. But Darren had more than played his part and dutifully stood back at the bar, waiting to serve Callie and Angie, who both asked for coffee.

'You are so lucky to be able to consume caffeine,' Felicity said. 'I wouldn't dare. I'd not be fit to be seen if I made a habit out of it. It dries the complexion out at an alarming rate. But still, you're older than me so I suppose you don't really...'

Felicity finally appeared to realise just how crass she was being. Her face flushed and she closed her mouth.

'Well, anyway,' Callie said, thinking she ought to bring the meeting to order. There was an outside chance that Felicity would think about something other than Darren when it was over and would wonder why Callie hadn't sought her opinion on the running of the place. After all, that was supposed to be the reason for her presence in Callie's inner sanctum.

'Tell me how you manage to juggle being a wife and mother as well as holding down a successful online career and being on so many charitable committees,' Callie said. 'You must have help with the children.'

'Well yes, we have an au pair but she isn't much use. Barely speaks a word of English but what can you do? Help is so hard to come by nowadays and really, I fail to see why I should stifle my creativity and stay at home all day just because I have children.'

'Quite so,' Callie said dutifully.

'I wouldn't ask my husband to be bound to the kitchen stove which is just as well since he can barely boil an egg.' She gave a ridiculous little laugh, as though she'd said something remarkable.

'Don't you worry that your husband might be... well, tempted to stray with a young woman living beneath his roof?' Angie asked disingenuously.

'Why on earth would he?' Darren smiled at Felicity from his

position at the back of the room, causing her to blush like a schoolgirl.

'Trust me, Mrs Renfrew—'

'Oh, please call me Callie.'

'Callie then. No, let's just say that I have absolutely no concerns on that score.'

Really? Callie shot Angie a curious look.

'If a wife can't keep her husband happy and ensure that he feels no need to stray then she can't be much of a wife, can she?' Felicity covered her mouth with her hand. 'Oh, so sorry. I forgot for a moment. You're both currently single, aren't you.'

You vicious cow!

Callie listened with half an ear to Felicity's impractical and unnecessary suggestions for improvements to the spa.

'I gather your husband is a rising star in the local political scene,' Callie said, when Felicity finally ran out of suggestions that Darren was pretending to make a note of. 'Does he have ambitions for even greater things?'

'I so admire a person who selflessly wants to make the world a better place,' Angie added. She bit her lip as she spoke, and Callie knew she must be trying very hard not to laugh.

'Oh, Daddy is delighted with his progress.'

'You must get to meet a lot of local dignitaries,' Callie said. 'Do you know George Markham? He's an associate of my husband's.'

'Markham? Does he belong to the golf club?' She screwed up her eyes in an effort to recollect, them appeared to remember that the gesture would create wrinkles and immediately straightened her expression. 'I don't think I know the name, but if he's an influencer in the locality, then Daddy or Morgan will certainly know him.'

It was obvious that Felicity knew absolutely nothing about

her husband's association with George, which had been Callie's main reason for getting her here alone. Having no further use for her, she was obliged to endure her self-promoting babble for another fifteen minutes before getting rid of her.

'Phew!' Darren escorted her off the premises and returned to Callie's office, wiping imaginary perspiration from his brow. 'Can I apply for danger money?'

'Thanks, Darren.' Callie smiled at him. 'You're a star. But anyway, guys, what did you make of her performance?'

'Other than disliking her intently,' Angie replied promptly, 'I'd say there's little love lost in her marriage, and I'd also advise Darren to make sure he never encounters her here at the spa without protection.'

They all laughed.

'I'm a big boy,' Darren assured them, seating himself across from the ladies and looking totally unfazed by Felicity's obvious interest in him.

'She'll be dining out on the fact that you asked for her help for weeks, Cal,' Angie warned.

'Yeah, but at least we're now aware that she doesn't know George so however her not-so-dear husband got involved with him, it wasn't through social circles.'

'What do you want me to do?' Darren asked.

'Not much you can do as things stand.' Callie sighed. 'We'll just have to hope that Dawn has more success doorstepping her husband.'

'Well, if anyone can get to the truth, it'll be Dawn,' Angie said. 'You know what she's like when she's on the trail of a story. She'd give a Rottweiler a run for its money.'

'Let's hope she gets some dirt on George that we can actually use.' Callie threw her head back and closed her eyes. 'Only six days left before he returns, demanding to use my rooms.'

'I've put feelers out amongst a few contacts,' Darren said. 'If we can find out what Gavin's next big project was supposed to be then we'll be halfway towards playing him at his own game.'

* * *

Morgan looked totally defeated. 'You knew all along,' he said, glowering at Dawn. 'I don't know how you found out. Did you get me here to gloat, or to try and put the squeeze on me? Well, you're too late for that. Someone else beat you to it. You were just stringing me along with all that "I'm-on-your-side" bullshit.'

'Actually, I didn't have a clue.' Dawn smiled at the man, liking him almost. 'I get the impression that you're not the sort that would easily accept a bribe. You *do* want to try and do what's right for the people of Brighton. I know how Markham operates and so it wasn't hard to decide that he *had* to have something on you that compelled you to dance to his tune. Then... well, something about your reaction caused all the pieces to fall into place.'

He shook his head. 'I thought that I'd been so careful.'

'Does Felicity know?'

'Yeah, and she doesn't care, just so long as Daddy doesn't find out. He's a card-carrying homophobic *and* still gives her a generous monthly allowance, even though she's an adult and married. You can imagine how that makes me feel.'

'Perhaps your father-in-law lives in the wrong town then,' Dawn replied, 'given that Brighton has such a thriving gay community.'

'He's the type that sees what he wants to see and mixes only with like-minded people.'

'You don't like him much, do you?'

Morgan shrugged. 'What's to like? He's a control freak who

uses his money and position of influence to get what he wants. Apart from anything else, he's a local magistrate.'

'He sounds like a bundle of fun.'

Morgan rolled his eyes. 'You have *no* idea!'

'Well anyway, how did Markham get onto you? And why you?'

'How do people who want something badly enough do anything?' He shrugged. 'I guess as chair of the planning committee, I was a prime target, given that the development in question was so controversial. I would have voted against it, given freedom of choice, by the way.' He let out a long breath. 'Markham followed me to a gay bar, one of the few places in town where I can let my hair down and be myself. What happens in that bar stays in that bar. That's the cast-iron rule. Most of the men there have careers. Some, like me, are married and haven't come out so the rule is to stay tight-lipped about anything we learn about the guys we meet.'

Dawn could see that frequenting such a place, no matter how well regulated, would make Morgan a prime target for people with other agendas but it didn't seem worth pointing the fact out now that the damage had been done.

'Isn't that a bit old hat? Being worried about coming out, I mean. Same-sex relationships are commonplace nowadays and no one bats an eyelid.'

'Ha! If you say so.' Morgan sent her a scathing look and Dawn knew she was seeing glimpses of the real man beneath the face he ordinarily put on to... well, face the world. He'd got the pretence down pat, Dawn conceded. No one would guess his secret unless, like her, they studied human reactions for a living. Besides, most people were too wrapped up with their own problems to care about anyone else's proclivities. She sensed too that he felt the relief of a burden shared and wished for a moment that she could follow his example. 'Anyway, people's sexuality is their own business. I fail to see why they should admit to being gay if they'd prefer not to.'

'I couldn't agree more.' Dawn gave his hand a reassuring pat. Morgan seemed surprised by the gesture but not unhappy about it. 'I assume Markham has photographic evidence of your preferences.'

'He does but he promised to destroy those pics if I did as he asked. I called his bluff and told him to do his worst but we both knew the revelation would destroy me. He mentioned Compton's name and I guess my face told its own story.'

'You held out for cash?'

'I did and he agreed without hesitation. Ten grand. Half upfront. It got me out of a severe jam, I don't mind telling you. Without it, I would have had to go to daddy dearest and undergone a severe grilling.' He snorted. 'I should have held out for more.'

'Didn't your conscience bother you?'

'It bothered me a lot.' He waggled a hand from side to side. 'At first. But what choice did I have? Besides, I might only be involved with politics at a local level, but that's been enough to give me glimpses of all the underhand bargaining that goes on. The political infighting, the backstabbing. Most of the councillors are in it for themselves, not to serve the community, so I thought why the fuck not?'

Dawn fiddled with a teaspoon as she mulled over what she'd just learned. 'It's a bit unrealistic to suppose that Markham will destroy the pictures he has of you. He could release them at any time, and you'd be screwed. In every sense of the word.' She held up a hand. 'Sorry. That was crass and unnecessary.'

'Don't you think I realise what a hold he has over me!' He shouted the words but then lowered his voice when several people looked up from their phones and sent him curious glances. 'But he had me boxed into a corner.'

'Didn't you ask him for proof... sorry.' Dawn held up a hand once again. 'Stupid question. There's no sure way of knowing that a digital picture has been permanently deleted.'

'Exactly, but he tells me that ordinarily local politics play no part in his business dealings, and I'm supposed to take his word for that. But still, all the time he might need me in the future, I guess it's not in his interests to expose my secret.' Morgan looked thoroughly dejected as he took his turn to fiddle with the table settings. 'Anyway, I don't have any other choice than to believe it.'

'Why do you carry on?' Dawn asked into the ensuing silence, leaning an elbow on the table and resting the side of her face on her splayed hand, watching him with growing sympathy.

'What do you mean?'

'Well, you're in what sounds like a loveless marriage that's ruled by your father-in-law. You're in local politics because he wants you to be. And he has greater things in mind for you, without having bothered to ask you how you feel about allowing him to live his own dream vicariously.'

Morgan nodded. 'You're very perceptive.'

'I'm guessing that he wanted a son to go into Parliament.' Dawn's research had thrown up the fact that Felicity was an only child. 'He's old school and it doesn't seem to have occurred to him that his daughter could just as easily have pursued that route and perhaps even made a success of it.'

'You're not wrong. Along with everything else, he's a misogynist, at least insofar as he doesn't think women have the brain power to make good politicians.' Morgan flashed the suggestion of a smile.

'So, my question stands: why not tell him to take a hike?'

Morgan laughed properly this time, apparently relaxed now

in her company. 'Felicity would have blue fit if her main source of income came to an end. And it would. If I didn't continue to toe the family line than Compton would cut her off until she came to her senses and went running back to him.'

'You could divorce her and go your own way.'

Morgan shook his head. 'The children,' he said. 'They're the one good thing to have come out of this mess and I love them unconditionally. Far more than Felicity does, which is ironic, when you think about it.'

'Why ironic? I know that a woman's maternal instinct is supposed to override all other considerations, but it doesn't always work that way.'

Dawn spoke from bitter experience. If she could have her time over, she liked to think that she would stand her ground and refuse to give Jago up. Since giving birth to him, not one day had passed without her regretting the way she'd acted, believing that Gavin would make good on his promise, leave Callie and be with her, if only she wasn't burdened with a child.

How selfish! How naïve she'd been. Dawn inwardly winced at the memory. Gavin had walked away anyway without a backward glance, leaving Dawn completely alone and with a lifetime of regrets.

'Ironic,' he said, fixing her with a direct look, 'because I'm not either of the children's biological father.'

8

Dawn gaped at Morgan. 'I beg your pardon. I thought you said that...'

'I know what I said.' Morgan ran a hand through his hair. 'God knows why I'm telling you all this. You're a reporter: the last person I ought to be revealing my dirty secrets to. But well, I dunno, you're easy to talk to, I guess. Perhaps I unconsciously want you to blow the whistle and make decisions that I'm too weak to make for myself.'

'Tell me why you're so sure that the kids aren't yours.'

'Simple. Felicity and I have never had full sex. Or any sex at all, come to that.'

'But you said that a drunken fumble resulted in her falling pregnant.'

'What I neglected to say is that we were at a student party. I'm sure you remember how wild they get. We were high and drunk – Larry, the guy I was chatting with, and me, that is. Felicity had her eye on Larry, but he hadn't returned her interest, which is the surest way, although he didn't realise it, to garner her attention. She found us lying on a bed together, smoking weed. She jumped into the middle of us and things went from there. I was keen to get my end away but well... I know now that I wasn't capable.'

'I still don't get it.' Dawn's expression probably reflected her confusion. 'If you both knew the child couldn't be yours, why did you let yourself get boxed in?'

'Like I say, Felicity and I were at the same uni. She came to me a few weeks after that party and told me of her predicament. I suggested an abortion, but she was having none of it. I was president of the student union and a leading light in the uni's political debating society. I was, like most students, ideological, ready to put the world to rights and although I didn't know it, perfect fodder for Felicity's ambitions.'

'A way to satisfy her father's ambitions, more like it.'

'Precisely. He had higher aspirations for his only child than a comparative nobody of my stature but if she was pregnant... well, she wouldn't have to dance to his tune. And she hasn't had to. Our marriage is conducted on her terms. I'm very much a supporting act, trotted out at appropriate times in a show of respectability.' Morgan's expression reflected his disgust at himself for playing along.

'I see.'

'We agreed to be discreet and lead separate lives without her father ever finding out, which is how she got pregnant the second time. Nothing to do with me. Even so, we agreed that I would be her children's father in all the ways that mattered. She wouldn't ask me how I occupied my spare time, and I wouldn't question her about her various liaisons.'

'But you knew you were gay, so why go through with it?'

'I've often asked myself the same question.' He rubbed his chin, implying that he hadn't come up with any answers that made sense. Dawn could empathise. It was always easier to suggest solutions to a situation that one wasn't personally involved with. 'Having to admit to myself that I'm weak-willed, I guess, amongst other things.'

'It's easy to be wise after the event,' she said with feeling.

'Yeah, if I had my time over… but then youth is wasted on the young.' Morgan stretched his arms above his head and yawned expansively. 'My problem, leaving aside the kids and the fact that they'd never see their dad again if I divorced Felicity, is that she is very happy with our situation. She's told me more than once that if I try to leave her then she'd force a paternity test. She'd do it too. She's like her dad in that regard. Everything has to be on her terms. And whilst I don't care about myself any more, I do care about the children, and she knows it.'

'Kids are resilient.'

'You're missing the point. I take far more interest in them than she does. They're just a fashion accessory as far as she's concerned. She trots them out when it suits her or uses them as an excuse if she doesn't want to do something. The rest of the time, she pretty much ignores them and leaves them to the au pair. And to me. They'd be lost without one parent taking an interest in their activities and she knows it.' He shrugged. 'So until they get older, I'm stuck.'

Morgan's frank admission threw up a dozen questions, the most obvious of which was why Felicity would settle for the status quo. Perhaps she enjoyed the security of a marriage while she played the field. More exciting that way, presumably, but Dawn didn't feel she could ask. She had already done more probing than she'd intended into Morgan's private life and now found herself both liking the guy and feeling sorry for his situation. It would be easy to blame him for being weak-willed, but you probably had to have been there.

'Okay,' he said. 'Your turn. What's your interest in Markham?'

Dawn hesitated. She had known he'd ask eventually and still

wasn't sure how much to tell him. She was the one accustomed to asking questions, not answering them. Callie didn't know why Markham was pressurising her to persuade Callie to let him use her private rooms. She wouldn't do it, didn't want to do it, but also had no choice. If Callie found out about her long-term affair with Gavin, she would be devastated. The thought of Jago's existence also being revealed simply didn't bear thinking about. Their friendship would never survive the feelings of betrayal that Callie would have every right to embrace.

Dawn forced herself to concentrate on the here and now, leaving the past where it belonged, hoping it would remain there. Interesting though Morgan's revelations had been, they hadn't got her any further forward in her quest to discover why Markham was so keen to use Callie's spa for his meetings. If Morgan knew anything else about Markham activities, he was unlikely to tell her unless she gave him something in return. She sensed that despite his love for his kids, he was teetering on the brink of a meltdown and might simply walk away from his family life so that he could be himself. That being the case, her assurance that she would keep his secret probably wouldn't be enough to satisfy him.

'You're familiar with the Frenchurch Falls Spa?'

He snorted. 'I'm familiar with its charges. Felicity's a member.'

'Its owner is Callie Renfrew.'

'Wife of the gangster.'

Dawn chuckled. 'Do people still use that term?'

Morgan shrugged. 'If the cap fits…'

'Whatever Callie's husband might or might not be, Callie herself is as pure as the driven.'

'Yeah, right!'

'She's a close friend of mine.'

'Sorry!' He held up a hand in apology.

'Take it from me, she's as honest as the day's long.' *More or less.* 'Markham is one of Gavin Renfrew's associates, for want of a better word.'

'In that case, I retract my apology for calling Renfrew a gangster.'

Dawn smiled, resenting the fact that despite the way Gavin had treated her, she still wanted to spring to his defence. She was truly pathetic!

'Gavin's on the missing list. Has been for several months and the sharks are moving in on his territory.'

'And that should concern me because...'

'Because Markham's one such shark. He wants to use Callie's spa to conduct private meetings with certain individuals. Individuals whom she'd much prefer not to give houseroom to.'

'I see.' Morgan rubbed his chin. 'I think.'

'It's purely coincidence that I discovered your connection to him. I was covering that council meeting for Sussex News and saw George there. I couldn't think what interest he'd have in the proceedings and so I followed him when he left the town hall and came across him with you in that alleyway.' She leaned forward. 'Now it seems to me that we have a common interest. Callie wants to find out why the use of her spa is so essential to Markham. She wants to sell the business, but it needs to be squeaky clean before she can think about doing so. Besides, she dislikes being manipulated.'

Morgan nodded. 'Yeah, I can relate to that.'

'So, if we can find out who asked him to intercede with that planning application, it might give us a starting point.' Dawn smiled at the younger man. 'Do you have any idea who, and why they'd turned to Markham for help?'

'Well, the developers seem like the obvious candidate.'

'Dorchester Consultants. Yeah, that's what I thought but I

haven't been in contact with them. Don't want to endanger you or anyone else by showing our hand until we know precisely who we're dealing with.'

'Can't you watch Dorchester's offices and see if Markham goes there?' Morgan asked.

'Why would he? He's served his purpose and probably earned a good payday. They will have no further use for him I don't suppose but I would like to know how he came to their attention.'

'You're a journalist, so I guess you always want answers.'

'Delving into that partnership is on my to-do list but I still would love to know why Markham picked on you to swing the vote for him. You have a reputation for playing by the book so...'

'Well, obviously, he had those incriminating pictures.'

'Only because he followed you. I don't think he caught you accidentally, unless he's gay himself and went there for reasons of his own, which I don't believe for a moment.' Dawn tapped her fingers. 'No, your paths must have crossed at some point. Try and think where you might have seen him.'

Morgan shook his head. 'I have done, time and time again, but I'm coming up blank. I go to all sorts of public places both as a councillor and in my day job.'

'Tell you what, Morgan. Do you think you can make some time to call at the spa and meet with Callie? If we put our heads together, it's possible that we'll come up with a way to get the better of Markham.'

'I'm not sure.' Morgan looked as uncertain as he sounded, giving Dawn a clearer idea of how he'd come to be Compton's poodle. But she also sensed a dormant part of him that was slowly coming to life as he dithered about fighting back. 'Markham won't come after me again. Better to let things rest.'

Dawn wanted to tell him to man up. Instead, she remained silent and subjected him to the type of cool appraisal that implied she found his attitude wanting. 'Keep telling yourself that. We both know it isn't true and that being obliged to dance to his tune will eat away at you. It's bad enough that you're living your father-in-law's dream vicariously. Do you really need a nasty piece of work like Markham pulling your strings as well?'

'You're right,' he said softly after a further prolonged pause, appearing to sit a little straighter in his chair, as though Dawn had given him the push he hadn't consciously realised he'd been waiting for. 'Come on then, before I change my mind.'

'I thought you said you had a full day's appointments?'

He lifted one brow. 'Did I? Anyway, you're right about Markham. He has got me where he wants me and what he wants me to do now affects your friend, Mrs Renfrew.'

'What is it?'

'I'll tell you both at the same time.'

Dawn smiled at him, rather liking the stronger-willed man emerging from the chrysalis of his father-in-law's ambitions. 'I'll call Callie and let her know we're on our way.'

* * *

Darren was just about to leave Callie's office when her phone rang.

'It's Dawn,' she said, checking the screen and taking the call. Aware of Darren loitering, she put the call on speaker so that he and Angie were both kept in the loop. 'Hi, babe, what's happening?'

'I'm with Morgan Fraser. We'd like to come over, if that's okay. He has stuff to tell you that you're gonna want to hear.'

Callie shot Angie a surprised look, although why she should be so surprised when she knew just how persuasive and tenacious Dawn could be, especially with the explosive material she held against Fraser, she could not have said. 'Excellent timing,' she said. 'Felicity has just gone bustling off to track some minor celebrity down to interview for her latest podcast. The coast is clear.'

'Okay, be there in a bit.'

'Well,' Angie said when Callie hung up. 'I shall be interested to see what we make of Felicity's husband. He can't be as pretentious as her, surely?'

Callie laughed. 'I wouldn't be against it.'

'You want me to hang around?' Darren asked.

'He might be grateful for a little non-judgemental male support, given that he's about to be interrogated by three assertive females,' Callie replied.

'Only two, I'm afraid,' Angie replied, genuine regret in her tone. 'I have a meeting with the dreaded auditors to prepare for.'

'Ah yes.' Callie smiled at her friend. 'Need to be ready for the Gestapo. Don't worry, we'll update you later. Go get 'em!'

'I'll get on too,' Darren said, 'and rejoin you when your visitors arrive, if that's okay.'

'Sure.'

Callie watched Darren go, wondering what had happened to create a hiatus in their friendship. She had kept him at arm's length all the time Gavin had been on the scene, their relationship friendly but businesslike, never crossing boundaries.

Just about every boundary known to man and a few that weren't had been crossed while they'd tracked down Angie's errant husband and put an end to O'Keefe's stranglehold over the local criminal fraternity. Only Darren knew what had really happened to O'Keefe and that he'd died at Callie's hand. He'd seemed impressed by her bravery at the time. She'd wanted to tell him that bravery played no part in actions driven by instinct and a strong will to survive. If she'd had time to think about it, her courage would have failed her. Unlike her husband, violence did not come naturally to her.

She and Darren had been seen in public several times during that period – once at a charity auction and again when he'd invited her out to dinner. She hadn't thought of it as a date but perhaps he had, and the ensuing gossip had scared him off. After all, he was not only an employee but also a good fifteen years younger than her. No one dated Gavin Renfrew's wife and got away with it, even if he had played fast and loose with half the female population of Brighton.

Whatever the reason, Darren's manner was once again strictly professional which was probably just as well. Callie didn't need a strong man with broad shoulders to lean on. She'd learned to fend for herself, put her own interests first, and depend on no one else's judgement other than her own during the course of a long marriage to a man who lived by no one's rules other than his own.

But despite all that, Darren's attitude hurt more than it should.

'Get a grip!' she muttered, annoyed with herself.

Callie forced herself to concentrate on the mountain of work awaiting her attention, but the threat posed by Markham was at the forefront of her thoughts, creating mayhem with her concentration. She was relieved when she heard voices from Darren's office that implied Dawn's arrival. The door to her own office opened and Dawn burst through it, a bundle of restless energy as always.

'Hey!' Dawn gave Callie a brief hug but appeared distracted and didn't meet her gaze. 'Let me make the introductions.'

Callie studied Fraser as she did so. Her initial impression wasn't favourable. He seemed unsure of himself, and his handshake was weak. She could easily imagine his wife manipulating him and wondered about the desire of such a unforthright individual to put himself forward in local political dogfights.

'Do sit down, Mr Fraser,' she said, indicating the comfortable chairs in front of the long windows. 'Would you like anything to drink?'

He asked for coffee and Darren did the honours for all of them.

'I hope you don't mind Darren sitting in,' Callie said once they had their beverages in front of them. She sat across from her visitor and crossed her long legs at the ankle. 'There's nothing you could say to me privately that you can't say in front of him.'

Fraser shrugged. 'Whatever,' he replied, rather like a sullen teenager.

'Okay,' Dawn said, smiling at the councillor, who looked as though he now regretted coming to see Callie. 'Tell Callie what you told me about George Markham's hold over you. Don't worry,' she added, touching Fraser's arm. 'There will be no judgement here.'

'We know you took a backhander from him,' Callie said, when Fraser remained silent. 'But as things stand, we have no intention of dropping you in it.'

'Oh, what the fuck!' Fraser threw up the hand holding his coffee. He splashed hot liquid over his wrist but didn't seem to realise. 'Where to start?'

Slowly, and in disjointed bursts, Fraser spilled the beans. Callie and Darren exchanged the occasional glance when he revealed the true nature of his family life and the fact that he hadn't fathered either of his kids. That being the case, Callie wasn't surprised when he admitted to his true sexual predilections. She felt rather sorry for a guy who'd boxed himself into a corner and was now at the mercy of an ambitious father-in-law and avaricious wife, unable to be himself.

'You can't leave because you love your kids,' Callie said, guessing the truth.

'Right.' Fraser had finished his coffee and now ran a hand abstractedly through his hair. 'If the truth ever comes to light then Felicity's dad will publicly disown me, even though it was Felicity who tricked me into marriage in the first place.'

'Surely you must have known that you couldn't have gotten her pregnant?' Darren made his first contribution to the conversation.

'I was wasted and still denying my sexuality at the time. I had a very hazy recollection of events that evening and wanted to believe that I'd managed to complete the act with a woman. Besides, why would Felicity have lied about it?' He waved his hands, something he seemed to do a lot when agitated. 'Perhaps because the guy who did the deed was a druggie, a total loser,' he added, answering his own question. 'He got sent down not long after that night and I never saw him again. But even if he'd hung around and accepted responsibility for the child, Daddy would not have approved.'

'Whereas you were a local guy with good prospects.' *And malleable*, Callie thought but did not add.

'Yep, I guess.'

'So, you pushed that planning application through, against a mountain of objections, and thought that would be the end of your dealings with Markham.'

'I know what you must be thinking.'

Undoubtedly, probably because Callie's expression implied that he'd been excessively naïve. 'You put your family's interests first,' she said. 'No one can blame you for that, but even so...'

'Yeah, I know, blackmailers never walk away but... well, I knew the scheme would be accepted eventually and I really needed that backhander. Everyone else seems to be on the take.

Having ethics isn't all it's cracked up to be, so I thought, what the hell!'

'Dorchester Consultants are the developers' local representatives. Fairclough Investments, based in Malaysia, are the actual guys pulling their strings,' Darren said. 'Presumably, someone from Dorchester recruited Markham to push the scheme through planning by whatever means necessary.'

Morgan shrugged. 'I have absolutely no idea.'

'Someone who knew Markham would do anything for a decent payday,' Callie added. 'But then his name is linked locally with Gavin's so it wouldn't be too hard to reach that conclusion.'

'I'm on it,' Dawn said.

'So...' Callie leaned back in her chair. 'What else? There's something, I can tell. Markham wants something else from you, doesn't he?'

Morgan nodded, looking miserable. 'He wants me to make sure your application to turn the land you just purchased into a golf course is denied,' he said.

9

Callie was rendered temporarily speechless.

'Why?' Darren asked. 'What possible reason could he have?'

Morgan shrugged. 'You're asking the wrong person.' He glanced at Dawn. 'That's what he and I were having such a heated debate about in that alleyway. He'd promised me that he wouldn't bother me again if I pushed the planning application through. Obviously, I feared that he would but what choice did I have? So I did as I was told and hoped he'd keep his word.'

'I hear you,' Dawn said softly, clearly feeling sympathy for the guy's situation.

'But, as it turns out, he couldn't wait to push the knife in. Didn't even give me any breathing space.'

'But also gave you a lot more cash upfront,' Callie said, an edge to her voice.

'Yeah, he did.' Morgan sat a little straighter. 'And I took it too. What else could I do?' He spread his hands in a supplicating gesture. 'He had me well and truly by the short and curlies. Not only could he prove that I'd accepted a bribe to push that planning application through, but he also knew about my private life and wouldn't have hesitated to ruin my reputation.'

'He could only destroy you by revealing his own part in the bribing,' Darren pointed out. 'He committed a criminal offence.'

'So did I. And like I say, he could not only ruin my political life, such as it is, but my family life too by revealing aspects of my sex life that I'd much prefer to keep private, which is why I was forced to take a bribe in the first place.'

'Did he give you any indication as to why he doesn't want me to have a golf course?' Callie asked.

'Nah, course not, and I didn't ask. He wouldn't have told me even if I had.'

'He might have wanted to use the refusal as a stick to hold over you, Callie,' Darren said. 'Cooperate, let me use your meeting rooms when I need them and your application will go through.'

Callie scowled. 'Seems a bit extreme.'

'Depends who he wants to meet with and why it has to be here,' Dawn remarked.

'I guess it does,' Callie replied. 'But more to the point, my application for change of use on the land is due before the planning committee any time now.'

'Next week,' Morgan said.

'And he's given me a week to make up my mind about giving him free access to this place,' Callie said, 'which is what granting him use of those rooms would amount to. The general membership doesn't ever step foot in them. I use them for private functions and, more to the point, Gavin used them for... well, for whatever he needed to speak to people about in complete confidentiality.'

'And his cohorts will know that,' Darren said. 'So will Markham's, which means whatever he has in mind, he wants to convince the people he meets with that he's doing so with Gavin's prior knowledge and approval.'

'He's trying to take over Gavin's territory,' Dawn said, tapping her fingers against the arm of her chair. 'And has to move quickly. We all know the various factions are gathering, threatening a turf war as they try to snatch control, what with both Gavin and O'Keefe being on the missing list.'

'Yeah, it looks that way.' Callie felt miserable, a little afraid and a lot out of her depth. 'But what to do about it?'

'That's something we need to think about.' Darren sent Fraser a sideways look and Callie got the message. It wouldn't be safe to discuss their plans in front of a man who could be so easily bought.

'Thanks for coming in, Mr Fraser, and for your candid revelations.' Callie stood to indicate that the interview was at an end and offered him her hand. 'Leave me a number that I can contact you on. We need to keep in touch.'

'What do you want me to do about your golf course?' he asked.

'Absolutely nothing. I intend to withdraw the application. For now. And that will resolve your problem.'

'Don't give Markham his dosh back,' Dawn advised, smiling at Fraser, who looked now as though the weight of the world had been lifted from his shoulders. 'You can't be held responsible for the application's withdrawal.'

Fraser took Callie's hand in a far firmer grip. 'Thanks,' he said.

'My pleasure. I don't like being manipulated any more than you do. There's no rush for the golf course. Besides, if I sell up, there won't be time to develop it. It will help to push the price up if I have permission but that's something we can discuss once we've neutralised the threat to us both posed by Markham.'

Darren left the room to show Morgan out, leaving Dawn and Callie on their own.

'Phew!' Callie wiped imaginary perspiration from her brow. 'The plot thickens.'

'And then some.'

Dawn found something to hold her interest in the picture on the wall behind Callie's head. Her friend was behaving very oddly but she did sometimes go off on a mental tangent when in pursuit of a hot story. And this story was potentially dynamite, at least insofar as the bribery of a local politician was concerned.

'What will you do about Fraser's backhander? Will you publicly expose him?'

'Damn, I wish I didn't have a conscience!' Both ladies laughed and the tension that Callie was probably imagining dissipated. 'My problem is that I like him and feel sorry for his situation. I mean, being gay nowadays is no big deal, but his wife and father-in-law will crush him if he dares to come out. She's selfish and enjoys the freedom that his predilections give her and he's homophobic. I don't think I can put him through all that.'

'It'll come out anyway sooner or later. These things usually do.'

'Yeah, perhaps, but it's not him I'm after. We're on a mission to find out what Markham's up to and don't need any distractions.'

'Another scoop bites the dust,' Callie said, sympathy in her tone. She knew how hard Dawn worked and that her position was under threat. This would be the saving of her and Callie admired her empathy in resisting the opportunity.

'Yeah, well, there's plenty more where this one came from. Probably.'

'You're too decent for your career choice. You need to toughen up. I feel sorry for Fraser too, but he did take a bribe with his eyes wide open.' Callie allowed a moment's reflection. 'I wonder if subconsciously, he wants his house of cards to come tumbling down but doesn't have the courage to operate the bulldozer himself. This way, the heavy lifting will be done for him.'

'Perhaps. Anyway, what are we doing to find out Markham's game?' Dawn asked.

'You've done your bit, babe. Leave it to Darren and me. This isn't your fight. You need to concentrate on getting your bosses to see the error of their thinking by giving them some kick-ass, controversial reports that get people talking. Do what you do best and leave us to chase the scumbags.'

'No, I want to help bring Markham to his knees.'

'You seem very keen to get involved and help me in my hour of need.' A slight crease troubled Callie's brow as she got up to hug Dawn. She, Angie and Callie had always been there for one another, but this time, Dawn's determination seemed almost manic. Perhaps a diversion from her career problems was just what she needed. 'You're a true friend.'

Dawn appeared to be embarrassed by an embrace that ordinarily she would have returned and struggled out of it. 'Yeah well, I won't have any qualms about exposing Markham, if we can get to the bottom of his latest scam.' Dawn sat a little straighter and adopted her serious TV face. 'The public have a right to know.'

They both laughed and once again, the tension that Callie felt with increasing regularity when Dawn was around fell away.

'Okay then.' Callie pressed the buzzer that brought Darren back. 'We need to decide how to go after Markham and get him off my back,' she told her assistant. 'Dawn is willing to put the might of the press behind our campaign.'

'Well then, he's dead meat!'

Callie couldn't help noticing that Darren fixed Dawn with the full-on, sexy smile that he used to bestow upon her but which she hadn't seen for a while. God forbid that he thought she'd been trying to encourage his personal interest in her. They were business colleagues and friends, but nothing more than that. She would have to find a way to ensure that he didn't think those particular goal posts had been moved.

'Okay, Darren,' she said briskly, 'so what has your sleuthing thrown up?'

* * *

Darren felt increasingly uncomfortable around a lady who happened to be his boss, but whose strength and determination he had come to admire in the months since her husband had gone missing. That situation had forced him to look at her in a very different light and brought out his protective instincts in spades.

Except Gavin wasn't missing, Darren reminded himself. He knew he was still alive and kicking because they spoke on a regular basis. Gavin had forced Darren into taking a position he didn't want to fill in order to keep an eye on his wife during Gavin's frequent absences and report back to Gavin at every turn. The rest of Darren's family were heavily involved in criminal enterprises, but Darren wanted no part in that world. His father was banged up, having committed crimes in Gavin's service. Gavin looked after Darren's mother financially, and Darren had known he would withdraw that support in a heartbeat if Darren didn't take the employment he was being offered.

He'd had no choice.

He knew that Gavin intended to return as soon as it was safe for him to do so. Safe from what, Darren had absolutely no idea. There was so much that he didn't know and he felt increasingly like a Judas for holding out on Callie when he saw her struggling to keep Gavin's various unsavoury contacts at bay.

What Callie didn't realise – one of the many things she didn't know – was that Gavin still kept an eye on his empire, which he ruled with a steadily weakening rod of iron. The longer he stayed away, the less effectual his reputation became, and Gavin knew it, which made it even harder for Darren to decide why he hadn't reappeared long since.

Gavin knew that Darren had taken his wife out to dinner and didn't like it one little bit. He had warned him off.

Very forcibly.

Talk about dog in the manger, Darren thought, silently seething. Gavin didn't care about leaving Callie in the mire to deal with the fallout from his various dodgy dealings with the sort of men it wasn't healthy to oppose. He'd done it more often than enough. But if another man looked at Callie twice then Gavin's revenge would be swift and brutal.

It was useless trying to convince Gavin that he didn't look upon Callie with romance in mind, even though it was true. Wasn't it? She was clever, sassy and didn't take shit from anyone. There was a lot to admire about the older woman. He knew what she'd done to O'Keefe and was full of respect for the way she'd reacted to the threat he'd posed. She hadn't fallen apart or resorted to counselling or any of that crap. She'd simply put it behind her and moved on. Whether she had nightmares, he couldn't have said. Nor was she likely to tell him even if he asked.

Darren had crossed a line by not telling Gavin when he asked what had become of his nemesis. He still wasn't sure why he'd kept shtum. He owed his family's comfort and his personal loyalty to Gavin and had faithfully reported Callie's every move to him up until that point. Gavin had indirectly been responsible for the pickle that Callie had become involved in, though and Darren found his casual neglect of his wife's wellbeing hard to forgive.

Gavin had really got his Y-fronts twisted when Darren told

him about George Markham's crude demands, but his partner's affrontery still hadn't brought Gavin scuttling back to defend his wife's corner. Of course it fucking hadn't! Gavin had been at the front of the queue when selfishness had been dished out. He hadn't explained Markham's reason for wanting use of the spa's private meeting rooms either, even though Darren was convinced he must know, or at least be in a position to make an educated guess. Before he'd taken off, Markham hadn't so much as sneezed without Gavin giving his permission.

'Just tell her to do it,' had been Gavin's casual advice, even though he knew Darren couldn't do that without revealing the fact that he was in contact with Gavin. And Gavin himself had warned Darren very forcibly not to say a word on that score. So, it seemed George was acting on Gavin's orders after all.

Even though he knew what a thug Markham was, it didn't seem to have occurred to Gavin that Callie would be on the receiving end of severe physical damage if she turned him down. Gavin might be old-fashioned enough to consider women and kids to be off limits, but Markham's conscience wouldn't be troubled if he felt compelled to give Callie a beating for being disrespectful.

So it was down to Darren to find a way to stop Markham in his tracks and to prevent Callie from doing anything rash, if that was even remotely possible. Darren chuckled to himself. Stopping a tidal wave would likely be easier.

'I've put feelers out,' he said, when he realised he'd been sitting in silent contemplation for a while and that both ladies were sending him quizzical looks. 'But none of my contacts have a clue what George is up to.' He shrugged. 'Sorry, but no one's heard a whisper, which in itself is a worry. The underworld could ordinarily give a sieve a run for its money when it comes to leaking stuff.'

'Must be something big then.' Callie looked stressed as she restlessly linked and then unlinked her fingers on the surface of her desk. 'Perhaps we could come at this from a different angle, given that Dawn's keen to help.'

'Whatever you need,' Dawn said promptly. 'Just name it.'

'Dorchester Consultants,' Darren replied, anticipating Callie's thoughts, which he appeared to do with increasing regularity. 'I've been looking into their management and one name stands out.' He paused, fixing Callie with a probing look that caused her cheeks to colour. 'Archie Taylor.'

Callie and Dawn exchanged a look.

'Doesn't mean anything to me,' Dawn said.

'I know the name.' Callie closed her eyes and threw her head back as she searched her memory banks. 'Gavin had dealings with him back in the day. He was a facilitator, if memory serves. Anything you want he can get. For a price, obviously.'

'Sounds about right,' Dawn said, a scathing edge to her voice. 'Gavin excels at facilitating.'

Callie and Darren both sent her curious looks.

'It's true and we all know it,' she said, shrugging defensively. 'Seems to me that he's dumped you right in it, Callie, but we're not allowed to tell it like it is. Well, I'm through pussyfooting around. The man's a jerk for treating you the way he does.' She folded her arms defiantly. 'There, I've said it. Someone needed to.'

'If you think I don't know that well enough then you really don't know me as well as you think you do.'

'Sorry, babe but sometimes...'

'Don't give it another thought.' Dawn's loyalty appeared to be off the chart today, but it was the first time Callie had realised that she disliked Gavin quite so much. Why? she wondered. 'Gavin's a piece of work and will soon be history, so let's concentrate on the business in hand.'

'Can you remember what precisely Taylor facilitated for Gavin?' Darren asked into the tense silence that was left in the wake of Dawn's outburst.

'Nope. I wouldn't have asked or been told if I had. But I do know that he wouldn't be averse to bending or even breaking the law to get what he wants so it doesn't surprise me that he latched onto George to get that planning application pushed through.' Callie paused. 'It sounds to me as though he's gone up in the world and had to prove himself, so he certainly wouldn't have let the inconvenience of a planning committee get in his way.'

'If Gavin worked with Taylor then George would have met him at some point, I dare say,' Darren said. 'That's one mystery solved.'

'Yeah.' Dawn nodded. 'To get something on poor old Morgan would have been child's play. George probably followed him to a gay bar and couldn't believe that he'd hit pay dirt so easily.'

'Do you think that Taylor's involved in whatever George wants to use my rooms for?' Callie addressed the question to Darren.

'I wouldn't bet against it,' Darren replied. 'If they're cooking up some scheme together then George probably offered to help Taylor with the planning application in return for… well, something. I did some digging on Taylor. He has a criminal record for GBH and demanding money with menaces. He served a year inside but that was more than ten years ago. He's obviously reinvented himself and somehow landed a position with Dorchester Consultants.'

'Which tells us all we need to know about their ethics.' Dawn sat forward, clearly sensing a story. 'They obviously didn't do their due diligence before putting such a man in a position of authority. Or then again, perhaps they did.'

'My people haven't been able to follow George,' Darren said, frustrated. 'He's too canny and can spot a tail at twenty paces with the wind in the wrong direction. But…' He grinned at the ladies and waited for them to join the dots.

'But,' Callie said, returning his smile, 'Archie Taylor doesn't know we're onto him.'

'Exactly.' Darren stood. 'I'll have him followed for a couple of days. If we can get some idea who he socialises with then perhaps we'll have a better idea of what George is up to. So, if there's nothing else, I'll get straight on it.'

'Yes, do that please, Darren, and thanks.'

'There is one other option available to us,' Darren said, pausing with his hand on the door to his office.

'Which is?' both ladies asked at the same time.

'You won't like it, but we could let George use the rooms once and see who turns up for his clandestine meeting.'

'Hmm.' Callie fiddled abstractedly with her mouse pad. 'I had considered that possibility but even if we recognise faces, we'll have no idea what they talk about. Those rooms are sound-proofed. Gavin insisted upon it.'

'Oh, I think that could be managed,' Darren said, grinning and waggling a hand from side to side.

'Very James Bond.' Dawn laughed at him. 'Bugs Are Us.'

Darren's grin widened. 'It's not as outlandish as it sounds. I know a man who knows a man…'

'Let's keep tabs on Taylor for a few days and see what that throws up,' Callie said. 'We'll resort to your suggestion, Darren, only if absolutely necessary. If I give in to George once, then I'll never get him off my back.'

'Point taken,' he replied, slipping quietly from the room.

No sooner had he returned to his desk than the phone he kept solely to communicate with Gavin vibrated in his pocket.

'What's the latest?' he asked. 'Has she agreed to let George use the meeting rooms?'

'She's digging her heels in.' *Why does it matter to you so much?* 'I've tried to persuade her...'

'Try fucking harder! She's getting above herself and needs to be slapped down.'

'I don't slap women.'

'I was talking metaphorically, you fucking moron. Just remember that what's being done for you and yours can just as easily be undone.'

'Don't threaten me.' Darren spoke quietly but with a hard edge to his voice. 'It's not helpful and doesn't achieve anything.'

'Sorry, son, it's all a bit stressful at the moment and I don't need to be worrying about Callie on top of everything else.'

You should have thought of that when you walked out on her over three months ago.

'Women can be emotional. Fuck it, they live on their emotions and don't think things through like we do.'

They don't run for the hills when the going gets tough either.

'I think it would help if she knew what Markham wants the rooms for.'

'It's none of her business. She just needs to do as she's told.'

'She's stubborn, but you don't need me to tell you that. If I push too hard, she reminds me in no uncertain terms that I'm the hired help. And dispensable. Can't help feeling that George wants to make it seem as though whatever he has in mind, he's doing it with your blessing, if you see what I mean.'

'Does he indeed.'

'Anything you'd thought about getting into before you took off that he might know about?' Darren asked, playing along. Gavin had already shown his hand and knew precisely what George was up to. It was obviously something big, which made it even harder to understand why Gavin continued to remain out of sight.

'Make something up, for fuck's sake! Something convincing. Do I have to do all the thinking? Callie listens to you.'

'Not always but I'll do my best.'

'Yeah, and don't forget who pays your wages.'

Callie does, you wanker, Darren thought when the line went dead. It was almost as though Gavin was trying too hard to prove to himself that he hadn't lost his edge. But by running away, that was precisely the message he gave out to his rivals and business associates.

Darren sat thinking for a long time after Gavin hung up, wondering yet again about George's reasons for using the spa's facilities and Gavin's determination to let him do so. Callie digging her heels in clearly hadn't crossed Gavin's mind. If Gavin was still around then it would have happened without recourse, but he'd blown his authority when he scarpered. It wasn't as if he could pick up the phone and tell Callie to do as he asked like a good girl. But it seemed he expected Darren to do something of that nature on his behalf, and didn't understand why the matter had become such a drama. He obviously didn't understand Callie nearly as well as he thought he did, despite their long years of marriage.

With a sigh, he picked up his regular phone and called a guy he trusted, asking him to arrange surveillance on Archie Taylor.

10

Dawn left the spa, her head spinning as she silently berated herself for allowing sentiment to overcome common sense. She knew that she'd overreacted, snapped at the constant references to Gavin, itching to spring to the defence of the defenceless. Callie had noticed her irrational behaviour and had looked at her askance.

Why now? she asked herself. She'd managed all these years to see Gavin and Callie together and not reveal the guilt that she bore over their clandestine relationship and its consequences. She sometimes thought that she deserved an Oscar for her performance, absolutely convinced that Gavin didn't realise she still carried a torch for him. How pathetic would she seem to him if he knew the truth?

Callie knew something was amiss with Dawn, but she didn't – couldn't possibly – suspect the truth. Dawn knew she was a rubbish friend. The aforementioned guilt which she'd previously kept firmly under lock and key now appeared determined to resurrect itself and remind her of the fact that friends, true friends, did not steal one another's husbands. It was no good telling herself that it took two to tango. She should never have responded to Gavin's flirtatious overtures and offers to kickstart her career for her, so the fault was all hers. She'd been too young to realise what she'd been getting herself into until it was impossible for her to back off. She was intoxicated by Gavin's attentions, his offers to help her make a mark for herself in the cut-throat world of journalism. She had been fascinated by Gavin's sophisticated circle of friends and blind to the warning bells that clanked loud inside her head.

Pulling her mind back to the here and now, she reclaimed her car and headed for central Brighton. She had an appointment with a lady in social services on the pretence of doing a piece about children in the care system for her cable channel. Most people reacted favourably when asked for an interview, anxious to show the world just how efficient and caring, albeit overworked and underappreciated, social services actually were.

Even though she was unable to park and therefore a few minutes late, she was still asked to wait for what turned out to be half an hour. Eventually, a harried lady came to greet her, hand outstretched.

'Sally Fairview... My God!' Dawn gaped when the lady introduced herself. 'You're Sally Dawes. We were at school together. I had no idea you worked here.'

Sally, a large, cheerful woman, grinned as she gave Dawn's hand a squeeze. 'I didn't think you high-flyers would remember us worker bees.'

'Of course I remember you. And I wouldn't describe what I do as high-flying. It's not as glamorous as you might think.'

'Is anything?'

Sally led them into a small, cluttered office that gave a lie to the modern, paperless world. There were files spilling from every available surface. More were stacked on the floor. As a meticulously tidy person herself, Dawn couldn't begin to imagine how Sally could find anything.

'Don't mind the mess,' Sally said airily, flapping a wrist. 'It's the maid's day off.'

'Is it really this bad, in your line of work?' Dawn asked, clearing files from a chair and placing them on the floor before sitting down. 'How on earth do you keep track?'

'I have a method, believe it or not.'

Dawn smiled as she watched Sally, momentarily preoccupied with something that had just pinged onto her computer screen. They were the same age but other than that, there were little or no similarities immediately evident and, Dawn conceded, the age thing would only be obvious to her. Sally had well and truly let herself go and clearly took little or no interest in her appearance. Her hair was lank and in need of a trim, she wore no make-up and sensible, drab clothing failed to conceal her bulk.

'Yours?' Dawn asked, nodding towards a photograph of a younger Sally with three teenage children.

'That's old news.' Sally laughed self-consciously. 'I've not long given birth to number four. Ron wants half a dozen, but I drew the line at three. Number four was a complete surprise. I thought I was too old but hey-ho.' She patted her belly. 'I'd like to say this is baby fat, but it would be a lie.'

'You look great.'

'False admiration doesn't become you, Dawn. You're gorgeous and you know it but then you're single, so your priorities are different. I do a job that I care about, juggle my home life and kids and so don't have the time or inclination to look in the mirror.' Sally's voice hardened. 'Each to their own is what I say.'

'You think I'm shallow?'

Dawn felt uncomfortable because Sally's dig hit a little too close to home. But then, she reasoned, if she hadn't taken care of her appearance, she wouldn't have gotten even as far as she had in the world of local journalism. As it was, it seemed her career was on the slide because of her age and fading looks. So yeah, she was shallow. She had always known it, but no one had ever pointed it out to her quite so bluntly before.

'It doesn't matter what I think.' Sally settled her bulk and eyed Dawn speculatively. 'What is it that you want, Dawn? I don't mean to be rude but as you can see…' She spread her hands across the swathes of paperwork that awaited her attention.

'Ron?' She glanced at the family picture on Sally's desk. 'Is that him? Didn't you and he date at school?'

'Yeah, that would be him. We're still joined at the hip, old-fashioned as that might sound to you, but this job, the damage I see done to kids when marriages break up and the parents declare war on one another, would be enough to keep me chained to a serial womaniser for ever. Fortunately, Ron doesn't have a roving eye. Anyway, what about you? I see you looking glamorous on the small screen from time to time, but I have no idea about your personal life. No ring,' she added, glancing at Dawn's hands, 'so I'm guessing no husband? Kids? Although, of course, marriage and kids don't necessarily go hand in hand, but like I say, I'm old-fashioned about that sort of thing and happen to believe that kids need a full set of parents.'

Dawn supressed a shudder at the mention of her childless state. 'Never found the right man.'

'Right well, that's us caught up and the small talk done with so what can I do for you? You said something in your email about interviewing some of my staff to highlight our daily struggle against financial restraints and red tape.'

'I'll level with you, Sally. Whilst you might think I'm glamorous, my station managers view things differently. They think I'm over the hill.'

'Ah, I see. Well, you did go into a profession where appearances matter. But then, I suppose, when we're young, we never think beyond the here and now. It sucks, doesn't it? I mean, the men don't get booted out if they have a few wrinkles.'

Dawn subconsciously touched her face, belatedly realising that the gesture would confirm Sally's opinion of her vanity. 'That about sums it up,' she said briskly. 'So, I'm looking for a local human-interest piece that will turn the spotlight on the pitfalls and challenges in the local child-welfare system. It will give you an opportunity to showcase the obstacles that you have to overcome every day so that next time a child slips through the net, something terrible happens to it and everyone's rightly outraged, pointing the finger at you, at least viewers will get a better insight into why it happened.'

'Hmm, I'm not sure.' Sally fixed Dawn with a probing look. 'Are you doing this because you really care or in a desperate effort to save your career?'

'Both,' Dawn shot back without hesitation, having expected the question. 'And to be fair to me, you wouldn't know my career was on the line if I hadn't come clean.'

'There is that but still, you're not a mother yourself so—'

'I'm not a criminal but I've done more pieces than I can recall on victims and how their lives have been turned upside down when the justice system lets them down.'

Sally nodded, her expression softening. 'I saw that one about the shopkeeper who was held at knifepoint. She hasn't been able to leave her house since. Your portrayal was sympathetic, I'll admit that much, and I had a tear in my eye at the end of it.'

'Jessica has got a clerical job now and is dating one of her colleagues.' A note of pride had entered Dawn's voice.

Sally elevated her brows. 'You kept in touch?'

'How could I not?' She decided against adding that Jessica's story had touched her too and she'd pulled a lot of strings to get Jess into a job that made her feel safe.

'Well, okay,' Sally said, 'perhaps we can work something out but every time a child is badly hurt or killed, and social services are called to account, someone like you always delves into our systems. What I'm saying is that it's been done before and we never come out of it smelling of roses. You can see just how hard we work.' She waved a hand towards the open-plan office outside her own, visible through the glass wall. All the desks were occupied with people either typing manically or talking on phones. The noise was loud, even through the glass.

'There are never enough hours in the day. We're understaffed, underpaid and underappreciated. The fall guy when something goes wrong, but nobody gives a rat's arse about the successes. So why would I agree to expose us to public criticism? Why will your piece be any different?'

Dawn leaned forward in her chair, grinning. 'Ah well, about that: I have an idea.'

'Why am I not surprised?' Sally rolled her eyes. 'You always did have an active imagination even at school; I remember that much about you. So come on, out with it: what is it that I'm not going to like?'

'Can I speak to a couple of graduates of your system? Talk to them directly about being put into care and their experiences. Ideally one who's made it good against all the odds, and one who's floundering through lack of support.'

Dawn expected a barrage of protests and so was surprised when Sally gave a thoughtful nod.

'That might just work,' she said.

'You can think of suitable people who'd be willing to talk to me?'

Sally made a sound that could either have been a raucous

laugh or a guffaw. 'Only about a hundred of each.' Sally leaned towards Dawn. 'You didn't hear this from me, but you might want to concentrate upon the vagaries of the foster-care system.'

'Why so?'

'Because, not to put too fine a point on it, some of our carers put themselves first.' When Dawn frowned, Sally expounded on the point. 'It takes a certain type of person to take on troubled kids, I'll be the first to admit it, which is one of the reasons why the financial rewards are worth having.'

'Ah, now I see.'

'Don't get me wrong. Foster parents earn every penny and it's hard for some not to get emotionally involved. But for others, it just mixes the kids up even more. I don't necessarily mean physical abuse, but it does go on, and those fosterers are dropped.'

'But not prosecuted?' Dawn frowned. 'Well, if they are then I've missed those stories.'

'Not my call. Basically, they're taken off our register and no more kids are sent to them.'

'But that's...'

'I know.' Sally threw up her hands. 'Putting them aside, we have a raft of fosterers who make a profit. Let me give you an example. I know of one couple with kids of their own. The foster child was given supermarket own-brand cereal for breakfast and often beans on toast for dinner. Their own kids shared the same dining table but had the best of everything. The contrast couldn't have been starker, or clearer to a child who's already been abandoned.'

'Making an already damaged child feel second best.'

'Right. She was never asked what she'd done at school, ferried to after-school activities or helped with her homework. Needless to say, the fosterer's own kids had every luxury.'

'How do you know this?'

'The girl told me, after she set fire to her bedroom.'

'Shit!'

'Right. I sat down with her for hours and eventually got her talking. Her mother was a drug addict, which was why she was taken into care. Father unknown. Foster life was supposed to be a fresh start, but she just got fed up with being an inconvenience.'

'A cry for attention.'

'Right.'

'I take it those fosterers are no longer on your register.'

Sally simply stared at Dawn, making her realise how naïve she was being.

'You have a lack of foster carers so can't afford to ditch them.'

'I do keep an eye on them, though, and as far as I can tell, at least the kids that are placed with them are eating properly. Well, the same as the people's own children. Whether they're made to feel like a part of the family is another matter. Anyway, I told you this because I took a personal interest in the fire-setting girl. The girl was quite clever. I placed her with someone I could trust, she did well in her exams and is now working full time for an animal charity.'

'Can I talk to her?' Dawn asked eagerly. 'She sounds ideal.'

'I'll see if I can set it up.'

Sally now seemed fully engaged with Dawn's proposal and they spent the next half-hour talking it through. Dawn got an insight into the stresses and pressure her old school friend lived with when they were interrupted half a dozen times by members of her team with critical situations requiring immediate resolution. Sally dealt with them all with the sort of swift and decisive efficiency that only comes with experience.

'How long do people survive in your profession?' Dawn asked when the latest emergency had been dealt with.

'There's a high turnover, which is part of the problem. You get someone trained up and then they either go on long-term sick leave due to the stress or they move on to something that pays better. You really have to care because the pay doesn't come close to reflecting the responsibility or the constant pressure, as you've already seen for yourself. And people who enter the care industry because... they care and want to make a difference are exploited quite shamelessly.'

'What about babies?' Dawn asked casually, getting round to the main reason why she'd decided to go down this route but glad too that she'd found a tear-jerking story to get her teeth into. Something that would strike a chord with the public and just perhaps see some adjustments to the system. Dawn wasn't naïve enough to suppose that would actually happen, but that wouldn't prevent her from giving it her best shot.

'What about them?'

'Babies that are abandoned or put up for adoption at birth. Is that part of your remit?'

'Blimey, don't you think I have enough to do.' Sally grinned, eternally good-natured which, Dawn supposed, one would have to be in her line of work. 'No, thankfully not. There's a queue of couples waiting to adopt so babies don't often enter the system.'

'How, as a matter of interest, would a parent who gave up a baby find out where he is now?'

Sally narrowed her eyes suspiciously, and Dawn knew that she hadn't been fooled by her casual question. 'You're asking me for a reason?'

'I know the child can ask to see his birth records when he turns eighteen, but what if he doesn't want to but his mother wants to see him? To explain.'

'Tough-titty, I'm afraid. I'm not in the blame business. I know there are dozens of valid reasons for a woman not keeping her baby. She probably spends every day after giving the child up, regretting her decision.' Sally paused. 'How old is he now?' she asked gently.

'What? No, I...' Dawn stopped speaking, aware that she'd given herself away by nodding in agreement with every word Sally spoke. Sally was too experienced to have missed the signs.

'It is a boy, I take it. You keep saying he.'

Tears trickled from the corners of Dawn's eyes. 'Yeah. I called him Jago, but I have no idea if he still goes by that name.' Making the admission felt cathartic. It wasn't as if she'd named his father, and nor would she. Not ever. 'I do know he was adopted, but that's all I know. And you're right, the guilt has never left me. He'll be about twenty-eight now so I guess if he wanted to get in touch then he would have done so long since.'

'I've known adopted kids to take a lot longer than that but yes, ordinarily, if they want to know then they make contact as soon as they legally can.'

Dawn was grateful to Sally for not sugarcoating it. 'I just want to know where he is, what he's doing, if I'm a grandmother. I won't actually approach him. You're a mother. Is what I want so very bad? I made a mistake all those years ago. His father was and still is a married man. He wanted me to abort the child and promised me we'd be together when the time was right. I know!' Dawn added when Sally rolled her eyes. 'I was young, naïve, and in love. I thought he returned my feelings.'

'Does he know that you had the child?'

'No, and I don't want him to. He turned his back on me the moment he'd given me money to abort, assuming I'd do as I was told because I always had up until that point. But... well, I just couldn't do it, but I wasn't in a position to keep him either. Well, that isn't true. I suppose I could have moved into a hostel or something, lived on benefits and done my best for us both but I'll admit, I was too selfish to even consider taking that path.'

Dawn gave herself a mental shake. Sally was far too easy to talk to and Dawn had revealed a great deal more than she'd intended to, painting herself as the selfish and ambitious woman that Sally had already pegged her as. Fair enough. After all, that's what she was. No wonder Sally was so good at her job, encouraging people to bare their souls without actually asking them to. She knew how to make pregnant silences work for her. Even so, she could tell by the firm set to her school friend's features that she wouldn't break the rules for Dawn, even though she would probably have access to the records pertaining to Jago's adoption.

'Look, I'm sorry,' Dawn said, extracting a tissue from the box that Sally produced from beneath her paperwork mountain. 'I didn't mean to tell you all that. I'm taking up your time when you have so many more important things to do. So, let's get back to the piece I'm planning. Who can I talk to here on record other than yourself? And what about graduates of the care system? The girl you referred to in particular. Who else would you recommend that I contact?'

Half an hour later, Dawn left Sally's office with a plan agreed between them. Despite her disappointment at not discovering Jago's whereabouts – had she really expected to? – Dawn left Sally's cramped office with a spring in her step. She was excited about the project she'd dreamed up in an effort to trace Jago and intended to do it justice, warts and all. Exposing local government for flaws in their system –highlighting the amount the money squandered on jollies whilst vulnerable children's needs were neglected was after all, what she did best.

She reached her tidy and empty apartment an hour later, wondering what sort of chaotic household Sally would return to at the end of her long day. She stroked Saffron, who seemed impervious to the attention, and felt lonely in a way that she'd forgotten was possible. Since giving birth and then being let down by Gavin, she'd buried herself in her work, leaving herself with no time to think about her empty life. But now, the futility of her existence compared to Sally's mad family life made her feel ashamed.

She fed Saffron but didn't herself feel hungry. Instead, she opened a bottle of wine and sat down at her laptop, typing up notes from her interview with Sally, in professional mode and totally focused on the job in hand.

'This is going to be the best thing I've ever done,' she told her cat, who appeared totally indifferent.

Two hours later, the wine bottle half-empty and Dawn's eyes drooping, she was just considering bed when her mobile pinged with an incoming text. She opened it without first bothering to see who it had come from and gasped.

'Jago Reid,' she read, glancing at the digital signature.

11

Left alone, Callie failed to knuckle down to the work that awaited her. There was something off about Dawn, she knew, and she felt concerned for her friend. She was jumpy, snappy even, short-tempered and defensive. Callie's own problems had prevented her from probing, as she otherwise would have. Callie knew Dawn was worried about being downsized or cancelled on the cable channel and she ought to have chatted with her about that situation. There could be updates that had further depressed Dawn, accounting for her withdrawn mood, but Callie had no way of knowing because she hadn't bothered to ask.

'You're a self-centred crap of a friend,' she told herself aloud.

Callie made a mental note to call Dawn that evening. Better yet, she might even call round to hers uninvited, have a girly evening drinking too much wine, discussing their relative problems and castigating men in general. As the wine flowed, the male sex would be blamed for woes real and imagined, regardless of whether or not that blame was appropriate. In Gavin's case, Callie reflected, there was no question about it being richly deserved.

He'd now been on the missing list for almost four months and, intuitive feelings to the contrary notwithstanding, Callie was obliged to face the unpalatable fact that he might actually be dead. No matter who he'd pissed off, he'd never leave his various business interests unattended for so long, aware that others would move in and take over, causing a massive loss of both face and income when he returned.

Others, like his partner and trusted friend, George Markham.

No one seemed to think O'Keefe was dead. His wife, Callie had heard on the grapevine, certainly refused to entertain the idea. Was Callie doing the same thing by so stubbornly insisting that Gavin must still be breathing? Did she want him to be? She was finding it increasingly difficult to think of any plausible reason for his continued radio silence. That had never happened before. Gavin always had to be in control, even from a distance.

'I have to go walkabout for a bit, doll,' had been his casual remark on the morning that he had taken off. 'Back soon. Keep the ship on an even keel, like you always do. You're the only one I can really depend upon.'

Callie hadn't bothered to ask where he was going, why he was going or how long he'd be gone. She knew he wouldn't tell her. He always said it was better if she didn't know. She'd been relieved to see the back of him at the time anyway, so hadn't pressed him. Gavin was always full-on. Selfish and self-centred, she was expected to follow wherever he led, no questions asked. It was lovely to be shot of him for a while. She appreciated the break: the opportunity to do as she pleased.

But warding off his business associates and enemies alike did not please her, and she'd had enough of juggling so many balls in the air without even knowing why she was doing it. She'd given him enough time to get himself sorted but he'd left her high and dry, so she'd be proactive. She'd find a way to get George off her case, put her clean books through an audit, and then put out feelers to see who'd be interested in purchasing her business. Then she'd sell the mansion she shared with Gavin. She would be a very wealthy woman indeed and could reinvent herself anywhere in the world she felt like settling.

She'd always liked the idea of Malta.

Her musings of a sun-drenched future were interrupted by Darren.

'You look like you've lost a fiver and found fifty pence, boss,' he said. 'Don't let the bastards get you down, that's what I say. Sorry,' he added hastily when she scowled at him. 'Not helpful.'

'No, it's okay, Darren.' Callie leaned back in her chair and let out a long sigh. 'I was just pondering George's demands. Obviously, he's trying to muscle in on Gavin's territory so it follows that he must know what's happened to him. He wouldn't have the balls to do it if he thought Gav might swan back any time soon so I'm thinking I must face the fact that my husband's pushing up daisies somewhere and put my own interests first.'

Darren looked away from her and Callie could have sworn that he blushed. What the hell was wrong with everyone today? First Dawn acting strange and now Darren. Was he so devoted to Gavin that he couldn't bear the thought of him having departed this world? Callie thought it unlikely.

'I'm gonna get George off my back, then sell up completely and take myself off to sunnier climes,' she said, articulating her earlier thoughts. Saying it out loud somehow made it seem more feasible. It *was* feasible, she reminded herself. Even if Gavin did reappear, the spa was still hers and she could do what she liked with it. As to the house... well, that was negotiable. Even without selling it, the proceeds from the spa meant she'd never have to worry about money ever again. Especially since she had access to Gavin's offshore accounts. His nest egg. If Gavin was being pressured by heavies, she wondered why he hadn't dipped into those accounts to get them off his back.

Because that was a line he would never cross, she told herself in answer to her own question. Those funds were there for a reason, he'd always insisted, only to be touched in a dire emergency. If he had to leave England in a hurry – always a distinct possibility in his line of work – then he didn't intend to live out his days as a pauper. He had scarpered, she reminded herself, so why hadn't he dipped into his stash?

Face it, girl. He's dead.

But Callie would never actually believe it until she saw his body. That was probably how Mrs O'Keefe felt, she reasoned, feeling a modicum of sympathy for her nemesis. Callie knew O'Keefe was dead but would be signing her own death warrant if she put the woman out of her misery.

By leaving her in the lurch for so long without a by your leave, Gavin had finally pushed her too far and forfeited the right to control her. Accepting that fact made it feel as though a ton weight had been lifted from her shoulders. She hadn't realised quite how comprehensively she'd been dancing to his tune all these years. It felt good to flex her muscles and make plans in which Gavin played no part.

'Good idea.' Darren nodded his approval. 'But in the meantime, you need a night out to take your mind off things. You work too hard and if you don't mind me saying so, you're as stressed as buggery.'

'Thanks, but best not.'

'I wasn't inviting you on a date.'

'Oh, sorry.' Callie felt her cheeks flood with colour, which infuriated her. She was no longer a gauche teenager, and women of her age simply didn't blush. She looked away from him and busied herself by tidying an already immaculately tidy desk.

'I put some feelers out, as you know, and I've discovered a pub in Brighton where Archie Taylor is known to be a regular. It's a big place that serves good food. Thought we could kill two birds with one stone. Have a bit of R&R and see if Taylor comes in and who he associates with. He's unlikely to spot us because the place is always crowded.'

'Good plan.' Callie stood and reached for her jacket. 'I'm not doing much of anything here. Might as well take myself home.'

'Okay. I'll pick you up at seven, if that suits.'

'Perfect,' she said, ignoring the fact that he winked at her as she walked through the door that he held open for her.

* * *

Dawn simply stared at Jago's name on her phone, feeling numb. Jago Reid. She assumed that he'd taken the surname of the people who'd adopted him. What were they like? Had they treated him well? Thoughts of Alice, the girl in foster care who'd been treated so badly that she'd felt compelled to start a fire in order to get some attention, sprang to the forefront of her mind.

Now wide awake, she felt nervous about having got a lead on her son's whereabouts. Just a name but with her contacts, it would be the work of a moment to find an address for him and learn so much more besides. This was what she'd wanted for as long as she could remember, wasn't it? So why was she hesitating? She wouldn't actually approach him. She'd forfeited that right when she gave him up. She just wanted to satisfy herself that he was well and doing okay for himself.

How will you handle it if he's not?

It was gone midnight. Nothing could be achieved that evening. She'd sleep on it, if sleep was remotely possible, and take action to find him the following day. Jago could have applied to the General Register for a copy of his original birth certificate and would therefore know who she was. But if he'd done that then why hadn't he gotten in touch? Perhaps because he was curious about his origins but didn't actually want anything to do with the woman who had so callously abandoned him, she supposed, answering her own question.

Dawn shivered, fully able to understand his grievance. She took herself off to bed, suspecting that even the larger than intended amount of wine she'd consumed wouldn't help her to sleep.

Early the following morning, after the largely sleepless night she'd anticipated, she called a member of the local plod whom she paid for information on any arrests that might interest her in her professional capacity. She gave him Jago's name and date of birth. He asked no questions about her need to know but called her back half an hour later with an address and national insurance number.

She looked at the address for a long time. Her son could have been anywhere in the country but lived a bare half-hour away from her. What were the chances? Google Maps identified his address as being in the middle of a line of identical bungalows positioned on a hill that led to the racecourse. She must have driven past his place a hundred times, perhaps even seen him without being aware.

But if that was the case, surely she would have felt the connection?

'What connection?' she asked aloud. 'You're delusional.'

Dawn didn't have any assignments that morning and despite being determined not to approach her son, wild horses couldn't have prevented her from driving up to his house and watching for any sign of him. She was in danger of becoming a stalker, she thought, shuddering. But that possibility didn't possess the power to make her abandon her plan. It was still early and perhaps she'd catch him taking himself off to work, she reasoned. That would be enough for her.

At least for now.

On emotional overload, she knew very well that she was in no state to make lasting decisions.

She fed Saffron but was too wound up to consider food herself, settling for black coffee. She'd had no dinner the night before and felt empty, but her stomach churned and she doubted whether she'd be able to keep any food down, even if she forced a slice of toast past her lips.

Dawn showered and dressed with care, paying special attention to her make-up and examining her image critically in the mirror. Age was creeping up on her, she accepted with a sigh, despite her best efforts to keep its ravages at bay. Fine lines around her mouth and eyes gave her away, which was one of the reasons why she planned to go under the knife. It didn't matter right now, though. She and her son would never come face to face, she reminded herself, not even accidentally.

Did he look more like her or Gavin? she wondered, as she drove her little car towards its destination. Thankfully, most residents seemed to park at the curb. A few had already taken themselves off to work and she found a space a few houses down from Jago's. She held her phone in her hand, as though conducting a conversation, just in case anyone wondered what she was doing loitering in a residential area. Not that anyone was likely to, she knew from experience, especially at this time of day when people were heading off to work, still half-asleep and oblivious to their surroundings. Besides, a woman wasn't considered to be a threat.

Half an hour passed with no activity that Dawn could see taking place in Jago's house. She'd been in one of the bungalows and knew that the kitchens were at the back, so she was unlikely to see anything anyway. Several dog walkers struggled to restrain excited mutts on their way to the downs. A delivery van double-parked and briefly shielded Jago's house from view.

'Come on!'

She tapped her fingers, thinking it would be typical of her luck if Jago appeared at that precise moment. Short of getting out of the car, she would never know. The van eventually moved away with a cloud of exhaust and all was again quiet.

Eight o'clock came and went. Then eight-thirty. Still no signs of life. Perhaps he worked shifts. Perhaps he didn't work at all. Perhaps he had the day off. Perhaps he was on holiday.

On the point of giving up, the front door opened and a tall man with a thatch of dark, unruly hair appeared, holding the hand of a blonde little girl. Dawn's heart leapt into her mouth. The child looked to be about five. She wore a backpack almost as big as she was and appeared to be chattering nonstop. The man, who could only be Jago – he was the image of Gavin – swept her into his arms and said something to her that made her giggle. Dawn could sense the closeness between them, even at a distance. He placed the child with care on a car seat in the back of a new-looking BMW. *Nice motor*, Dawn noticed, her thoughts a chaotic ramble.

The child could have been Dawn at that age, she sensed from the brief glimpse she'd caught of her. She had Dawn's hair. She knew that they would have the same eye colour, and that the little girl would have a fiercely independent spirit, as evidenced by the manner in which she possessively clutched a cuddly rabbit by one of its ears and continued to talk at a rate of knots; much as Dawn tended to chatter when she was with friends.

It took every vestige of her self-control not to leap from her car and demand access to her granddaughter.

'My granddaughter,' she muttered, her eyes wide with

wonder. Considering the possibility, as she often had, was one thing but having it confirmed knocked her sideways. And frightened her. Perhaps the fear was a product of her not being an actual mother, not in the real sense of the word. She hadn't been there to change nappies, have the disturbed nights that were part of the job, tend to scraped knees, help with homework, freeze to death on the touchline watching football...

The list went on. Dawn had missed all of that, but it was obvious that Jago didn't intend to shortchange his own child. That demonstrated a degree of responsibility and care, she thought with pride. Perhaps his own upbringing had been so traumatic that he was determined his daughter would never know anything other than deep, paternal love.

Feeling wretched and wishing for the millionth time that she could have her time over – how differently she would have done things – Dawn wondered if coming here had been such a good idea. So what if George Markham told Jago who she was? What harm could it do? If Jago wanted to know, he could have found out long since. Perhaps he already had.

But if he told Callie... well, that was a different kettle of fish entirely.

She watched the car pull away with mixed feelings, automatically making a note of the licence number. Then she started her engine and drove off too, wondering why the child's mother hadn't come to the door to see them off. Presumably, Jago was taking her to school before going off to work but it didn't seem right that a mother would let her child go without a final wave from the doorway.

'Who am I to judge motherly behaviour?' she asked aloud as she headed for home, now in a position to find out a great deal more about her son and his life.

She vowed that she would only delve out of curiosity and

reminded herself that she had no intention of contacting Jago. Well, she mentally amended, she'd had no intention before learning that she was a grandmother. Now images of that little girl would stay with her. Perhaps the existence of the child would prove to be an opportunity to mend a few bridges that would never be fully secure and make amends in some small way.

Her head told her to back off and let things be. Jago clearly had no need of her, and she doubted whether the child did either. Besides, what did she know about kids? But her heart was having none of it and she knew that she would at the very least find out everything there was to know about her son and his family.

12

Callie dressed casually for her evening out, but spent a lot of time fussing over her hair and make-up in an effort to make it seem as though she'd made no effort at all. She wasn't sure precisely why Darren had asked her out but didn't want him to think she'd gotten the wrong end of the stick and expected more from him than was on offer. His attentions had awoken dormant feelings in her, that much was undeniable, but she wasn't ready for an affair, even if that's what he was angling for.

Was she?

Darren arrived right on time and drove her into central Brighton. They didn't talk about anything of consequence during the journey. Callie found that he was an easy person to be with and that he didn't feel the need to fill silences with banal chatter. She liked that and so many other things about him and was really glad to have such a loyal employee in her corner.

Hold that thought!

'We're gonna have to park in the multi-storey and walk to the pub,' Darren said, as he indicated to turn into the car park in question. 'The pub's in the Lanes and it will be impossible to park any closer.'

'I think I can manage to walk that far,' she replied, smiling at him.

As always seemed to be the case, there was a strong sea breeze that wreaked havoc with Callie's hair. She really would look *au naturel* now, she thought with a sardonic little smile, grabbing a band from her bag and pulling her hair inelegantly into a ponytail to avoid further damage. Darren took her arm in an old-fashioned gesture, presumably because he thought she couldn't withstand a battering from the wind and still balance on her heels. He was wrong but she decided against insisting that she didn't need to lean on him. It felt good to be cherished, just for a while.

'I take it this is it,' Callie said, when they turned into a narrow lane where a crowd had spilled onto the pavement outside a bar with a trendy awning. They were not, she could see, only the smokers cluttering up the lane, but a whole gaggle of mostly younger people, probably students. Callie wondered how they could afford the prices, but she assumed that being seen at the latest 'in' place was worth the expense.

'Hope they aren't waiting to get in,' Darren remarked.

Inside was mostly full but they found a vacant table in the bar and Darren gave their drinks order to a waitress sporting a wooden smile when she approached them. She left them with menus and sashayed away, having assured them that she'd be right back with their drinks, and to take their order.

'Not a place to relax,' Callie remarked. 'They obviously want us in and out quick.'

'Yeah, but don't let her rush you. We're here to enjoy ourselves.'

'Oh, and there was me thinking we were on a mission.'

'The two aren't mutually exclusive.' Darren leaned towards her, sending a waft of expensive cologne in her direction. 'Don't feel guilty for having fun. Gavin sure as hell won't be. Sorry,' he added, holding up a hand by way of apology. 'That was crass of me.'

'No apology necessary for speaking the truth.'

Darren's gaze roamed around the bar. All the tables were occupied in it and the adjoining dining room. A large crowd of businessmen, ties loosened, occupied the bar stools, their conversation getting louder and coarser as the booze flowed.

'This table was vacant because it's close to the toilets and the door,' Darren said when a blast of cold air swished past them, causing Callie to shiver and change her mind about removing her jacket. 'But it serves our purpose well because it gives us an unimpeded view of the bar, without ourselves being too obvious.'

'And the facilities,' Callie added, nodding towards the door to the gents. 'If Taylor comes in, the chances are he'll pay a visit at some point. Most men feel the need when they get on the beer.'

'It's a prostate thing, I'm told,' Darren replied, grinning.

Their waitress returned, tutting when they admitted that they hadn't yet looked at the menu.

'I'll come back in five,' she said with a disapproving look.

'I feel like I've just been told off,' Callie said, giggling.

'Don't let her bother you.' He picked up his menu. 'She's probably told to hurry things along. Anyway, what do you fancy?'

They made their choices and gave their order to the pouty waitress when she returned the next time.

'I assume you know what Taylor looks like,' Callie said.

'Sure.' Darren pulled his phone from his pocket and brought up a picture of a middle-aged man with thinning, salt-and-pepper hair and an air of self-importance that oozed from the small screen.

'Okay. Let's hope he looks that way in real life.'

'Oh, I think he's the type that likes to make an entrance and be noticed. Ego, and all that. That crowd at the bar will be off to their home lives soon, I'm betting, and then the big boys will come out to play.'

The arrival of their food prevented further speculation.

'This is extremely good,' Callie said, nodding approval at her fancy fish dish. 'I can see why the place has a good reputation.'

'Restaurants are everywhere in this town so if a new boy wants to make a mark in such a competitive industry, then he has to be a cut above.' Darren closed his eyes as he savoured his steak poivre. 'The chef claims to be French but who knows, he's probably from Peckham.'

Callie laughed. 'You're such a cynic!'

They cleared their plates and ordered more drinks from the waitress when she returned to collect them.

'Did she just tut again?' Callie asked when the girl walked away.

'Wouldn't surprise me. She probably works mostly for tips and so needs a fast turnaround.'

Callie's wine was plonked in front of her. Darren had ordered sparkling water, due to his driving duties, but insisted upon Callie having a refill.

'No sense in us both suffering,' he reasoned. 'What's on your mind?' he added when she fell silent for a prolonged moment.

'Oh, sorry, I was thinking about Dawn. I'm probably being silly, but she doesn't seem like her usual sunny self at present and I can't help wondering what's wrong. Or why she hasn't discussed it with me, for that matter. We don't have any secrets from one another. She helped no end when Angie needed her, and if she has problems then I'd like to repay the favour.'

'She has been less bubbly than usual, I suppose,' Darren

replied, 'but don't forget that her career is under threat. That's bound to be playing on her mind.'

'Yeah, I know, but...'

'It's all she has.'

Callie shrugged. 'A bit like me, you mean.' She was aware of an edge to her voice. 'If men remain single, no one bats an eyelid, but if women are alone and career-focused, it's assumed that they're abnormal not to want kids. Or that they're lesbians, or... well, something.'

'Right.' If he felt chastised by her tone, he gave no sign, causing Callie to realise that she'd been unnecessarily prickly. 'Life isn't fair. If it was then Dawn would be judged by her abilities, not her looks, which are still dynamic, by the way.'

'Glad you noticed.'

'I'm a man. Noticing beautiful women is part of the job description.' He sent her a sexy smile across the space that separated them. 'Why else would I be here with you?'

It was the first time that he'd paid her such a lavish compliment or flirted quite so blatantly, and Callie was unsure how to deal with it. A part of her hoped he was being genuine, but an annoying little voice at the back of her head wanted to know why he felt the need to flatter.

'Game time!'

Callie was glad of the distraction when she saw a man who was unmistakably Archie Taylor swagger through the door in the company of two other men. He paused to glance around the bar, presumably to ensure that his arrival had been noted, and then headed for the bar. As if by magic, the rowdy men still occupying the stools downed the remnants of their drinks and quietly left the gastropub.

'Who are the men with him?' Callie asked. 'And why is that man who I think is the manager kowtowing to Taylor?'

'Who indeed? I'm going to try and get a picture to run through facial recognition.'

'I'm not even going to ask how you can do that.'

He winked at her. 'That's probably for the best.' He pulled his phone out again. 'Turn your chair slightly so your back's completely to those guys.'

Callie did as he asked and Darren shot off several snaps, supposedly of her, but she knew he would have zoomed in on the men behind her.

'He certainly appears to rule the roost,' she remarked, glancing over her shoulder at Taylor. 'He's behaving like royalty.'

It was true. Taylor was loud and demonstrative, putting a beefy arm around their waitress and giving her a smacking kiss on the cheek. The girl clearly resented the gesture but didn't say a word. That surprised Callie, given her spiky attitude towards them.

'I thought men knew better than to behave like that nowadays,' Callie remarked, wrinkling her nose in disgust. 'It's entirely inappropriate; why didn't she knee him in the balls?'

'Why indeed.' Darren drank the last of his water. 'Have you seen enough? If so, let's get out of here. Taylor's holding court and hasn't seen you yet. But if he's as bent as we think then he will know Gavin and recognise you.'

That thought hadn't occurred to Callie. She watched Darren signal for the bill as she finished her drink. Their waitress appeared with lightning speed, toting the card machine. Darren left a large tip in cash, presumably because he felt sorry for the treatment she'd had to endure.

'Who's the guy at the bar?' he asked.

The girl, seeing how much Darren had left her, was now all smiles. 'The owner,' she replied, sniffing. 'Well, one of them.'

'Even so, you don't have to put up with that treatment,' Callie said quietly. 'We saw what he did to you.'

'I need the money,' she replied starkly, friendly now and willing to chat due to Darren's financial inducement. 'I'm at uni in my final year and the debts are growing by the minute. It's all for show, what he does. If he tried it in private, he'd live to regret it, and he knows it.'

'Attagirl!' Callie smiled at her.

Darren, large and protective, stationed himself between her and the men at the bar as she stood up.

'Thanks,' Callie said as they walked back to the car against an even stronger wind. 'Put it on expenses. You can't keep feeding me out of your own pocket.'

'Don't worry about it.'

'That young guy with Taylor,' she said, once they were back in the car and on the road to Frenchurch. 'There was something familiar about him but I'm sure I've never met him.' She chuckled. 'I'd remember. What?' she added, when Darren took his eyes off the road and shot her an amused, sideways look. 'I'm married, but I'm not dead and I can appreciate a handsome face when I see one as well as the next woman.'

'Absolutely! Glad you're not holding a candle for your missing worse half. Sorry. None of my business. It's just that I don't approve of the way that Gavin's left you to hold the fort without so much as a by your leave.'

'Yeah well, I'm gonna have to face up to the fact that he's most likely dead. He wouldn't have done it otherwise. Besides, if he was running from heavies then they would have put the squeeze on me before now and apart from O'Keefe and Stafford, no one's come anywhere near.'

'Has it occurred to you that he might have gone AWOL in order to protect you?'

Callie swivelled her head sharply in his direction. 'What do you mean?'

'Perhaps, like Paul Dalton, he's dancing to the tune of whoever wants something from him.' He shrugged one broad shoulder. 'It's just a thought.'

'And one that hadn't occurred to me,' Callie admitted. 'It should have done. It's just that even when Gavin gets overconfident and screws up, he always finds a way out and never lets anyone else govern his movements. So...' She let out a protracted sigh. 'He *has* to be dead.'

Darren grunted and seemed to Callie to be concentrating a little too much on the road in front of him. 'Well, anyway, I'll see what comes from those snaps I took of Taylor's cohorts.'

'It's interesting that he's part-owner of that bar,' Callie said. 'I wonder who his partners are.'

'I'm all over it,' he said, pulling up outside Callie's house.

Darren leaned towards her and Callie thought at first that he intended to kiss her. Properly kiss her. Not the customary peck on the cheek. She wondered how she would respond, aware that she shouldn't cross that line but still aching for the contact of his lips on hers. She was not strong enough to resist the growing attraction, she knew, and it would complicate everything. Even so, she was unsure if she was more relieved or disgruntled when he settled for a brief touch of his lips on the side of her face.

'I'll wait until I see the lights go on inside,' he said.

'Stop spooking me!'

'That wasn't my intention, but I have a feeling that matters are coming to a head, so be careful. Make sure you double lock the door behind you.'

'Yes, sir!' She gave him a mock salute as she left the car, in control of herself once again, after a fashion.

'I'll send those pics I took to Dawn,' he said, before leaning across to pull her door closed behind her. 'She knows everyone locally in her line of work and might recognise them.'

'Good idea.' Callie smiled at her assistant. 'Night, and thanks again.'

* * *

Dawn planned to make good use of her day off. Now that she had a name and address for her son, nothing would stop her from finding out as much about him as there was to know. She drove straight home from her morning's snooping, checked her email and then got to work on her laptop.

Within ten minutes, she knew that he had moved into his bungalow four years previously. The deeds were in his sole name.

'No wife then,' she muttered, tapping a pen against her keyboard.

She was shocked out of her complacency when she realised that he had no mortgage either. How was that even possible? She sat back to think the situation through. How did a twenty-four-year-old, as he would have been at the time of purchase, find the cash to buy a property outright? There could be any number of explanations, she supposed. Perhaps one or both of his adoptive parents had died and left him a legacy. But that would only work if he'd had no siblings, she reasoned. His bungalow was modest, but they still sold for eye-watering amounts, giving the trendy nature of Brighton's location.

She phoned the TV channel and sweet-talked one of the researchers into cracking births, deaths and marriages. Ten minutes later, she knew her granddaughter's name.

Lisa Reid was just over five. Jago was on record as being her father. Her mother was shown on the birth certificate as being Caroline Parsons.

'What happened to you, Caroline?' Dawn asked aloud, in full sleuthing mode.

Had history repeated itself, after a fashion, she wondered. She had walked out on Jago. Had Lisa's mother done the same thing?

A prolonged online search threw up no person of the right age anywhere in the Brighton area. She could well have moved elsewhere but Dawn had no national insurance number and so it would be the equivalent of a needle in the haystack scenario. Dawn tried another tack. She called her long-suffering colleague back and asked him to check deaths for any trace of Caroline's premature demise, preferring to think that unlike Dawn herself, only a tragedy of that nature would prevent Caroline from being with her child.

Perhaps she *was* still with her, Dawn reasoned as she awaited a return call. Perhaps she had chosen to watch Jago on a day when he happened to have charge of his daughter. But somehow, she doubted it. That brief glimpse she'd caught of father and daughter implied a close understanding that only came from daily familiarity.

Probably.

She really wasn't in a position to know for sure.

Dawn returned her attention to her laptop and googled Jago's name, wondering what if anything the internet would throw up. Reid was a common name, but Jago wasn't. Dawn had chosen it for that reason and was ridiculously pleased that his adoptive parents had stuck with it. The one thing she had said to the adoption lady during that brief, blissful period when she was permitted to hold her baby for a few precious seconds, was that she wanted him to be called Jago. But she'd never known if that desire had been taken into account when the child was placed with his new parents.

'Bingo!' she cried, punching the air when she hit upon a

modest website sporting Jago's unmistakably handsome face on the homepage. He was an IT expert, apparently, able to sort out just about any problem a person might have with a computer. He could also build websites and set up any sort of mailing list a business might require. There was a brief bio that told her he'd graduated from Brighton university with a first in data science, which he assured potential clients made him indispensable in the modern digital marketplace.

Dawn, who didn't doubt it, felt monumental maternal pride in her son's achievements. He had, loosely at any rate, followed in her footsteps insofar as they were both in the communications business. There was the usual form to complete if she wanted a quote for his services and it took a massive effort on her part to not fill it in.

He presumably worked from home, giving him time to attend to his daughter's needs, if Caroline wasn't part of the picture. A phone call from the station confirmed that she was not. Dawn had been right to suppose that Caroline was no more. She'd been murdered, stabbed in the street, whilst walking home with her baby in a buggy. The child had not been hurt, as Dawn already knew, even before pulling up the newspaper reports of a crime that had never been solved. The general consensus was either a case of mistaken identity or Caroline had been in the wrong place at the wrong time.

'You poor, poor thing!'

Dawn sighed, her sympathy all for her son. She had abandoned him and then the woman who had given birth to his daughter had been murdered. How the hell did anyone get past so many tragedies? Always supposing that Jago looked upon Dawn's abandonment of him as a tragedy, of course. What you've never had, you tend not to miss. Her journalistic antenna twitched like it had incurred a severe bout of St Vitus Dance.

Caroline's murder had occurred five years ago almost to the day. It would now be relegated to cold-case status, no one expecting the perpetrator to be brought to book. But investigating impossible cases was what she did best, wasn't it? Besides, if she could crack it then it would make it near on impossible for the station to downgrade her status.

And if by any chance she succeeded, it would give her a legitimate reason to be in touch with Jago. She didn't have to reveal her identity.

Pleased with herself, only an urgent need for the bathroom and an empty belly caused Dawn to realise that she'd spent the entire day researching her son. And then his partner's murder. She stood up and stretched her arms above her head, swivelling her hips to restore the circulation. She'd been sitting in one place for far too long and had lost most of the feeling in her buttocks.

On the point of heading for the kitchen to knock up a sandwich, her phone pinged with an incoming email. Dawn never ignored her messages. It was often to do with work, and she wouldn't let an opportunity pass her by only for one of her younger, prettier colleagues to pick it up.

It was an email from Darren, explaining what he'd done with Callie that evening. They'd run Taylor to ground but wondered if she recognised any of his cronies. Dawn stared at the picture attached to the email and her jaw literally dropped.

The youngest member of Taylor's set was Jago.

Her son.

13

Darren knew he'd crossed a line with Callie the previous evening. It bothered him that his iron will had deserted him at a time when he ought to have been especially cautious. Gavin seemed determined to return and when he did, Darren's debt to him would have been more than paid. Darren's plan had always been to leave the spa once he was off Gavin's hook. It hadn't been part of his game plan to admire Callie's strength and determination and feel an increasingly compelling need to remain with her and protect her from all the crap that came her way on a daily basis.

There was absolutely no way that he would be able to do so; not once she realised that he'd known all along where Gavin was. Well, he didn't know his precise location, why he'd scarpered or even if he was still in the UK, but he *did* know that he was still breathing. Callie would be devastated by the betrayal. She put loyalty above all other considerations, and it had taken Darren a long time to win her trust. He still wasn't absolutely sure that she did actually trust him completely, but she had begun to ask his opinion and lean on him more frequently. She confided in him, sharing her fears and expectations and sometimes even acting on his advice.

Darren would be well rewarded financially by Gavin when he returned, but money wasn't what had motivated him. It wasn't as if he'd had much choice but to accede to Gavin's demands, thinly veiled as an offer. He was required to keep an eye on Callie and let him know everything that went on in the spa. It had seemed a harmless enough assignment: an easy way to get himself and his family out from Gavin's toxic control. How difficult could it be to keep one female's activities in his sights? Besides, it was legitimate employment, far away from the murky activities in the criminal world occupied by his father and brothers, into which he was in constant danger of being drawn.

The problem was, Darren hadn't expected to be trapped in the position for five years. More to the point, he hadn't expected to feel so disloyal for deceiving Callie. He'd seen the way she'd struggled to keep the business she loved profitable, whilst fighting off the more determined of Gavin's associates, all of whom wanted to muscle in on Gavin's territory now that he'd been on the run for a protracted period.

Darren hadn't made a conscious decision not to keep Gavin fully informed. It was a situation that had arisen slowly. The odd snippet not reported soon turned into a flood of withheld information. As a result of his reticence, Gavin was not aware that the man he feared more than any other was dead.

Dead by his own wife's hand.

It was a vital piece of information – the death, that is. Gavin didn't need to know who'd killed O'Keefe. Darren had promised Callie that he wouldn't tell a soul and that was one promise he was determined to keep. If she wanted Gavin to know then she would tell him herself when he returned. Was Darren protecting

Callie by withholding that not insignificant piece of information or was he subconsciously attempting to delay Gavin's return?

It was impossible for Darren to be sure.

He didn't know why Gavin had taken off, but he did know that knowledge of O'Keefe's demise would bring him scuttling back to protect his empire before the predators moved in, and where would that leave Callie? In the middle of a turf war was where, Darren knew, because Gavin would be eyeing up O'Keefe's territory without taking into account the vindictive nature of the man's grieving widow.

As though summoned by the nature of his thoughts, Darren's second mobile rang. Gavin checking in. Again.

'Hey,' Darren said by way of greeting as he took the call.

'I was expecting to hear from you before now.' Gavin's gravelly voice echoed down the line, dark and threatening. 'What's happening?'

'You told me to call only if I had something to report and only then if it was a matter of urgency. I don't have anything and you prefer me not to call you anyway. Callie's wound up about Dawn, whose career is under threat, but I didn't figure that would be of much interest to you.'

Gavin harrumphed.

'I told you about Markham wanting to use her meeting rooms. What do you know about Archie Taylor?'

'A shark. If George is doing business with him then Taylor will shaft him as soon as look at him.' There was a pause, during which Darren could hear Gavin's heavy breathing. He was annoyed, perhaps because George had become so independent. 'What is it you think they're into?'

'No idea.' Darren could have sent Gavin the picture of Taylor and his cohorts taken in the bar the night before. He was pretty sure that Gavin would know who the mystery men were, but something held him back. Apart from anything else, he'd have to explain to Callie how he'd identified them, and he was through with lying to her any more than was absolutely necessary. Besides, Gavin wouldn't be happy if he knew Darren had taken Callie out again, albeit innocently enough. He'd already warned him off once.

His mate on the force would do the facial-recognition thing for him. Only once he knew who the men were would he decide whether or not to enlighten Gavin.

'Any sign of O'Keefe?' Gavin posed the question casually but there was an edge to his voice that implied panic. Darren's hard-as-nails boss was afraid of another man. Either that or he'd crossed him and was wary of the consequences, which would account for his prolonged absence.

'None. The sharks are gathering, boss. You need to be here.'

'Since when did you get to tell me what to do?' Gavin barked. 'Just do what I fucking pay you to do and keep an eye on my wife. Let me know if she dates anyone and I'll cut his balls off with a blunt knife.'

Darren rolled his eyes and refrained from making any comment. He knew he wasn't expected to. Gavin was letting off steam. Wherever he was, he was itching to get back into the action and Darren would dearly love to know what was holding him back. It had to be something pretty cataclysmic.

'What do you want me to do about Markham's demands?' he asked.

'Find out what game he's playing but be careful. Taylor doesn't take prisoners.' Darren heard a female voice in the background calling Gavin's name. No surprise there. 'I have to go. I'll call tomorrow for an update.'

The line went dead. Darren remained where he was with phone in hand for several minutes, thinking the conversation over. Gavin was rattled, probably bored and definitely a little scared. How to exploit that weakness?

Darren phoned his mate on the force – a guy he'd been at school with – and sent him the picture and asked for identities. It would cost him a few readies – the man had a young family to support – that he'd pay out of his own pocket. That would help, in some small way, to assuage his guilty conscience.

That done, with a promise of results within the hour, Darren sat back and pondered the Gavin situation. He was definitely on the verge of returning. He kept saying he'd be back imminently, but something about his tone was different today and Darren sensed that this time, he meant it. O'Keefe hadn't surfaced so it followed he was the man who'd driven Gavin out: the man he had the good sense to be afraid of.

Darren needed to find a way to defer his return, he decided. The longer he was away, the more time Callie would have to sell the spa for a decent profit, sell the house she shared with Gavin, perhaps clear out his offshore accounts while she was at it and retire somewhere warm and exclusive, an exceedingly wealthy woman, safe even from Gavin's long reach.

That was something she deserved. The *only* way out of the mire for her that Darren could see. The net was closing in. Gavin's protection from the police was crumbling, mainly because Fallow had got cold feet and wanted out. With him gone, Gavin's protection at a senior level would be eradicated and then it would be open day on Gavin. And with him in the wind, the next best target would be Callie.

'Not happening!' he told the ceiling.

His business phone rang. Dawn's name flashed up on the screen and he took the call, hoping she'd have information for him about the mystery men.

'Hiya,' he said. 'Any ideas about those identities?' he asked.

'Sorry, don't know the younger, good-looking one but the other guy is Chris Ambrose. I interviewed him once. He was given a suspended sentence for whacking his girlfriend. A real charmer. The stupid girl stuck by him. Said it was her fault, and he got away with a suspended sentence.'

'What does he do now?'

'Apart from hitting women? Who knows? I think he's a doorman at one of Brighton's seedier clubs, but don't quote me on that.'

'A bouncer?'

'If you like.'

'Why would Taylor need private muscle?'

'Well, there's a question.' Darren expected Dawn to expand with a dozen theories of her own, as was her way, and so he was surprised when she abruptly ended the call.

'Odd,' Darren remarked, shrugging and turning his attention to his computer.

He commenced a search of Chris Ambrose's name and came up with a welter of hits. It seemed that he was an aficionado of a local boxing club. Darren prided himself on keeping fit himself and had been known to don the gloves on occasion. He rubbed his chin, thinking that if it became necessary, it would be as good a way as any to bump accidentally into Ambrose.

* * *

Dawn hung up, feeling dismal. It seemed she had graduated from lying to her best friend to also being economical with the truth with her PA. She hung her head, ashamed and frustrated. She knew time wasn't on her side. Darren would discover Jago's identity soon enough, even if he wouldn't realise the connection between her and her son. Unless he was thorough and got access to Jago's birth certificate.

Dawn's blood ran cold at the thought.

She had called in sick to the station, something she'd never done before, and so her excuse of a heavy cold for missing an assignment was accepted without question. She tried not to resent the fact that a younger colleague, keen and ambitious, would fill in for her, much as she herself had done years before. *Never mind all that*, she told herself. Dawn had more important fish to fry which could well result in a scoop that secured her career, or perhaps even enhanced it. She had not given up on her dream of a national TV spot, albeit increasingly unlikely as the years passed.

Why on earth was her son connected to a dodgy character like Taylor? She needed to find out and, if necessary, rescue him from his own folly. That was something that she could and would do for the son she had abandoned. But to put her determination into practise, she needed to know a great deal more about him, which was something she would have delved into even if there wasn't a crisis looming. She simply couldn't help herself.

Her first port of call was social media. It still amazed Dawn how much people gave away about their private affairs to perfect strangers online. She had heard people say that their lives were open books, they had nothing to hide and no reason to conceal their activities. Hadn't they heard of scammers, who cloned accounts, stole their data, or worse?

She found Jago's Facebook account and browsed through his friends. There was a large number of them but from the few posts visible to her, a Joan Reid continuously commented on posts that mostly featured his little girl.

Dawn's granddaughter.

Wiping away an emotional tear, Dawn forced herself to

concentrate on the job in hand. Joan was, presumably, Jago's adoptive mother. She visited Joan's own account to be confronted by a kind, homely face. She quickly discovered that her husband had died a year previously. Dawn's curiosity was piqued. What had been wrong with him? Had he left Jago a legacy that enabled him to purchase his home outright? No, that wouldn't have been possible since Jago had bought it before the man had left this world. Perhaps the child's mother had had life insurance. That seemed more likely.

In several posts, Joan referred to activities, family parties and what have you, naming the street she lived in. Dawn rolled her eyes, even as she silently praised the lady's trusting nature. A picture of little Lisa posed in front of a gatepost even gave Dawn the number of Joan's house. A quick search of Google Maps confirmed that the street in question was not that far away from Jago's new home.

'Right, what next?'

Dawn tapped her fingers, wondering if she dared to confront Joan in her professional capacity. Well, of course she did! A thick skin was the first requirement of any halfway decent reporter. Besides, this was a matter of urgency and so she pushed aside a guilty conscience that had chosen a most inconvenient time to make its presence felt. Dawn was now a woman on a mission. She packed all the things she might need into her oversized bag, grabbed her car keys, gave an indifferent Saffron a quick kiss on the head and left her apartment.

She drove to Joan's home, willing herself to think like the journalist she was trained to be. If Joan was naïve and if Dawn was convincing enough, this might just work. What was the worst that could happen?

Dawn preferred not to dwell upon that particular question as she found a parking space close to number seventeen, took a deep breath and walked towards the house in which her son had likely spent his early years. It looked well cared for in a road of similarly cared for properties: a quintessential English suburb where the neighbours probably knew one another's names and looked out for each other. Dawn had spent years wondering where her son had been raised and was relieved to see that he had grown up in a decent home in a good neighbourhood.

So why is he associating with the likes of Taylor?

Dawn walked up the path, noticing how well the garden was tended, how sparkling clean the windows were. The paintwork was peeling in places, though and a downpipe was coming away from the wall. She wielded the brass knocker, and the door was opened almost immediately by the lady she'd seen online.

'You're early... oh, hello. Sorry.' Joan blinked at Dawn from behind oversized glasses. 'I thought you were someone else. I'm expecting my friend. We go to bridge club together on a Thursday.' The smile was wide and welcoming. 'What can I do for you, my dear?'

'You're Mrs Reid?'

'I am? What is this about? Are you selling something? I don't mean to be rude but—'

'I'm a journalist with—'

'With *Sussex News!*' Joan's smile grew even wider, something Dawn wouldn't have thought possible. 'I watch you all the time. Your name is Dawn.'

'Dawn Frobisher.' Dawn returned the lady's smile, relieved that she hadn't made the connection to Jago's parentage. Presumably, she hadn't seen his original birth certificate, in accordance with Dawn's wishes. She had emphasised to the adoption agency that she didn't want any contact with her child, thinking it would deter Gavin's interest in her. Ha! But in retrospect, perhaps her selfishness had inadvertently been the best thing for her son. 'I wonder if you could spare me a few moments. The channel is planning a segment about adoptive parents and your name came up.'

'Oh.' Joan didn't ask any of the obvious questions. 'Well, in that case, you'd better come in.' She glanced at her watch. 'My friend isn't due for fifteen minutes and she's always late anyway.'

Joan led the way into a scrupulously tidy lounge, albeit slightly old-fashioned. There were net curtains at the window and chairbacks on worn, leather seating. Nick-nacks decorated every surface, as did pictures of Jago, his daughter and a young woman – presumably Caroline. The house was in dire need of a little TLC. Joan was clearly houseproud and so Dawn wondered if a lack of finance held her back. Either that or she didn't notice the shabbiness. People became complacent after a while, she knew. Then again, perhaps she had kept everything as it had always been as a testament to her late husband. Any changes would eradicate his presence.

'You have a lovely home,' Dawn said, sinking into the chair that Joan indicated.

'Thank you. Would you like tea?'

'No, please don't bother. I know you're about to go out and I don't want to hold you up.' Dawn took her recorder out of her bag and placed it on the table beside her. 'Do you mind if I record our talk? I won't use anything you say without your prior approval. Besides, if we go ahead, I'll have to come back with a cameraman.'

'Oh no, I don't mind at all.' Joan sat opposite Dawn, all smiles. 'This is so exciting! I've never been interviewed before.'

'This segment is still in the planning stage and might not be broadcast in the end. It's not my decision. This interview is purely exploratory.'

'It needs to be interesting, I suppose.'

It was Dawn's turn to smile, which was no great hardship. The woman's good and trusting nature was infectious. She had done a much better job of raising Jago than Dawn would ever have done – she already knew that much – and felt nothing but gratitude and goodwill towards her.

'I am absolutely sure that you will have something interesting to tell us.'

A cat stalked into the room, tail rigid and, finding nothing to interest it, disappeared as quickly as it had arrived. 'May I start by asking what made you decide to adopt?'

'Oh, the usual, I suppose. We tried for years to conceive naturally. I desperately wanted to be a mother.'

'I'm sure you were a good one,' Dawn said, meaning it.

'Well, I hope so. Ben and I married late. He was in his thirties, and I was twenty-nine. We tried for three years to conceive, then had IVF, which didn't work. Adoption was our final hope and thankfully, we were deemed suitable parents for baby Jago.'

'That's him.' Dawn stated the obvious by pointing towards the pictorial montage.

'Yes.' Joan once again beamed. 'And he never gave me a moment's regret. He was a perfect baby and child in every sense of the word. Caring, considerate, loving. A good student too, with an enquiring mind.' *He gets that from me!* 'Well, I say enquiring. Perhaps too enquiring.' Joan smiled again. 'He's always had a way with computers, as so many young people do. Well, they're brought up with them, unlike my generation. Anyway, he was in trouble for getting into places that he shouldn't. The dark web, I think.' She held up a hand as she sprang to his defence. 'But only to prove that he could, he told me. He never intended for it to go any further. He said he could probably break through a bank's firewall if he put his mind to it but, of course, he'd never do such a thing.' Joan beamed with pride. 'Such a talented boy.'

'I assume he knows that he's adopted.'

'Oh yes, we told him when he was eleven. It seemed the right age. He was a sensible boy and had started asking questions. He took it well. Told us we would always be his mum and dad, and he didn't care who actually gave birth to him.'

'Did he ever express curiosity about his birth parents?' Dawn held her breath as she posed the question.

'No, not once. Well, not in my hearing, anyway. If he was curious, and I expect he was, I mean, it's only natural to want to know who you are, isn't it? But anyway, he wouldn't have told me, if only to spare my feelings. Not that I would have minded. Nor do I blame his birth mother for giving him up.' Dawn inhaled sharply, causing Joan to send her a curious glance. 'I dare say she had her reasons and anyway, if she hadn't then we wouldn't have had the pleasure of Jago in our lives.'

'According to my research, your Jago used his computer skills to set up his own company and is doing well and at such a young age.'

'He is.' Joan beamed. 'He works mostly from home too so that he can be there for Lisa. He has help, of course. Lisa's mother is dead, you know.' She swiped at an errant tear. 'Such a tragedy.'

'Yes, that came up in my research. I'm so sorry.'

'Well anyway, about Jago: he has one of those *au pairs,* a nice girl, and Lisa loves her, but I said to him, he didn't need to go to the expense. I could have Lisa whenever he needs me to, but he said she was a handful and that I deserved a little peace. Jago is *so* thoughtful that way.'

'I assume you and Ben helped him with the funds to purchase his bungalow.'

'Oh, good heavens, no! We would have, of course, if we'd had the money to spare, but it's always been tight. No, Jago has made it completely on his own.'

'Did Caroline have life insurance?'

'No. Well, you don't at that age, do you? You tend to think you're invincible. No, Jago's business has taken off big time. He turns clients away on a regular basis and made enough to buy his bungalow.'

Dawn wanted to believe it, but something wasn't right. Dawn would have to take a look at his company's accounts, but she would be very surprised if a start-up had made enough for its owner to be able to purchase an expensive property outright. There had to be another explanation that didn't involve criminal activity. *He could have broken through a bank's firewall, if he'd wanted to.*

No, not possible, she silently deemed. Dawn wasn't ready to accept that her son may not be whiter than white, even if he did mix with questionable company.

'Our research brought up the murder of Jago's partner,' Dawn said gently, 'which is one of the reasons why we thought we would include you in the piece.'

'Ah.' Joan nodded. 'I thought that might be the case.'

Not quite as naïve as she seemed then, Dawn thought. 'What happened?' she asked gently. 'I've read the reports, but I'd like to hear what you have to say. I gather the poor girl was stabbed in the street and no one was ever arrested.'

Joan nodded. 'It was a terrible time. Little Lisa was just three months old, the poor mite.'

'No one knows why she was targeted?'

Joan looked away, evasive for the first time. 'We don't think she was. She couldn't possibly have been. She was just an ordinary girl, in love with my son, planning their wedding. That's where she was going to on the day she died: to look at a venue for the wedding. My Ben was with her.'

'Your husband?' Dawn hadn't realised that.

'Oh yes. He knew they couldn't afford the venue they'd set their hearts on, so Ben wanted to see if it would be the right place for them. If so, we'd have found the money from somewhere and treated them as their wedding present. Caroline grew up in care and didn't have any family to help her, so Ben sort of adopted her too. The pair of them were inseparable.' She shook her head, having made direct reference to their obvious financial restraints. 'Now they're both gone. It's so terribly sad.'

'He's dead too?' Dawn reached forward to touch Joan's hand. 'I am so sorry.'

'Well, yes.' Joan blinked behind her glasses. 'I thought you knew. He tried to protect Caroline and Lisa from the attack. He struggled with the knifeman, who pushed him out the way and Caroline was fatally stabbed in the struggle. He fell and hit his head and sustained serious brain damage.' A tear trickled down behind Joan's glasses. 'He was never the same again and it was almost a relief when he died a year ago.'

'What did he do for a living?'

'Ben?' Dawn seemed surprised by the question. 'He worked for an important man. My Ben was a boxer in his younger days. He worked out all the time at Murphy's gym.'

'Murphy's gym?' Dawn's heartrate accelerated. The place was owned by O'Keefe's family – a hive of criminal activity and a no-go area for the local plod. 'Did your husband work for the owner?'

'Oh yes, and he was very highly thought of. He introduced Jago to his boss. Mr O'Keefe was very impressed with his skills, which is how he got his start.'

Damn!

Ben Reid wasn't so highly thought of that he was paid a decent wedge, Dawn thought, her gaze roving round the shabby room with its outdated furniture and inexpensive ornaments. 'What did he do for him, just as a matter of interest?'

'He ended up being Mr O'Keefe's bodyguard.' Joan sat a little straighter. 'I'm not sure why he needed one, but Ben explained people were jealous of the Irishman's success and that he'd made enemies on his way to the top, as generally happens. Mr O'Keefe and my Ben were the best of friends, until near the end.' She frowned. 'Something happened between them. I never was able to discover what. But anyway, Mrs O'Keefe was lovely. Always had time for a chat and a cuppa whenever we met. A real family lady, through and through.'

'Jago must have been very young when his daughter was born. Probably not long out of uni. Were he and Caroline childhood sweethearts?'

'Oh no, nothing like that. She worked in the university bar. They met there and hit it off at once. I don't think marriage or babies were on their agenda but... well, these things happen, and Jago was determined not to abandon his child in the same way that he'd been abandoned.' *Ouch!* 'Caroline was brought up in care so obviously, she felt the same way, but—' The doorbell sounded. 'Ah, that will be Jane.' Joan glanced at the clock in the corner of the room, ticking loudly away, and smiled. 'Late as always. Now, you really must excuse me.'

'Thank you very much, Mrs Reid.'

'Oh, please, call me Joan.'

'Joan then. Thank you. I will be in touch again. Enjoy the bridge.'

Dawn drove away, barely able to see the road in front of her, so preoccupied was she with untangling what she had just heard and attempting to make sense of it. She didn't believe in coincidences and was convinced that Ben had been the knifeman's real target. One simply didn't fall out with O'Keefe and live to tell the tale, especially a trusted, long-standing employee whose loyalty ought to have been beyond doubt. As to Jago being involved with criminal activity, she felt hugely disappointed but not surprised. There was obviously a great deal of his father in him.

Dawn thumped the steering wheel in frustration, wondering how to explain this latest breakthrough to Callie without exposing her connection to Jago.

14

Callie had back-to-back meetings on the morning following her dinner with Darren. That was no bad thing, she decided, since her concentration was required and there was no time to dwell upon her more pressing problems.

Finally clear of the demands of suppliers *et al* by lunchtime, Darren tapped at her door, bearing a platter of sandwiches.

'I knew you'd forget to eat,' he said, flashing a businesslike smile.

Callie had avoided him that day, using her meetings as an excuse. Something had changed between them the previous night. She couldn't have said what precisely. Something about Darren's attitude, perhaps. He'd seemed remote and yet flirtatious, preoccupied but attentive – if that made any sense – causing her to wonder if the dynamics of their relationship had been inexorably altered.

It seemed she needn't have worried, though, since he'd set the tone by returning to his normal self. Perhaps she'd imagined his personal interest in her, which would be just as well. He was Gavin's man through and through and if her husband returned and Darren was forced to choose between them, she was under no illusions as to the direction he'd take. Anyway, Callie had more immediate concerns that left no time for her to dwell upon romantic interludes.

Or lack thereof.

'Good progress with the gym equipment?' he asked.

'I managed to get the price down a little.' She waggled a hand from side to side. 'Well, quite a bit, as it happens, so now I'm wondering what's wrong with this super new equipment and why they're so keen to offload it.'

Darren's laugh eased the tension that was probably the product of Callie's imagination. 'Have you considered that it's your negotiating skills that wore them down?'

'Not even remotely.'

Darren went to the machine and made her coffee just the way she liked it, placing a steaming mug in front of her.

'Thanks.'

He sat across from her, sipping his own brew.

'Any progress on the names of the people with Taylor last night?' she asked.

'Some. The older one is Chris Ambrose, amateur boxer and bouncer. I've put feelers out, trying to find which club he minds the door at. It was Dawn who recognised him but that was all she could tell me. She seemed to be in a bit of a hurry.'

Callie smiled. 'When isn't she?'

'I sent that picture to a contact of mine on the force. He confirmed Ambrose's identity. He has form for AGH, GBH, and just about all the other letters in the alphabet. He's bad news. Muscle for hire, if you like and, I'm told, not too fussy who he works for or what he does, just so long as the price is right.' Darren paused. 'The younger guy's a bust. He's not on the police database so he remains a mystery.'

'See if you can dig up any connection between George and Archie Taylor please, Darren. Something other than the planning permission George pushed through on his behalf.' Callie frowned. 'I can't help thinking that was some sort of test. An initiation thing, if you like. Fix this and we can do business. It sounds off the wall but also makes perfect sense.'

Darren nodded. 'I hear you.'

'It's a shame George didn't show his face last night.'

'Chances are *he* would have noticed us, so probably better that he wasn't there.'

'If he'd seen us and thought we were onto him, it might have given him pause.'

Darren's expression told her she was being naïve. Perhaps she was. Hard men like George and Taylor didn't back off because a woman might be on their case.

'Anyway, if we can get a handle on what Taylor, Ambrose and the mystery younger man are up to, then we'll have a better idea why George wants to use my rooms for his private shenanigans. If we know that, then we're halfway towards undermining him.'

'Already on it.'

'Of course you are. Sorry.' Callie tapped her fingers. 'We should be doing something more. I've asked Fallow to call in and look at that picture. We could have sent it to him, but I want to see his reaction when he looks at it. That way, if he tries to say he doesn't know the younger man's identity, I will know that he's holding out on me.'

'Yeah, he knows the net's closing in, which is why he's thinking of putting in his papers before his collar's felt. We can only depend on Fallow to put his own interests first now that Gavin's in the wind. It doesn't hurt to keep that in mind.'

'I know. Anyway, send me that picture. Let me have a good look at it.'

Darren nodded and shortly thereafter, her phone pinged with an incoming message. She enlarged the picture and took a long, hard look at the younger man's profile.

'I only caught a brief glimpse of him last night,' she said, frowning. 'I thought then that there was something familiar about him and I am even more sure of it now. I know him from somewhere, but I just can't think…'

The thoughts in question were interrupted when Fallow put his head round the door.

'Morning,' he said, sitting down and nodding towards the coffee machine. Darren got up and did the honours. There was none of the bombastic attitude about him today: the resentment that so annoyed Callie. He was the one to have taken a bribe when his career was in its infancy. He hadn't stopped doing so all these years later. He couldn't. Gavin had too much on him. Be that as it may, he now seemed to put the blame for his situation on everyone other than on himself. 'What can I do for you?'

'We wondered if you could identify a person for us,' Darren said, pulling up the picture on his phone and handing it to Fallow.

'Archie Taylor, a real snake in the grass and a nasty piece of work. Chris Ambrose, muscle for hire, and the young guy's Jago Reid. Thanks,' he added, taking his coffee from Darren and inhaling half the mug in one inelegant swallow. 'Bugger, I needed that!'

'Who's Jago Reid?' Callie and Darren asked together.

'A computer whizz who we've spoken to once or twice. Convinced he's been involved in cybercrime but can't prove it.'

'Any idea why these three would be putting their heads together in a popular watering hole?' Darren asked.

Fallow shrugged a beefy shoulder. 'Might just be a social

occasion, but I doubt it. They aren't the sort to have much in common, other than criminal activity.'

Callie glanced at Darren, suppressing her amusement as pots and kettles sprang to mind. A high-ranking policeman who'd been on the take for years, shamelessly abusing his position, was arguably the lowest form of villain.

'Have you heard any whispers?' Darren asked.

'If there are any rumours then they haven't reached me yet. But then, they wouldn't unless there's something concrete. I don't get involved in the detail nowadays.' He sat a little straighter, seeming to think there was something to admire about the power he wielded and misused within the ranks of the police.

'If they're planning some sort of online scam, why would they need hired muscle?' Callie asked on a quizzical note.

'You've got me there.' Fallow drained his coffee and stood. 'But now, if there's nothing else...'

'Let us know if you hear anything about those three,' Callie said.

'I'll keep my ear to the ground.' He offered them a mock salute and was gone.

'I'm going to do a little digging into Jago Reid,' Darren said.

'And I have more meetings.' Callie rolled her eyes. 'Lucky me.'

Callie remained where she was for a long time after Darren left her, staring at the picture of Jago Reid.

'Where do I know you from?' she asked aloud.

* * *

Dawn and John recorded a puff piece for the channel about a child with cancer and the funds raised by the local community to send her to a specialist unit in America. It was tear-jerking stuff, but Dawn knew the station managers would only use it on a slow news day. She sighed, wondering why she bothered.

Finally finished for the day, she returned home and concentrated her mind on what she'd learned about her son. And more specifically, pondering upon where he could have acquired the funds to pay cash for his home. Joan could see no harm in him and was proud of his achievements but then she clearly didn't know how O'Keefe made a living, or that her son had been drawn such a murky world by his foster father.

She could see that he had every reason to be resentful, what with his future wife having been murdered so brutally and needlessly. But the worrying throwaway line that Joan had put out there, about his being able to break through a bank's firewall if he felt so inclined, had rung alarm bells. He had probably been boasting, she tried to tell herself, since he'd made the statement not long after he graduated; not that long before his life had been turned on its head by the senseless murder of the mother of his child.

Would it be such a bad thing if he did rip off some faceless establishment like a bank that itself routinely ripped off its customers with its extortionate overdraft interest rates? A victimless crime? The majority of her viewers would, she knew, applaud his ingenuity, but did that make it right?

Dawn shook her head, aware that she was in no position to adopt the moral high ground. Being abandoned by her had probably played a part in the direction Jago's career had taken, she knew. Not knowing who you were or anything about your heritage would play upon a person's confidence, she suspected. Dawn was well aware, now that she appreciated the nature of his skills, that he wouldn't have needed to approach the adoption agency to ask about her. It would have left a trail and made it appear as though he gave a shit. If he could hack into a bank then breaching the online defences of an overworked agency would be... well, child's play.

Dawn leaned back in her chair, nodding to herself as she accepted that Jago must know who she was and that he had absolutely no interest in meeting her, or hearing why she'd had no choice but to give him up. Except that she had had a choice, she accepted now. There were always choices, but had selfishly put her ambitions and personal interests ahead of the welfare of her child.

No wonder he didn't want to know her.

She didn't like herself very much at that precise moment. Telling herself that she was now mature, a very different person to the lost young woman who'd found herself pregnant and then abandoned by the man she'd foolishly believed when he'd spun her a line, didn't help much.

She chastised herself for a momentary bout of self-pity. She had brought her woes upon herself and had long since learned to live with her past by burying it. Gavin's disappearance and Jago being thrust into her life in such an unexpected way had forced her to face up to it again. She now had decisions to make. Darren was looking into Jago's background. He was no slouch when it came to computers either and she knew it would only be a matter of time before he discovered the name of Jago's birth mother.

Dawn swallowed as she faced up to the unpalatable inevitable. She would have to call on Callie and try to explain. It would destroy a friendship that meant so much to her but if she was going to find out anyway, it would be better coming from her and was the least she could do to soften the blow.

Before she could talk herself out of it, Dawn grabbed her mobile and called Callie.

'Hey,' Callie said cheerfully as she picked up. 'How are things?'

'Things could be better.' Dawn paused, finding it hard to speak past the lump that had lodged itself in her throat. 'Anyway, I need to talk to you.' She glanced at her watch. It was later than she'd realised. 'Are you about to head home?'

'I was, actually. Dawn, are you okay? You don't sound right.'

'I'll be round at yours in an hour and all will be revealed.'

'I'll open the wine.'

'Good plan.'

Dawn had a feeling she was going to need it, but whether or not Callie would literally throw it in her face when she discovered the tawdry truth remained to be seen. God alone knew, she deserved all the shit that was about to come her way, for which she had no one to blame other than herself.

Before she could lose her nerve, Dawn changed into casual clothes and touched up her make-up. Not that it mattered what she looked like, she realised, but disguising herself behind warpaint had become her go-to defence mechanism – a way to hide a lack of confidence that no one had ever accused her of possessing – ever since she'd first graced the small screen.

Her lack of faith in herself often made her wonder why she'd chosen a profession where there was nowhere for her *to* actually hide. Had she been attempting to prove something to herself? She'd been admired in her younger days for her looks and style, but when she glanced in the mirror, Dawn could only see her myriad flaws. Perhaps that was why Gavin had found it so easy to seduce her when she'd been young and inexperienced. She liked to think it wouldn't happen today but then a man of Gavin's ilk would never make a move on a person of her age. Predators, because that's what he was, she now realised, liked them young, insecure and malleable. He couldn't have targeted a more compliant victim, she thought, and she had been living with the consequences of her stupidity– her regrets and self-recriminations – for almost three decades.

At least the business with Jago had given Dawn time to reassess her thought process. The torch she had continued, inexplicably, to carry for Gavin all these years was now flickering and in imminent danger of being completely extinguished.

Her jumbled thoughts whirled through her brain like a hurricane as she drove towards Callie's sprawling house. As she pulled up on the driveway, Callie emerged from inside, also dressed casually, and wrapped Dawn in a fierce hug that she didn't deserve and would probably never experience again once she'd told Callie everything.

'You've got me worried,' she said, taking Dawn's hand and leading her into the house. 'You haven't been yourself for a while so I'm glad you've decided to confide in me.' She led them into the conservatory with its sparkling swimming pool, subdued lighting and fully stocked bar and pushed Dawn towards one of the comfortable armchairs. 'Let's open a bottle and you can tell me what's got your knickers in such a twist.'

'Sure.' Dawn couldn't look at her friend but Callie, busy with a corkscrew, didn't seem to notice.

'Actually, I'm glad you're here,' Callie said, handing Dawn a glass. 'This place gets lonely when I'm rattling around in it on my own, and I can't spend *all* my time at the spa. I used to enjoy having it to myself when Gavin went walkabouts, but it's been too long this time. I'm thinking of offloading the place. I mean, it's obvious he isn't coming back any time soon, isn't it?' Callie paused to draw breath. 'Listen to me, prattling on when it's obvious that you have something bothering you. So come on, out with it.' Callie leaned towards her expectantly. 'What's the problem?'

The sound of light rain on the conservatory roof perfectly reflected Dawn's sombre mood. 'The problem is Jago Reid.'

'Ah, so you've found out who he is.' Callie smiled at Dawn. 'Fallow told us. I should have called to update you, but it seems that wasn't necessary. His name's been in the frame for cyber-crime but nothing's stuck so far.'

Dawn felt tears trickling down her cheeks as she turned to look at Callie. She'd promised herself that she wouldn't cry. It would seem like an attempt to invoke Callie's sympathy: sympathy that she didn't deserve. But on emotional overload and almost glad to be on the point of unburdening herself of a secret that she'd borne the weight of for too long, the tears appeared to have a mind of their own.

'I didn't need to do any delving. I already knew who he was,' Dawn said, dabbing at her eyes with a tissue she pulled from her bag.

'Dawn, you're frightening me.' Callie clasped her hand. 'How did you know him?'

'I've imagined this conversation, what I'd say, how I'd justify myself a thousand times, but now that the time's come...'

'Dawn, I'm one of your best friends. You can tell me anything. I promise not to judge. Whatever you've done, or think you've uncovered, I've probably been there before you, so give.'

Dawn swallowed and found the strength from somewhere to meet Callie's curious gaze. 'Jago's my son,' she admitted.

15

Callie's jaw fell open. Whatever she'd expected Dawn to say, the possibility of her having a secret child that she'd never thought to mention during the course of a thirty-year friendship hadn't once crossed her mind.

'Your son,' she repeated stupidly.

Dawn, with tears streaming down her face, nodded emphatically. 'Yeah, my son,' she emphasised. 'How about that?'

'Are... are you sure?' Callie remained bemused as she crouched beside Dawn and took her hand. 'Well, I suppose you must be. Stupid question. Why have you never said anything before now? Come on, babe, I want to know it all. Presumably, the child was put up for adoption. You must have been pretty young yourself at the time and if the father didn't stand by you then I can understand why you had no choice other than to take that decision. It must have broken your heart, though. I know it would have done mine. Anyway, who is the father?'

Dawn flashed a watery smile, clearly struggling with her emotions as she held up a hand to stem Callie's flow of words.

'I was eighteen,' she said, 'and a child wasn't part of my plans.

Jago was an accident, obviously, and the father was adamant that I have an abortion. He gave me the money to make it happen and just assumed that I'd do as I was told. No discussion, nothing.'

'But you didn't...' Callie squeezed her hand, doing all she could to support her friend. 'Good for you! It takes two and the man should have taken your views into account.'

Dawn snorted. 'Yeah, right!'

'He was married, I take it.'

Dawn nodded, seemingly too choked up to speak.

'Was it rape?' Callie asked, her voice oozing empathy. 'Is that why you didn't say anything?'

Dawn hiccupped as she reached into her bag, extracted a tissue and blew her nose. She then turned towards Callie, fresh determination appearing to prevent more tears from falling.

'Yes, he was married and yes, I was besotted. An older, sophisticated man who could energise a room simply by walking into it. A man who could do anything he set his mind to. He was glamorous, generous, dangerous and fun and I was totally in awe of him, unable to decide why he'd chosen me.'

'I understand. Better than you possibly realise.'

Callie's remark, intended to soothe and reassure, appeared to have the opposite effect and Dawn became quite agitated again.

'I was in love. And in spite of the way he treated me, a part of me still loves him.' Dawn spread her hands. 'How pathetic does that make me?'

'Our heads and hearts aren't always on the same page,' Callie replied. 'Take it from one who knows. Besides, deep down, we all love a bad boy. The danger is intoxicating. Life is never dull or routine when you're around one of them. But Dawn, you still haven't told me why you've kept this to yourself for so long and, more to the point, why you're telling me about it now. Well, I suppose, Jago coming up in this investigation gave you quite a shock.' Callie felt for her friend. 'Does he know who you are? Have you met? There's so much you need to tell me.'

'Actually, Callie, there's only one thing you need to know and then everything will become obvious.'

'You're frightening me, Dawn. I've never seen you this way before.' She again clutched Dawn's hand. 'It's me you're talking to. It can't be that bad. Just say it.'

'It's worse than bad. Once you know the truth our friendship will be history and...' Dawn choked on a sob. 'I don't think I can bear it.'

Callie's mind went into overdrive. She conjured up Jago's image, reinforcing the feeling that he looked familiar, and it all clicked into place with astounding clarity.

'Gavin,' she said slowly, dropping Dawn's hand like it had scorched her. 'Jago is Gavin's child.'

The deafening silence that greeted Callie's assertion – an assertion that she prayed, against all the odds, would be false – was all the confirmation that she needed. A raft of conflicting emotions swirled through her brain as she got up and paced the length of the conservatory, oblivious to her surroundings as a red mist of anger blurred her vision. Of all the people to target, Gavin had to choose Callie's friend. It defied belief and yet made a perfect kind of sense. Dawn had been a real babe at eighteen: all long legs, long hair and impressive boobs, even though she herself couldn't see it and her confidence was non-existent. Despite her blinding rage, Callie could see that Dawn would have presented the ultimate challenge to her rat of a husband. What it said about her ability to satisfy Gavin's needs when they'd been married less than two years at the time was a question she'd prefer not to dwell upon.

'It's pointless saying I'm sorry and that I didn't mean for it to happen,' Dawn said. 'I was young but still knew it was wrong, yet I couldn't seem to help myself.'

'But a child...'

'I know you couldn't have them. Even so, I kept a low profile when I could no longer hide my condition, pretending to be off on glamorous assignments. You've never said about your inability to conceive so I figured it was a sensitive subject, but Gavin told me and said that it didn't bother you.'

'Ha!' Callie threw up her hands. 'I got tested. There was nothing wrong with me and no earthly reason why I shouldn't conceive. I wanted a large family, did you know that? Well no, you wouldn't have. I've never told anyone and perpetrated the myth that motherhood wasn't for me because I assumed Gavin was the one at fault. He refused to be tested, you see. Probably thought it wouldn't be macho if he knew he was firing blanks, but I know now that he didn't need to have a clinician tell him because he already knew he was virile.'

'I had no idea you wanted children,' Dawn said softly. 'Thinking that you didn't helped to ease my guilt, just a little.' She blinked back tears. 'I am so very, very sorry, Callie. If I had my time over, I'd like to be able to assure you that I'd behave very differently, but truth to tell, I'm not so sure that I would, simply because Gavin's allure, his charm, the sophisticated places he took me, to were simply overwhelming for an eighteen-year-old and I loved every minute of the time I spent on his arm.'

'I have no doubt.' Callie resumed a chair, a fair distance away from Dawn, as she took a moment to examine her feelings.

'Gavin persuaded me to give TV reporting a go. I was content to remain with print. I didn't have the confidence to put myself in front of a camera, but he was like a steamroller, calling in favours and getting me a screen test. I couldn't refuse him because... well, because I'd have walked over hot coals for him.'

'Yeah,' Callie said on a heavy sigh. 'I hear you.' Her initial shock and devastating sense of betrayal had dissipated, and she now simply felt numb. 'Does Gavin know that you didn't abort your child?'

'Not as far as I'm aware. He simply assumed that I'd do as I was told, and I almost did. I went to the clinic and was on the verge of doing it, but in the end, I just couldn't. Gavin promised me that we'd always be together, but he wasn't ready to have a family. He also persuaded me that a child would hold me back in my career. I believed him, probably because I wanted to, and had no idea how I'd tell him that I couldn't go through with an abortion. I convinced myself that he'd be glad, once he got over his anger, but I never got the chance to find out. He walked away and I never saw him alone again. Of course, I tried to call him and in the end, he took a call from me, just to get me off his back, I suppose. He said it had been fun, but all good things come to an end. I had my career, and he had his business. It was time to go our separate ways.'

'You would still have been pregnant at the time. Didn't that change your mind and make you want to keep the baby?'

'How could I? I was a junior reporter, earning minimum wage. I could barely support myself, much less a child. I told myself he'd be better off adopted by a couple who could give him all the care he needed.'

'And forgot all about him.' There was a bitter edge to Callie's voice.

Dawn stared directly at Callie. 'I have thought about him every single day since giving birth, wondering if he's happy, what he's doing, if he has children. I'm a grandmother, by the way.'

Callie couldn't believe that she felt sorry for the woman who'd screwed her husband, but she did. Even by Gavin's standards, he'd treated her appallingly, abandoning her in her hour of greatest need. 'Congratulations,' she said in a hollow voice.

'I guess I should go.' Dawn gathered up her bag. 'I'll understand if you never want to see my face again.'

'It's not *your* face that I want to pulverise. I can't say I'm thrilled by what I've just learned. It feels like the ultimate betrayal. I need time to process. But the blame isn't entirely yours. When Gavin turns on the charm, I know how hard he'd be to resist. That doesn't make it right but what's done is done. Thanks for telling me.' Callie paused. 'I think.'

'I didn't do so to ease my own conscience. If I'd wanted to do that then I'd have said something years ago. I figured it was my guilty secret and that I needed to bear the weight of it alone without burdening you. That was the one thing I could do for you. But you see, the situation has changed insofar as George found out about Jago somehow—'

'Well, if Jago and George are both mixing with Archie Taylor, presumably Jago told him.'

Dawn shook her head. 'He's not applied to the adoption agency to see his birth certificate.'

'Is Gavin named on it as his father?'

Dawn shook her head. 'The thing is, though, Jago's a whizz with computers. I interviewed his adoptive mother, Joan Reid, on the pretext of doing a segment on the adoption service. Jago graduated with a first in data science and boasted to Joan that he could get past a bank's firewall if needs be.'

'So hacking into the adoption records would be a breeze for him.'

'Right. But if he did that then he hasn't felt the need to contact me. Not that I can exactly blame him for that. I mean, he probably thinks I abandoned him. Well, there's no "think" about it. I did, selfishly, in order to pursue both my career and my love life. A child would have held me back.'

'He's an adult now and must know that these things aren't always black and white. In his place, I'd want to know why you did what you did.'

'I didn't even know his name until a couple of days ago. Well, I knew I'd called him Jago but had no idea if his adoptive parents had kept that name. He's a devoted father himself now, by the looks of things.'

Callie listened as Dawn explained Jago's family background and the fact that the woman he intended to marry had been murdered in broad daylight.

'He doesn't have much luck, does he, the poor kid?'

'I think he is into something dodgy, perhaps because he's angry with the world and wants his revenge.' Dawn scowled. 'He paid cash for his bungalow up near the downs. That and the company he keeps only points one way. Anyway, the reason why I started looking for him and the past has been dredged up is that George came to see me at about the same time as he asked to use your meeting rooms.' Dawn paused. 'Callie, he knew all about Jago and threatened to tell you if I didn't persuade you to let him have his way.'

'You didn't try to persuade me though, quite the opposite, although I do understand now why you've been so introspective recently.' Callie let out a long breath. 'I'm glad you didn't give in to George. That's something.'

'Whatever you might think of me and, trust me, you can't have a lower opinion of me than I have of myself, we need to work together to get to the bottom of George's shenanigans. Then, if you never want to see me again, I'll understand.'

'If I never spoke to any of Gavin's conquests then half the female population of Brighton would be on my hit list. I'll confess that his betrayal with you hurts more than the others, but I don't hold you responsible. Well, not entirely. You were young and ambitious. Gavin would have picked up on that and you'd have been putty in his hands.'

'I think I'd prefer it if you shouted at me and threw things. You're being far too reasonable.'

'Well anyway, what you've just told me has made my mind up for definite. I no longer care if Gavin's alive or dead but if he is still breathing then he no longer has a wife.' Callie leaned towards Dawn, trying to feel the same way about her that she always had, suspecting that her eyes were sparkling with a combination of determination and barely suppressed malice. 'And I intend to take him for every penny I can lay my hands on. I know where all the funds are buried.' She smiled at Dawn, her disappointment momentarily put aside. There would be plenty of time to examine what she'd just learned once they'd dealt with more pressing matters. 'Anyway, first things first. We need to decide how best to get George off our backs, then I shall be speaking to an estate agent.'

'I'm glad you said "we".' Dawn smiled. 'I am on your side, Callie, even if it doesn't seem that way.'

'I know.' Callie waved Dawn's assurances aside. 'I can't think about our friendship right now. What I do need is for you, me and Darren to put our heads together, combine our knowledge and see what we come up with. Darren stayed on late to try and find out more about Jago. I'll call him now, tell him we're ahead of him on that one and get him to come over. Him, I'm increasingly certain, I *can* depend on.'

'Ouch!' Dawn muttered so quietly that Callie barely caught the word.

Accustomed to Gavin's indiscretions, even if this one hurt

more than most, she wouldn't let her feelings stand in her way. She picked up her phone and dialled Darren's number.

'Damn, it's engaged. I'll try him again in a minute. Shall we open another bottle? I think we could both use more wine.'

* * *

'Holy shit!' Darren sat back in his chair and scratched his head. 'There has to be some mistake.'

He rechecked the record of Jago Reid's birth that he'd just accessed thanks to a little creative hacking and let out a long breath, already aware that no mistake had been made and that he'd just opened a can of worms.

'Dawn has a kid.' He shook his head, trying to figure out why he'd been given up for adoption and why she hadn't said a word for all these years. He stared at the picture he'd taken of Jago's profile for a long time, unwilling to accept what was now glaringly obvious. The kid was the spitting image of Gavin as he must have looked in his younger days. 'What the fuck!'

He tried Dawn's mobile. He needed to talk to her before he decided what to do with his newfound knowledge. Knowledge that would knock Callie for six and Darren wasn't about to have her more upset than she already was if he could possibly help it. The strength of the protective feelings he harboured towards his boss at that moment surprised even him.

'Damn!'

The call went straight to voicemail. He left a message, asking Dawn to ring him as a matter of urgency. He then continued to look into Jago's background and what he discovered turned his blood cold.

'Fucking hell! It can't possibly be.'

But Darren knew that he'd hit pay dirt and, more to the point, that Gavin had royally played him. His mind went from talking to Dawn to visiting Callie. What he now knew couldn't wait for the morning and Callie would have to be told immediately.

His phone rang twice whilst he drove towards Callie's house. It was her calling on both occasions, but he declined the calls. What he had to say to her would be best said face to face.

He swore when he arrived and found Dawn's car on the drive. A moment's thought was sufficient for him to realise that it would be just as well to get both ladies together. He could only trust to luck that Callie was strong enough to withstand what he had to tell her, as well as learning about Jago's parentage. For all her bravado about enjoying a childless life, Darren had never believed it. Beneath the polished façade, he'd seen glimpses in unguarded moments of a woman who would have loved a family and would likely have made a great mum.

Not allowing himself the time to change his mind, turn tail and run, Darren climbed from his car and pressed Callie's doorbell.

'Oh, hi,' she said, when she answered it. 'I've been trying to call you. Come in. Dawn and I have stuff to tell you.'

Darren greeted a subdued Dawn, who had clearly been crying, and accepted an offer of beer from Callie. He had a feeling he'd need it.

He listened as Callie succinctly repeated what Dawn had obviously just told her, admiring Callie's fortitude when she kept her emotions under tight control. She could have been talking about the weather, and it was obvious that she hadn't shed a tear.

Yet.

Darren suspected that the floodgates would open when she was alone. Despite all the affairs, he knew that Callie still had feelings for her waste-of-space husband. All the women he took up with seemed to react towards him in the exact same way.

Darren had fended off more of them than he could recall when Gavin got fed up and ditched them. What was it about the man? He treated them well, then appallingly, but they remained unswervingly loyal. It made absolutely no sense.

'You've done your own research, Darren, haven't you?' Callie asked. 'I'm guessing that you took a peek at Jago's birth certificate too.'

'You know?' he asked, glancing at Dawn.

'She just told me. I'm still processing.'

'Then I'm sorry to overburden you, but there's more.' He splayed his legs and rested his forearms on his thighs, dropping his head to stare at the floor beneath him. 'I wish like hell that I didn't have to tell you this, Callie, now of all times. One shock is more than enough, but…'

'But,' Callie replied, fixing Darren with a ballistic stare. 'Gavin's still breathing and you're in touch with him.'

16

When Darren failed to hold her gaze, Callie knew that her suspicions were on the button. She should probably be falling apart, given all the shocks she'd received over the past hour, but instead, she felt calm and in control. It was as though her mind had closed down in order to protect the rest of her from the pain of disloyalty.

At the same time, she was almost relieved to have her suspicions about Darren's duplicity confirmed.

'How did you know?' Darren asked, finally lifting his head and looking at her, sheepish and subdued.

'I didn't, not for sure. I suspected but wanted to be wrong, so I tried to ignore all the small clues. I'd grown to rely on you as being someone who put my interests first and foremost and didn't want to believe that I'd got it wrong. That you were playing a part.' Callie heaved in a massive breath. 'Okay then, out with it. Where is he and why has he stayed away for so long?'

'As to where he is, I have absolutely no idea. No, honest!' He held up a hand, pushing it palm-first towards Callie, warding off her protests. 'I don't even know if he's still in the country but somehow suspect that he isn't.'

Callie eyed him speculatively, feeling dead inside. Another betrayal. It was almost more than she could withstand, and yet she felt oddly detached from reality, immune to disappointment and stronger than she had ever been. Not knowing whether her husband was dead or alive had held her back. Aware that he was still breathing and that he didn't give a toss about the shambles he'd left her to deal with killed off any lingering feelings she might otherwise have maintained for the bastard.

The truth was almost liberating.

'How do you keep in contact with Gavin?' Dawn asked.

'Burner phone,' Darren replied succinctly. 'He called as recently as yesterday and said he would be back soon.'

'How nice.' Callie flashed a sarcastic smile.

'Have you told him about George's demands, and does he know what his partner is planning?' Dawn asked.

'I have told him about George and he claims to be completely in the dark but says I should persuade you to let him use your rooms.'

'Ha! So much for being in the dark.' Callie frowned at her PA before pointedly lowering her head. 'I expect he pays you well enough to be his lapdog.'

'It's not that simple.' Darren paused until she lifted her head again and glowered at him. 'I'll explain why I felt it necessary to come over here and break cover. Yes, I did look at Jago Reid's birth certificate and put two and two together, but that wasn't the reason.'

Callie continued to hold Darren in a death glare, feeling all sorts of regrets, and didn't say a word, compelling him to break the heavy silence.

'You're aware that my dad's banged up.'

Both ladies nodded.

'My two brothers are as bad as him, if not worse. Dad was working for Gavin when he got his collar felt. He didn't drop Gavin in it and in return, Gavin looks after my mum. To be honest—'

'That would make a pleasant change,' Callie remarked scathingly.

'Ouch! I deserved that.'

He tried a smile, but Callie was now immune to his charm. It had all been a massive lie, she realised, and he'd probably flirted with her on Gavin's orders, laughing at her behind her back for being such a pushover. What a sap she must seem like. What had she been thinking, letting her guard down with him recently? She knew better than that. Had a little flirtation with a handsome younger guy really turned her head to the extent that she'd put her suspicions about his motivation aside? She really should have trusted her instincts, she knew now, but hindsight was bloody irritating.

'My mum is the only member of my family that I have any time for. Annoyingly, though, she can see no harm in my old man and the way he makes a living. Which is the same way that my brothers earn a crust, I might add.'

'You chose the path of the straight and narrow,' Callie said, flapping a hand, her tone cold, hostile. 'Yeah, yeah, I've heard it all before. That's old news. Not that you can be *that* straight, not if you take orders from my husband. Anyway, get to the point.' Callie wasn't in a good place right then and so chose not to accept that the same could be said of her.

'I'd had enough getting on for six years ago and took myself off abroad, bumming around, doing bar work. Picking fruit. Stuff like that. Moving from country to country while I tried to decide what to do with myself. Then after about a year, I got a frantic call from Mum. My oldest brother Colin was in deep trouble with the law, and I was needed to get him out of it. Again. Colin knew that if he called me, he'd be wasting his time because I wouldn't have given him the time of day, but I never could refuse my mum anything.' He drew a deep breath. 'And so I went home to a shit storm.'

'Hang on,' Dawn said, holding up a hand. 'If you're on the side of the angels, why did you mother think you could get your brother off from criminal charges?'

'What was he accused of doing?' Callie asked at the same time.

'I had no idea of the details and never wanted to know. The one thing I'd learned growing up in a criminal family was never to ask questions. That way, if you're pulled in, you can't tell what you don't know. All I knew at the time was that there had been a serious incident, involving a knife, and a witness had given a good description of Colin. A grainy image had been caught on CCTV as well, so the plod thought they had their man, even though his features weren't clear.'

'Jesus!' Callie muttered.

'The witness was all that stood between Colin going down for murder and him getting off. The CCTV wouldn't have been enough.'

'Please don't tell me the witness disappeared,' Callie said, clutching her head in her hands. She had absolutely no idea that Gavin's activities had extended to arranging hits and intimidating witnesses.

'She had a severe case of amnesia.'

'You didn't buy her off for Gavin?' Callie asked.

'Me? No. But I could be useful to Gavin, and he saw Colin's problems as an opportunity. Someone like me who has a foot in both camps, so to speak. Gavin had tried to recruit me before, which is one of the reasons why I went abroad, out of his reach. Colin would take an enforced holiday, well away from UK justice until the heat died down, or until it was safe for him to come home, Gavin assured me. Mum would continue to be looked after but in return, I had to take a job working for Gavin.'

Callie probably looked as astounded as she felt. Darren sounded so plausible and looked totally sincere, but it couldn't possibly be true.

Could it?

'Why have you decided to come clean now?' she asked.

'Orders from Gavin, I suppose.'

Darren's focus was on Dawn and when Callie glanced at her, she could see why. Her face was now chalk white and her entire body appeared to have gone into spasm. Callie didn't want to care but instinctively reached for her friend's hand.

'You okay?' she asked.

'It was Caroline, wasn't it?' Dawn said in a barely audible voice. 'Your brother killed my son's fiancée. The mother of his daughter.' She shook her head. 'What are the chances?'

Not that favourable, Callie thought but didn't say, when mixing with local villains. It was a small, insular world.

'I deliberately didn't want to know what Colin had done, cowardly though it sounds. On my life!' he added when Callie sent him a sceptical look. 'I found myself between a rock and the proverbial hard place. I didn't want to get involved with criminal activities, but I did want to protect my mum. What choice did I have?'

Callie never thought that she would look upon Darren – always so solid and dependable, so tough and resourceful – as weak, but that was the way that he now came across. He'd tried to get away from his family's activities by bumming around the world, but he hadn't settled on a career that would have made his intentions clear and provide him with independence. It was almost as though he'd been torn between the two camps. If Callie had been in a reasonable frame of mind, then perhaps she would have conceded that it hadn't been as easy for him as it appeared to be to an outsider.

Fairness was out of the question as things stood. Darren had been set to keep an eye on her, her every move reported back to Gavin, and she wasn't sure that she'd ever be able to forgive his duplicity. She wasn't sure if she felt angry, upset or just plain disappointed. She had been *so* close letting him get past her defences, but something had held her back. Well, lesson learned. From now on, she would listen to and act upon her instincts and emotion would play no part in future decisions.

'Anyway,' Darren said. 'I had to face my demons today, once I delved into Jago's background and found out about Caroline. I knew at once that must be the crime that Colin had committed. The stupid bastard bungled it, of course. Reid had been the target, but Caroline stepped in front of him when Colin wielded the knife. He killed an innocent young woman, and it didn't even seem to bother him.' Darren's expression oozed the disgust that Callie felt. 'He only cared about avoiding getting nicked for murder.'

'You know this how?' Callie asked.

'When Gavin got hold of me, after I'd come back and gotten involved, he spelled it out. Obviously, I didn't know until now about Jago and his connection to the murdered lady. I wanted to leave Colin hanging in the wind, but I knew that if I did that then my mum's life would be ruined. She'd be ostracised by her friends and Gavin would withdraw his financial support.' He spread his hands. 'I had no choice. Besides, the position Gavin offered me at the spa was legitimate and I actually grew to enjoy it, although I don't expect you to believe that.'

'Just as well,' Callie muttered, jiggling her knees because sitting still without exploding with anger seemed like an impossible ambition.

'Why did Gavin want Reid dead?' Dawn asked. 'I thought he was low down the food chain with O'Keefe's mob.'

'Gavin and O'Keefe were working together on something. Don't ask me what because I have absolutely no idea. Reading between the lines, I think Gavin was being tested when O'Keefe asked him to deal with Reid.'

'O'Keefe was the bigger man,' Dawn said, nodding. 'Perhaps Gavin hoped to take over his position by working with him on the inside to begin with. O'Keefe had been making noises about retiring.'

'Yeah, but it was a family business. He wouldn't have handed the reins to an outsider,' Darren said.

'Okay, but if Gavin somehow crossed O'Keefe, it would explain why he's gone to ground now.'

'Yeah, I thought the same thing,' Darren replied. 'O'Keefe is the only man I've ever known Gavin to be afraid of.'

'Is Colin still abroad?' Callie asked.

'As far as I know. Mum doesn't know why he took off but hears from him occasionally. She thinks he's making a new life for himself overseas, even if she doesn't know where, or what he's doing. Mum is very good at burying her head and believing only what she wants to believe. Anyway, even if Colin has returned, he knows better than to get in touch with me.'

'I suppose you've updated your paymaster on the latest developments,' Callie said, an edge to her voice.

'No, actually. I stopped telling him everything a while back.' Darren held up a hand. 'I don't expect you to believe me, but it's true. He's had his pound of flesh. I'm out for myself now and really want to help you, Callie.'

His intense look was almost convincing.

Feeling deflated, her trust abused by both her best friend and by her PA, Callie turned away without answering.

'Why would Jago continue to work for the man who killed Caroline?'

Dawn's question was obviously rhetorical, and Callie didn't attempt to answer it, even though it seemed obvious to her. Jago either didn't know who had killed his future wife or else it wasn't a case of mistaken identity. Jago, with his cyber skills, would be invaluable to the criminal fraternity given the modern-day nature of crime. Blaggers no longer needed to take the risk of holding up banks physically but instead stole from them online. If Caroline discovered what he'd been doing and threatened to turn him in, or told Reid what she knew, not wanting her child's father to become a criminal, and if O'Keefe found out then she'd have signed her own death warrant. And Reid's.

Why would Gavin agree to have a woman murdered, though? Callie sucked her lip as she thought it through. He had standards, after a fashion, and females were strictly off limits when it came to violence. But then again, he'd grown more ambitious with the passing of the years and Callie no longer knew what drove him. Perhaps, in his determination to impress O'Keefe, he had changed, become more ruthless. Why would she have noticed if that was the case? she asked herself. She made a point of *not* knowing anything about his criminal activities. Did that make her complicit by default? Ignorance, she knew, was no defence in the eyes of the law.

'It's a little late to show motherly concern,' Callie said, her words intended to wound. Dawn flinched, indicating that they had done so, and Callie immediately regretted her pettiness. 'Anyway, you said yourself that Reid introduced him to O'Keefe after he graduated. If he was already in, there would be no way out and he'd have known it.'

Dawn nodded. 'True enough.'

'Anyway, my primary objective is still to find out why George wants to use my rooms so that I can get him off my back and set about selling the business. Can I trust either of you to help me? If you're concerned about your son, Dawn, then it would be in your best interests to do so.'

'Absolutely,' she replied without hesitation. 'Jago is clearly no choir boy, and I'd like to save him from his own folly, greed, or whatever before he gets in too deep.'

'I owe Gavin nothing,' Darren said, his expression resolute.

'Okay, so what do we know?' Callie asked, in business mode with her emotions shut off in a place where she couldn't reach them. There would be time enough to reflect upon Dawn and Darren's dual betrayal at a later time, when she was feeling less raw and vulnerable. Whenever Gavin had been lairy or unreasonable, which was a lot of the time, burying herself in her work had been her escape route. She'd fall back on it now in an effort to take charge of her own life.

'Archie Taylor, George, Chris Ambrose and Jago are involved in something almost certainly criminal,' Dawn said. 'Not sure why Ambrose would be needed, though. He's the brawn and Jago's field of expertise is non-confrontational. The question is, who are they working for? O'Keefe, presumably. Gavin's on the missing list because, we think, he's done something to cross O'Keefe. There's no other explanation and the chances are he won't return until he makes his peace with O'Keefe.'

'Into spiritualism, is he?' Callie asked. 'Seems you know more about my husband's habits than I do.'

'What do you mean?'

'O'Keefe's dead.'

Dawn looked stunned. 'How can you be so sure?'

Callie sent Dawn an aloof look. 'Because I killed him.'

'Come again,' Dawn said, swallowing. 'What? When? Why didn't you say?'

'The whys and wherefores don't matter. And I didn't tell you because I thought you were my friend, as well as being a journalist. I was protecting your interests and didn't want you to have to choose between the scoop of the century and what I thought was a solid, no-secrets-withheld friendship.' Callie turned her hostile gaze towards Darren. 'I suppose Gavin knows.'

'Nope. God's honest, I didn't tell him.'

Callie grunted.

'You knew about this?' Dawn pointed a finger at Darren.

'You only need to know that O'Keefe will never resurface,' Callie said in an authoritative tone. 'And I guess if you'd told Gavin then my not-so-lamented husband would have come swaggering back into my life like nothing had happened,' she added, turning to Darren. 'So, with O'Keefe and Gavin both out of the way, we have to assume that Taylor and George, with the cyber assistance of Gavin's son, are making a bold move to take over their territory, combining both operations under one umbrella.'

'Leaving aside the not-to-be-messed-with Mrs O'Keefe,' Darren pointed out.

'Without Ryan O'Keefe to carry out her every wish, she's lost her power to intimidate and must know it.'

Darren nodded. 'Fair point. She's certainly been keeping a low profile since O'Keefe joined the missing list.'

'Okay,' Callie said. 'So, we know they're up to something. Suggestions as to finding out what?'

'I could have a word with Jago.'

Callie laughed aloud. 'You've never spoken to the boy. What's the plan, Dawn? Walk up to him, stick a microphone beneath his nose and introduce yourself, expecting him to spill the beans?'

'You obviously want to meet the lad,' Darren said, his voice more sympathetic than Callie's, 'but there's no way that he isn't aware of your identity. You must realise that. If he wanted to know you, he'd have been in touch long since.'

Dawn dropped her head and examined her manicure. 'Yeah, I guess.' She couldn't recall another time in her life when she had ever felt so low. So disgusted with herself. Callie's cold attitude cut her to the quick, although what else she could have expected, she was at a loss to know.

'Let's think what Gavin and O'Keefe had going and where their operations overlapped. Neither was into drugs, but both had interests in prostitution, moneylending and...'

'And people smuggling,' Dawn said. 'We know that Melody and some of the other girls at Phoenix were brought into the country illegally.'

'None of which would require input from a cyber expert,' Darren pointed out.

'I think the plan is to go legitimate,' Dawn said, staring off into the distance.

'Gavin's been working towards that end for a while,' Callie snapped. 'What is it that you think they want to legitimise exactly? There are plenty of kosher moneylenders. The type of people that O'Keefe and Gavin lend to are the ones who don't have the collateral necessary to satisfy a legitimate source.'

'I think you might be onto something, Dawn,' Darren replied in a pensive tone. 'But whatever it is, it's big and bold. We know Gavin is alive and O'Keefe isn't, but George *et al* don't, so they have to move quickly and make it appear as though they're doing so with Gavin's prior knowledge and approval. Hence the vital need for your rooms at the spa, Callie. All the people that Gavin works with know that he does business from there, so it makes sense.'

'No. It has to have something to do with cyberspace,' Callie insisted. 'That's the only part that makes any sense of Jago's involvement.'

'I could have him followed, if you like, Callie.' Darren smiled at her. 'Say the word and it's done.'

'If whatever he's up to happens online, then physically following him won't do a thing,' Callie replied.

'What else do we have?'

Callie took a moment to consider the matter, then tilted her head. 'Okay, we'll try that for a couple of days but make sure your people are discreet. I don't want him spooked.'

'I hear you,' Darren replied.

'I wonder if what they're planning was in the works with either O'Keefe or Gavin, perhaps both because we know Gavin was cozying up to O'Keefe before they went on the missing list.' Dawn followed Callie's example and canted her head, in journalistic mode and thinking outside the box. 'O'Keefe was into property, so it stands to reason he'd have someone like Archie Taylor in his pocket.'

'Perhaps.' Callie conceded the point with an abrupt nod. 'But I think it's something bigger than property. And yes, I do think that the sharks are gathering. Those who knew what Gavin or O'Keefe had planned, and whatever it was that sent Gavin into hiding, are attempting to pick up the reins. See if any of the people connected to your family have heard whispers, Darren.'

'I'll do some deep online digging,' Dawn said, 'to see if I can find out where Jago has been browsing.'

Callie glowered at her. 'You think he won't have set traps to prevent any such snooping?'

'Yeah, perhaps you're right.' She sighed, feeling unsettled and frustrated, hating Callie's semi-hostile attitude even though she had expected worse and knew she deserved everything she got. 'Jago is apparently a regular visitor to the dark web. Well, I'm not sure if it's a regular thing but his mother – his adoptive mother – said he boasted about his ability in that regard.'

'Christ, I hope it's not some form of nasty porn!' Callie said, shuddering.

They talked around the subject for another half-hour without coming up with anything solid. Dawn felt she'd more than overstayed her welcome and so gathered up her bag, thinking Callie and Darren needed to clear the air. Worried about Callie's ability to withstand two betrayals in one day and wishing she could hug her spontaneously in the way she'd been doing for years.

But those day were gone, at least for now. Perhaps forever.

She took her leave, promised to keep in touch and left Callie's house, possibly for the last time. Tears blurred her vision as she climbed into her car, started the engine and pulled away.

17

Once Dawn had left, Darren felt the full weight of the crystalline silence that prevailed. Callie acted as though he wasn't there, the bruised look in her eye affecting him like a punch in the solar plexus. He wondered if he should leave too and allow Callie time to come to terms with the double betrayal she'd just endured. Dawn and Gavin... he shook his head, unable to believe it. Despite being well aware of Gavin's womanising, he would never have supposed him capable of being that cruel so early on in his marriage. Dawn was a real babe, but she was also one of Callie's closest friends, and therefore off limits to any person with even limited scruples. Any lingering respect which Darren might otherwise have still entertained for Gavin was now dead in the water.

He wanted to ask Callie how she was coping but knew it was a fucking stupid question that would be met with the open hostility it deserved. She was tough, he reminded himself. She'd had to be in order to remain married to a selfish misogynist of Gavin's ilk, but even she had her limits. He felt like a shit for having had to come clean, especially so soon after Dawn's revelation. The disappointment in her expression had hit square between the eyes, even if her knowing was kind of cathartic. There would be no secrets between them now and he'd do all he could to make her see that he really was on her side. *If* she continued to give him the time of day.

And that was a very big if.

'Let's think about where we go from here to stop George,' he said briskly, deciding that keeping it businesslike and not showing unwelcome sympathy would be the best way forward.

'Why don't you ask your boss.' She sent him a scathing look. 'I'm sure he'll be full of ideas.'

'I'm not going to keep apologising for being boxed into a corner and taking the only way out that was available to me at the time. All I will say is that things have changed since then and I really am on your side. If you want me to be. I realise that the trust is gone, and that I have a lot of ground to make up, but let's not waste precious time talking about what can't be changed. Looking forward and finding out what the hell's going on would be the smart move.'

'That's just it. You hit the nail on the head. It all comes down to trust, but you've been deceiving me for five years so how can I believe a word you say? You claim to be going straight but—'

'The world isn't *that* black and white, Callie.' He leaned towards her, somehow resisting the urge to touch her. Persuading her to give him another chance was all that mattered. 'You claim not to be involved in criminal activity but are well aware that your business was being used to launder dirty money, so...'

'*Touché!*' She heaved in a huge breath. 'We've both done what we've needed to in order to survive. I get that. At least I think I do, but like I say, it's a trust issue.'

'You've never fully trusted me because you thought I worked for Gavin. Well, I did. You knew that he'd hired me and weren't happy about it, but you didn't fight his decision because you wanted to show him that you could run the business and make a success of it. Respect. That hadn't been part of Gavin's game plan. He underestimated your intelligence and will to succeed. You've found your forte and given him pause.' Darren spread his hands. Taking a tough attitude had been the right way to go, he now knew. Instead of feeling betrayed, she was ready to fight her corner.

'Yeah, okay. Point taken.' She paused. 'So, do you really believe that Gavin doesn't know, or at least suspect, what George is up to?'

'I'm pretty sure that he *does* know, which makes it that much harder to decide why he isn't at least talking to George direct.'

'He probably didn't expect George to try and take control.'

'That's his own fault for staying away for so long. Something big is in the offing but for some reason, Gavin can't come back and so he's getting desperate. He's calling me daily rather than weekly and does not sound happy.'

'Hmm.' Callie leaned her elbow on her knee and cupped her chin in her hand. 'What can be so sensitive that he won't share with you?'

'There's always been stuff he doesn't share with me. I've made it clear that I don't want to know anything about his criminal activities. Anyway, this latest thing has to be to do with his joint venture with O'Keefe, I'm thinking.'

She glanced up at him, her expression speculative. 'You really didn't tell him that O'Keefe's dead, did you? Why not?'

'I promised not to tell.' He winked at her. 'Besides, he didn't need to know.'

'When he finds out, if he does, he will look upon it as the ultimate betrayal and then your neck will be on the line.'

'I'll worry about that when the time comes.' Darren stared at the swimming pool, fascinated by the rays refracted by the underwater lighting that created a rippling, turquoise kaleidoscope on the water's surface. 'As to why I didn't mention it, perhaps because I saw the effect his disappearance had on you, leaving you to deal with the fallout without even bothering to tell you what to expect. Just assuming you'd handle whatever came your way. That was cowardly. Besides, if he knew O'Keefe was no longer, then he'd be back.'

She looked at him, reluctant surprise reflected in her expression and was slow to lower her gaze again. 'Really?'

'Yes, really. I don't think either of us are in any hurry to see him again. He claims to be going legit, but the means he's using to get there won't bear scrutiny, especially with O'Keefe gone, leaving him free to do as he pleases.'

'Okay,' Callie said briskly. 'I'm ready to nail the bastard with or without your help. I'm done with making excuses for him and my feelings for him won't survive this latest betrayal. So, how do we go about it?'

'Seems to me you hold all the aces. Unless he has money stashed away somewhere that you know nothing about, which seems likely. Otherwise, how's he been living these past months?'

'Good point. He hasn't touched his offshore accounts. I've been keeping an eye on them.'

'The business and this house are in your name too?'

Callie nodded.

'Well then. We find out what George is up to and scupper his plans. In the meantime, put out quiet feelers about the sale of the business. Nothing public that Gavin will see to bring him running home. It can be done, if you trust me to arrange it. Same with the house.'

'I'm with you. We put a stop to George, because we know whatever he has planned was Gavin's original idea. Once it becomes obvious that O'Keefe isn't coming back then Gavin will return and there will be a turf war—'

'That I don't want you caught up in. If he finds out that we knew O'Keefe was dead—'

'That I killed him.'

'And I didn't tell him, then neither of us will be safe, which is why you need to be ready to disappear fast.'

She glanced up at him. 'What about you?'

Darren flashed a careless smile. 'I'm a big boy. I can take care of myself.'

'You're thinking, and I am too, that whatever George is attempting to muscle in on is the big one that would have seen Gavin set for life and that it was a joint venture with O'Keefe.'

Darren nodded. 'Looks that way to me.'

'Then I want to stop him.'

Darren had never seen Callie half so calm yet determined before. Gavin's affair with Dawn had been the catalyst, he suspected, that had pushed her over the edge. Darren had watched her over the years and knew that as much as Gavin exasperated her, a large part of her was still in love with him. But everyone had a breaking point, a time in their lives when they had to face reality, and Callie had reached hers.

'Okay.' She got up, poured herself a large glass of wine and, without asking if he wanted one, opened a bottle of beer and handed it to him. Darren took it as a sign that he'd not been forgiven exactly but that she wasn't intending to throw him out on his ear either. She was intelligent enough to know that she needed him. At least for now. Darren would do everything in his power in the time available to him to demonstrate his loyalty. 'So, how do we go about cracking George's plans?' she asked.

'I'm thinking that Jago Reid is pivotal. Sorry,' he added, holding up a hand when she winced at the sound of his name.

'Don't mind my finer feelings. I'm immune to disappointment. And I agree with you, as it happens. As far as we're aware, Jago is a cyber rather than hands-on criminal, so whatever they have planned is virtual, so to speak, and he's intrinsic.'

'Right, so I have him followed for a few days and see where he leads. He will have to leave his cyber cave sometimes.'

'Can we have George followed too?'

'Best not. He'll be on his guard.' Darren took a moment to mull the matter over. 'Might be better to have Chris Ambrose tailed. Seems to me that if muscle is required as well as cyber skills, the scam will involve presence "in real time".'

'What the hell can they be into?' Callie asked, frowning.

'That's what we aim to find out,' Darren said, sounding more confident than he actually felt. He could think of a dozen things off the cuff that could go wrong, but he saw no point in worrying Callie more than she already was.

'Do you really think your brother killed that poor girl?' Callie asked after a short pause.

'Yeah, it looks that way.' Darren stared at the rug beneath his feet. 'If I hadn't been so set upon... well, setting myself apart from my criminal roots at the time then I would have found the courage to look into his crime, ask him about it and then probably turned him in myself.' He looked up at Callie, shaking his head, not liking himself much at that moment. 'He crossed a line and has never spent a day behind bars to make amends. That's on me and I have to live with it.'

'So this might be an opportunity to make amends?'

'By showing Jago up as a partner in crime?'

'I was thinking more in terms of warning him off. God alone knows how he got involved with criminal activity in the first place, but then perhaps it's in his genes. I mean, Gavin is his father.'

'Dawn said that his foster dad worked for O'Keefe, so there's your answer. I understand your desire to keep the kid out of trouble, but how the hell are we supposed to do that?'

She sent him a fragile smile. 'I'm sure you'll think of something.'

'For you, I'll see what I can do.'

'Next time you hear from my beloved, let me know what he has to say for himself.' She waggled a finger at him. 'No more secrets.'

'No ma'am!'

Callie stood up, appearing unsteady on her feet. Darren jumped up too and reached out a hand to steady her, but she shook him off. 'Get out of here,' she said.

'See you tomorrow,' he said, looking back over his shoulder as he left the house and waiting until he heard the locks click into place before he climbed into his car and drove away.

* * *

Early the following morning, Dawn paid a visit to the spa. She suspected that Callie wouldn't have slept any better than she had and wanted to at least clear the air between them. She knew that Darren and Callie would probably work together to try and figure out what game George, and by implication Jago, was playing. She hoped they wouldn't cut her out of their investigation. She needed to know too. Nothing concrete had been agreed when she'd been with them the night before, other than it wouldn't be safe for Dawn to dabble with the dark web.

'Can I come in?' she asked, tapping at Callie's office door. 'Darren isn't here to keep me out so...'

'Sure.' Callie's tone was brisk, businesslike, as though she was speaking to a stranger. In some respects, that's probably what Dawn was to her now, she supposed.

'Is Darren...'

'Yeah, he's still working here. He's probably popped out for a moment.' Callie sat back and eyed Dawn in a manner that made her feel deeply uncomfortable. 'What do you want, Dawn? If it's forgiveness, then you're being naïve. The trust is gone, and we can neither of us change the past. You'll just have to live with your guilt, if you feel any.'

'I was thinking more of getting to the bottom of Jago's involvement in George's affairs,' Dawn replied, matching Callie's brisk tone.

Callie raised a sceptical brow. 'Worried that your son's in too deep?' she asked provocatively.

Dawn decided against apologising. Again. 'I was wondering about engaging the services of a computer expert I know. He's worked for the station sometimes, delving into places he has no right to be without leaving a trace. He's a safe pair of hands because he's not actually on the station's payroll and therefore deniable. Anyway, I thought I should run the idea past you first, just in case you and Darren have decided upon a different course.'

Darren put his head round the door at that moment.

'Come in,' Callie said, her tone as impersonal with him as it had been with Dawn. 'Dawn has a computer expert who she thinks might be able to see what Jago's been up to online.'

'Does he have any direct links to you?'

Dawn shook her head. 'No, he's an independent. He's worked for the channel before, but his involvement has never been made public.'

'It can't hurt, I suppose.' Darren glanced at Callie for approval.

'Darren has arranged for Jago to be followed,' she said, 'but

I'm not sure what help that will be. Not if whatever they're doing is online so yeah, if you think this guy can delve without leaving a footprint, go for it. But be careful. The people Jago's mixing with are no boy scouts.'

Callie's internal phone buzzed.

'George Markham here to see you, Callie,' the receptionist said when she picked up. 'He says you're expecting him.'

'Not yet, I'm not,' she muttered beneath her breath. She still had a couple of days' grace. Dawn and Darren had both heard the call and Dawn wasn't surprised when she glanced at Darren, clearly unsure what to do and seeking guidance. Dawn wondered if her friend realised just how much she'd come to depend upon her handsome PA.

'Best to see what he wants,' Darren said quietly.

'Okay, Ellie, send him up please.' Callie cut the connection. 'You two, skedaddle,' she said. 'Dawn, leave the back way so he doesn't see you. Darren, stay at your desk in case I need you. I'll leave the intercom open,' she added, flipping a switch.

Dawn stood, only just preventing herself from leaning over to hug Callie. She knew the gesture would be neither welcome nor reciprocated. 'I'll keep in touch and let you know what my guy finds out.'

18

Callie watched Dawn leave, the rancid scent of betrayal eating away at her like a virus. It would be a long time before she could properly forgive her for the damage she had done to their friendship. The affair wouldn't have mattered so much but for the fact that Dawn had borne Gavin's son. That knowledge cut to the quick. She had lost count of the sleepless nights she'd spent, hugging her knees to her chest, lamenting the fact that she'd never fallen pregnant. She had perfected an attitude of indifference and learned to keep her feelings to herself. But the ache, the churning need to embrace motherhood, had never gone away.

And throughout Callie's angst, Gavin's son had been growing up in a household not ten miles away. She wondered whether Gavin had known or if Callie was right and he simply assumed that she'd aborted his child, ending his life like it meant nothing at all and never thinking about him ever again. Given Gavin's selfish nature, she reckoned that was likely the case.

Her introspective thoughts were brought to an abrupt halt when Darren put his head round the door and ushered George in.

'What can I do for you?' Callie asked coldly, not bothering to get up from her chair, or offering George her hand. She noticed how stressed he seemed and hoped that implied his plans were not going smoothly. There was a reason, Callie knew, why Gavin had always referred to him as a follower, never a leader. The stress involved in taking over something dangerously ambitious was obvious for all to see.

'I came to ask you a question.' He sat in the chair that Darren had recently occupied and fixed her with a contemplative look. 'And to issue a warning.'

'A warning about what?'

'You're aware that Gavin and O'Keefe were involved with joint projects.'

'Nope.' Callie shook her head decisively. 'How am I supposed to know that? I play no part in Gavin's activities and have no desire to. All I'm good for is fending off people like you when Gavin takes a holiday, and they think they can encroach on his territory.'

'I keep my ear to the ground and word is that Gavin and O'Keefe had a falling out. Mrs O'Keefe is convinced that her husband is dead, and that Gavin had a hand in his demise, so she's out for revenge. Without Gavin here to take the heat, you're in the direct line of fire. I thought you should know.'

'I see.' Callie linked her fingers together in her lap, if only to disguise the fact that her hands were shaking, as she wondered about George's real purpose in coming to her. 'It's kind of you to consider that possibility.'

If George noticed her sarcasm then he chose to ignore it.

'It seems to me though that your worries are misplaced. If Mrs O'Keefe is involved with her husband's business affairs, and I'm told that she is very much in the driving seat in that respect, then she will be aware that the same can't be said for me.'

'Yeah, but she thinks you must know where Gavin is and why he's lying low. She urgently needs to talk to him.'

'Then she will have to join the queue.'

'She's a dangerous woman to cross.'

Callie fixed George with a hard stare. 'So am I. That might be worth bearing in mind before you try more of your strong-arm tactics.'

George held up a hand. 'Look, I'm trying to help. I don't have any other agenda.'

Like hell you don't!

'Well anyway, regarding Gavin, I suspect that he's dead too, otherwise he would have resurfaced before now. Especially,' she added emphatically, suspecting that George was fishing for information, 'if he had O'Keefe killed. He wouldn't have stayed away this long, leaving his empire and O'Keefe's up for grabs because the field would be clear for him to take complete control.'

'Perhaps but we go way back, Callie, and I'm worried about you. You're vulnerable. There are a lot of people wanting a word with Gavin and they won't wait forever. Sooner or later, they'll all turn their attention towards you.'

'You're motivated entirely by concerns for my welfare.' Callie leaned back in her chair and sent him a caustic look. 'How touching.'

'Believe it or not, your choice, but it's true. I knew you before Gavin set his sights on you and if memory serves, I tried to warn you off. Gavin was never going to be the monogamous type.'

'So, if O'Keefe and Gavin did have business interests in common, they would have been beneficial financially to both parties. And, presumably, they needed to work together, combine their influence, in order to bring the scheme to fruition, so it really wouldn't be in Gavin's interests to bump his partner off. I'm sure Mrs O'Keefe would be aware of that since I happen to know that Ryan ran all his schemes past her and if she didn't approve, it didn't happen.'

'There is such a thing as falling out amongst thieves, to coin a phrase.'

George's argument sounded weak, presumably because he hadn't expected Callie to dismiss his warning. Did he really think she was so easily intimidated? George was right to say that they'd known one another for a long time, so if he bothered to think about it, he'd realise that she wouldn't have survived the last three months without Gavin's protection had she been the wilting-violet type.

'Okay, Mrs O'Keefe's suspicions notwithstanding, who's Gavin's latest squeeze? Chances are he'll be shacked up with her.'

George looked away. 'I'm not sure I...'

Callie thumped the surface of her desk hard with her fisted hand, making both George and the objects on it jump violently. 'You started this conversation, George. You want to know where Gavin is. Personally, I don't give a shit any more but if you're dead set on finding him, help me out here.'

'He... Word is that he had a dalliance with O'Keefe's elder daughter,' he said with patent reluctance.

'Fucking hell!' George's revelation had shocked Callie out of her complacency. 'Jackie, you mean. I thought she was happily married with a brood of kids.' And drop-dead gorgeous, Callie recalled, having seen her once or twice at social events arranged by Gavin. She had that long, black hair, green-eyed Irish look going, complete with dotted freckles across a cute little snub nose and was a real traffic stopper.

'Married, sure, but to one of O'Keefe's foot soldiers. Sean Barlow. Not sure he was the guy that her pa had in mind for her.'

'What?!' Callie shook her head. 'Come on, George. I know

O'Keefe is a control freak but even so, this is the twenty-first century.'

'I suspect she was up the duff, and Mrs O'Keefe wasn't about to have any child of hers giving birth out of wedlock, so Jackie wouldn't have had much choice but to marry a guy who she'd probably only turned to for rebellious reasons, unless she wanted to be drummed out of the family and for Sean to lose vital body parts. But a gofer wasn't what O'Keefe had in mind for his little girl, that much I do know.'

'Right.' That made a bit more sense, Callie thought. Jackie had a reputation for being hot-headed, spoiled by a doting father and determined to have her own way. But Daddy would have his limits and would support his wife's views of single-parenthood, Callie assumed, what with him being a card-carrying family man and all that.

'As to Jackie and Gavin, Sean is currently doing a stretch at His Majesty's pleasure, so the field was clear, and Gavin probably couldn't resist. Sorry.' George held up a hand when Callie winced.

'What's he banged up for?' she asked briskly, annoyed to have shown any reaction to Gavin's latest indiscretion. Nothing he did could surprise her any more. Not really.

George shrugged. 'No idea.'

'No wonder Mrs O'Keefe is out for Gavin's hide, the stupid bastard!' Callie paused. 'Where would they have gone?'

'Absolutely no idea. That's why I'm here. Gavin sniffing around Jackie was fairly common knowledge, but I figured you probably wouldn't know, and if you're looking for him, Jackie's friends might be a good place to start.'

Gavin's prolonged disappearance now made a ton more sense. He probably couldn't resist hitting on Jackie – the more dangerous the situation, the harder it would be for Gavin to back away, as evidenced by his affair with Dawn. He wouldn't have meant for this latest affair to get so serious. Presumably, O'Keefe had found out, which would explain why Gavin had agreed to sell the spa to him, albeit for a generous price. Perhaps Jackie had come on to Gavin at O'Keefe's suggestion, simply to weaken his bargaining position? O'Keefe had wanted the land behind the spa very badly and ordinarily, Gavin would not have agreed to sell.

Not at any price.

Why George had suddenly decided to come clean was less clear. Perhaps whatever scam he was planning had reached a critical point, and he was getting cold feet, worried that O'Keefe or Gavin might reappear and scupper the plans in question. Then again, perhaps he suspected that O'Keefe was no more and needed it confirmed. That would make more sense, except there was no reason for Callie to know, unless he thought she was in regular contact with Gavin and that he'd told her he'd done the killing.

Gavin had previous when it came to taking off without notice. But O'Keefe, the poster boy for family life, was another matter. By putting out feelers, Mrs O'Keefe had shown her hand. She didn't know where her husband was, which was unheard of, leaving her with just one conclusion to draw.

'If the affair was no secret, then those wanting an urgent word with Gav will have already followed that trail,' Callie pointed out.

'I dunno, do I.' George looked evasive. 'It's just that we need him home, Callie.'

No, you don't! You just want to make sure that he won't be back any time soon. 'Speak for yourself, George. I have no further use for the cheating rat. Thanks for stopping by. Don't let me keep you.'

'While I'm here, about that other business.'

'Nope.' She stood, arms akimbo, and looked George straight in the eye, her expression resolute. With her heels on, she was the same height as him and had an up-close view of his thinning hair and bald spot. She'd had enough of being manipulated and was through with buying time. 'Not happening.'

'Now just a minute!' He waved a finger at her. Callie took hold of it and bent it backwards, causing George to howl.

'I'm through with being bullied by big, strong men.' She put extra force on his finger before releasing it, just to make a point. 'Tell me why you need the rooms and I might reconsider, otherwise it's no dice.'

'Better you don't know.' George puffed out cheeks puce with barely suppressed rage. A woman had assaulted him physically and his ego would never recover. Only Callie could get away with such a thing, she realised. Unless or until Gavin turned up dead, his cohorts would always fear him. Callie was at a loss to know why she had attacked George's finger, other than that he'd caught her on a bad day. She'd always resented anyone who poked fingers in her direction and something inside of her had snapped. She was nearing the end of her tether and had had enough of being bullied, but even so, if she'd taken a moment to consider, she never would have done it.

'In that case, I want no part of it. Now get out!'

George glowered at her, still nursing the damaged finger in his other hand. Callie idly wondered if she'd broken it. 'You'll live to regret this!' he growled. 'Gavin's been gone for too long, the predators are gathering, and you'll get caught in the crossfire. Don't expect me to protect you when that happens. You're on your own.'

She gave a significant nod towards his injured finger. 'Your sort of protection I can do without. Now get out and leave me alone. I have work to do.'

Darren joined her the moment George left.

'What did you do to him exactly?' he asked, laughing. 'He looked like he was ready to commit murder.'

'He shouldn't have pointed a finger at me,' she growled.

'It's a bit late to suggest that you should have exercised restraint,' he replied, still smiling.

'I know. But hell, it felt good!' Her expression sobered. 'Gavin taught me that trick. When confronted by an angry person, they inevitably point a finger for some reason, making the finger in question vulnerable, easy to bend back.'

'Right.' Darren held his hands close to his chest, making them both smile.

'Did you know about Gavin and the O'Keefe girl?'

Darren waggled a hand from side to side. 'I'd heard rumours but no, I didn't know. Not for sure. Gavin is many things, but I've never known him to have a death wish before.'

'What's Sean Barlow banged up for? Do you know?'

'Not a clue. Want me to find out?'

'Please.' Callie tapped her fingers restlessly on the surface of her desk. 'Can't help thinking he'd become an inconvenience.'

'Gavin wouldn't have grassed him up just to get a clear run at his wife. There is a certain code about that sort of thing that's never broken.'

'Honour amongst thieves?' She raised a brow. 'I thought that went out in the eighties.'

'I'm wondering if someone in O'Keefe's organisation fitted him up. I mean, he got the favoured daughter pregnant, and he never really fit into the family circle. Word is, the marriage wasn't going so well.'

'O'Keefe pushed Gavin and Jackie together in the hopes of getting the spa?' Callie nodded in response to her own question. 'I was thinking the exact same thing. It would certainly explain why Gavin agreed to sell without bothering to run the proposal past me.' She snarled the words. 'So typical of him!'

Darren made a quick call on his mobile, waited a few minutes then offered thanks and hung up.

'That was one of Gavin's tame cops,' he said. 'You're right about Barlow. He was caught shifting drugs and not only are drugs a big no-no in O'Keefe's operation, but you were right about him being grassed up too. He was only caught because of an anonymous tip-off and you wouldn't get odds against that tip coming from inside O'Keefe's organisation.'

'The plot thickens.'

'Indeed.' Darren paused. 'Why did you stand up to George? I thought we were playing for time.'

'Because he's worried and nervous. Things are coming to a head, and I got the impression that they're doing so faster than he anticipated. He's losing control and so I wanted to put a spoke in the works. He can threaten all he likes but what can he actually do to me? A physical attack or worse won't open up the place to him. And anyway, it felt good to tell him to take a hike.'

'You realise he'll go to Dawn now and put pressure on her. You didn't tell him that you know about Jago.'

'No, because we know Jago's involved in whatever's going on and I didn't want to show our hand. But you're right. I need to warn Dawn not to let the cat out of the bag either.'

'Right.' Darren remained where he was. 'Is there something else?' Callie asked, phone in hand.

'Just one thing.' He looked her straight in the eye. 'On my mother's life, I did not tell anyone about O'Keefe's death. I know George's visit made you think I had.'

He then stood up and left the room without saying another word.

* * *

Dawn took Callie's call, listening as she related in an emotionless tone the details of her meeting with George.

'Okay, thanks for the update,' she said when Callie ran out of words. 'I'll expect the pleasure of a call from George and won't let on about Jago.'

Dawn waited for small talk that didn't materialise, realising that the call had already been disconnected. Callie hadn't even said goodbye.

Sighing, Dawn returned her attention to her laptop, where she was endeavouring to find out everything she could about her son's activities. Her contact at the paper was already delving into the dark web on her behalf. She half-dreaded what he might find but urgently needed to know. The truth couldn't be any worse than the scenarios playing themselves out inside her head.

She delved into the public posts on his various social media accounts, discovering that he was a dedicated gamer. A game called Enrarvis that she'd never heard of featured prominently. She logged onto its promo site to find out what it was all about. It appeared to be the usual thing. Teams trying to get the better of one another by violent means. Gaming, she knew, was massive business. The social lives of half the young people on the planet, and many of the not so young, revolved around playing solitary games on a screen. No wonder social skills were on the decline. There had to be a story in there somewhere, she thought absently.

Shuddering in reaction to what little she had learned about the violent nature of this latest craze, Dawn was hesitant to sign up. Eventually though, curiosity overcame caution. Using a generic email address – one of many she'd had occasion to use in her day job and which, she was assured, couldn't be traced back to her – and calling herself LucyB, she joined the game. Having paid a fee with a credit card that wasn't in her name, she read the rules.

'Fucking hell!'

She knew it was fantasy but wondered what sort of people would want to involve themselves with something so visually abhorrent. She knew gaming was addictive and people went to greater and greater extremes to get their kicks, but this was sick. Disgusting. The killings were so realistic that she could smell the blood as stomachs were torn open and the guts spilled out, and she was only able to see level one. There were five more levels above that, but she really didn't want to think how much worse it got.

Dawn felt physically ill as she logged out and gulped fresh air into her lungs. How could her son involve himself with anything so extreme, she wondered, reminding herself that Jago wasn't actually her son insofar as she'd never had anything to do with his upbringing. She'd given birth to him and then given him away, having no part in the shaping of his mind. She found it hard to imagine that Mrs Reid would have encouraged an interest in violence but then, that was the problem with cyberspace, she knew. You got drawn into things and no one else knew what you were up to. Besides, his foster father worked for O'Keefe and had introduced Jago to him.

Enough said.

Having had more than enough virtual blood and guts, Dawn idly searched for more mentions of Enrarvis, which appeared to be everywhere. Clearly, it was top of the charts amongst gamers, perhaps because it was so extreme, pushing boundaries of good taste that would never pass muster in the real world, and thereby giving players a vicarious thrill. That, she supposed, was the entire point. Domination of the world from the comfort of your own home. What was wrong with the younger generation nowadays? Dawn wondered. A bit of weed and kicking back against authority had been more than enough in her day.

Dawn scrolled through all the testimonials for the game but halted when she came upon notice of an Enrarvis symposium right here in a Brighton hotel. It opened the following day. That had to mean something for Jago, she reasoned, given that he was such a massive fan. It stood to reason that he'd be there at some point. What did enthusiasts do at a gaming symposium? God forbid that they should emerge from their personal caves, talk to a person rather than a machine, and play in the real world. Not that they could set about killing one another – obviously. But she figured that mock battles would fill a need in people who had nothing better to do with their time and who enjoyed a little gratuitous violence simply for violence's sake.

She picked up her phone to call Callie, glad that she'd made progress of sorts and keen to talk it over with someone.

'Interesting, but I can't see the relevance,' Callie said in reply. 'Jago probably thinks that being a cyber whizz means he can beat the odds, go up a few levels, or whatever it is that gamers try to do. Anyway, if it's already scoring big with gamers, I don't see why it would interest George and his cronies. That ship has sailed and there won't be any money to make out of it.'

'Yeah, it's probably nothing but I might just stroll down to the Majestic and see what all the fuss is about. The journalist in me needs to know. I imagine they'll be setting up for it right now and I can pretend to be there in my professional mode.'

'Do that,' Callie said, sounding distracted. 'Let me know what you find out.'

'Will do.'

Dawn checked her appearance and then set off for the hotel. There was a lot of frenzied activity in the foyer when she arrived.

Posters of people in weird costumes, all wearing masks and wielding swordlike weapons. Someone was inflating a giant-sized figure that looked a bit bionic.

''Scuse me, love.'

A burly man carrying a ladder barged past her. Another, wielding an iPad, referred to it constantly and shouted instructions that no one appeared to hear. Disorganised chaos didn't come close to describing the scene.

'What's going on?' she asked a harried girl.

'Enrarvis symposium, obvs. The venue's been changed and the date brought forward, so it's all a bit of a hustle.'

'I can see that.' But Dawn was talking to herself. The girl had already hurried off.

Unsure if there was anything to learn from the chaotic scene, Dawn was about to turn tail and head home when she noticed a discreet side door. And standing guard over it was a man she recognised from pictures Darren had taken in that pub the night before. The man in question folded massive arms over a toned torso as he guarded the door and kept an eye on proceedings.

Dawn ducked out of sight, her heart racing. It was Chris Ambrose, the hired muscle.

She had clearly hit pay dirt and retired to a quiet spot to call Callie again. What could possibly be behind that door that required guarding? Dawn felt that prickling sensation at the back of her neck that she always got when she was on the point of breaking a big story. *Well, big by local standards*, she mentally amended, but everyone had to start somewhere.

Callie answered on the first ring.

'Find something out?' she asked.

Dawn explained. She heard a sharp intake of breath at the other end of the phone. 'Get out of there! Don't let Ambrose see you.'

'He won't suspect me. I'm a journalist. It's my job to poke my nose in where it doesn't belong.'

'Have you got a death wish?'

'It's just a stupid, violent game they're playing, Cal. It's not real.'

'Even so. I know where that hotel is. There's a café down the road. Wait for Darren and me there. We'll be twenty minutes tops.'

Dawn definitely wanted to investigate but this was also her chance to mend fences with Callie and she had no intention of wasting the opportunity. There was probably nothing more sinister behind that door than a few anoraks putting the final touches to the symposium anyway. Nothing to see here.

With a sigh, she emerged from the alcove where she'd made the call and stepped straight into a brick wall. She gasped when a heavy hand came down on her shoulder and she looked up into the handsome, unsmiling face of her son.

'What the fuck are you doing here?' he demanded to know.

19

Darren drove Callie towards the Majestic hotel at high speed, clearly sensing the urgency every bit as much as Callie herself did.

'I did a bit of digging when Dawn came back with the name of that game, Callie,' he said, indicating to overtake a slow van. 'It's nasty stuff and very realistic but I can't figure out what possible interest Jago and his friends can have in it.'

'Unless Jago wrote it.'

'Yeah, that possibility crossed my mind, but I don't see it myself. I mean, if he did and it's already making a fortune, what good would that be for George? These things are like fashion. They only stay in vogue until the next craze comes along. They have a short shelf life and George has missed the boat in that respect. Besides, why would Jago sell a going concern if he himself is making a mint?'

'Is it easily accessible to all?'

'Not sure. I didn't sign up. They wanted a credit card, and I was being cautious. You know, just in case they suspect we're onto them and my name raises a red flag.'

'I can't believe how popular this gaming lark is,' Callie said pensively. 'It's big business, obviously, but why does it have to be so violent?'

'A voyeuristic thrill? Frustrated people wanting to take themselves out of their dreary lives? Why do grown men go to boxing matches to watch other grown men knocking six bales of shit out of one another?' Darren took one hand off the wheel and waved it towards Callie. 'I'm not the right person to ask.'

'I hate over-regulation, but I do think this stuff could be damaging young minds and there ought to be some limitations put on it.'

'It's addictive, like gambling, like bingo, like alcohol… the list is endless. Where do you start with your regulations, and where do you draw the line? Like everything, I'm guessing that the vast majority are responsible and know when to call a halt. It's those with addictive personalities who go too far.'

'But that's the clever part, don't you think? You can go up a level, presumably once you reach a certain stage, and the curiosity to know what comes next keeps the punters playing. Or conducting virtual fights. Or whatever it is that they do.'

'Well, we're here. If I can find somewhere to park, we'll meet Dawn and see what she's found out, then go into the hotel and see what we can see. Anyway, how do you want to play this?'

'I have a cunning plan.'

Darren chuckled. 'Of course you do.'

They parked in a multi-storey and walked back to the hotel. There was already a crowd of young people outside, even though the symposium didn't start until the following day.

'Are they really planning to queue all night?' she wondered aloud. 'Blimey, there's dedication for you.'

They were dressed in lairy costumes, wearing masks and wielding worryingly realistic-looking weapons. The odd thing was that no one appeared to be talking to anyone else. It seemed to Callie as though they didn't know how to socialise. Either that or it was a rule of the game, in which case it definitely needed intervention from authority.

'I'm scared to speak,' she said in an undertone.

Darren laughed. 'Morning guys,' he said loudly, saluting the crowd. 'Nice day for it,' he added as rain started to fall.

Hardly anyone turned to look at him.

'Have they taken a vow of silence or have they forgotten how to speak?' Callie asked, shaking her head in mystification.

'Are they human beneath those masks?'

They were both laughing as they passed the hotel and headed for the café where they'd agreed to meet Dawn.

'Where is she?' An anxious edge crept into Callie's tone as she glanced around the packed café and Dawn was nowhere in sight. 'She should have been here ages ago. Something isn't right.'

'Don't panic yet. You know Dawn. She probably couldn't resist having a little look-see back at the hotel. She'll come barging in at any moment, apologising and running her mouth just like always. Just a mo.'

Darren effortlessly caught the attention of a busy barista. A quick conversation resulted in the girl shrugging and shaking her head.

'She doesn't remember seeing anyone who resembles Dawn,' he said. 'Doesn't mean she wasn't here, though. The place is popular, and I dare say that one face looks much like another to her.'

Callie extracted her mobile and called Dawn's number. 'Voicemail,' she complained, leaving a message asking Dawn to call her urgently. 'If she'd been here, she'd have waited for us.' Callie dragged at Darren's hand. 'Come on. We need to be at that hotel.'

'Try not to worry.' Darren kept hold of her hand and squeezed it. 'She's a journalist so has ideal cover.'

'Unless Jago sees her. I have a feeling that he harbours antagonistic feelings towards his birth mother.'

'You can't possibly know that,' Darren replied, dropping her hand as they neared the hotel. Callie wouldn't have made the admission under the threat of torture, but she'd have felt much better about... well, everything if he'd kept hold of it. There was something both comforting and reassuring about the feel of a man's hand wrapped protectively around hers. But now, she reminded herself, was no time to lean on Darren. On any man.

The hotel's foyer was chaotic. Callie glanced around but there wasn't the slightest possibility of spotting Dawn amongst all the comings and goings. None of the participants had been admitted but the crowd waiting outside seemed to have grown in size during the short time that Callie and Darren had been in the café. Orderly and introspective, it would be hard to realise anyone was there, were they not so visible in their colourful outfits.

'Come on!'

Callie marched straight up to the reception desk.

'Hi,' she said. 'We have a room booked for two nights. The name's Renfrew.'

The girl checked her computer, hit a few keys, shook her head and smiled up at Callie.

'Sorry,' she said. 'We don't appear to have a reservation under that name.'

'But... but you must have. My assistant made the booking.'

'At this hotel? There are a lot of others in Brighton.'

'No, definitely this one.'

'Well, I'm sorry, but as you can see, we're very busy this weekend. It would be quieter elsewhere.'

'No, no. We have a specific reason for needing to be here. I'll kill my PA when I get my hands on him,' she said, glancing up at Darren. It felt good to smile at him, even though she was still angry and upset by his deception. 'Can you find us a room?'

'Well, I'm not sure. Two nights, you say.' More keys were punched. 'We only have a penthouse suite and that's five hundred a night.'

Darren let out a low whistle. 'No wonder it isn't taken.'

'We'll have it,' Callie said, producing a credit card.

The girl looked surprised but booked them in quickly, as though afraid they might change their minds, and handed Callie a card key.

'Put the key in the slot in the lift and it will take you straight up to the top floor,' she said.

'Dawn won't be up here. Shouldn't we go look for her?'

'In a mo. I just want to check out the lie of the land.'

'I don't want you to think I'm complaining,' Darren said as they pushed their way through the crowd to the elevators, 'but is there a specific reason why you've booked us a room that you haven't shared with me yet?'

'Get your mind out the gutter,' Callie replied, suppressing another grin. 'Whatever's going down with George and Jago is happening at this hotel and we need to be here if only to scupper George's plans and get him off my back.'

'Oh, is that all? Should have it cracked by lunchtime then.'

'Don't be so defeatist. I'm fed up with being bullied and need to stand up for myself. And you,' she added, poking a finger into the middle of his chest to emphasise her point, 'are going to help me.'

'Yes, ma'am!'

They were still laughing when the lift whizzed them to the top floor, and they let themselves into a sumptuous suite with a panoramic view over Brighton.

'Wow! I could get used to this,' Darren said. 'How long are we staying again?'

'We're not,' Callie replied. 'It's simply a means to an end. A justifiable reason to be here.' She paced the length of the room feeling a combination of impatience and anticipation. 'George is up to his ears in whatever's going on here, but that's beside the point. We need to find Dawn first, then lay our plans. I'm worried that something's happened to her.'

Callie rang Dawn's mobile, tutting when it went straight to voicemail. Again.

'Come on.' She threw her phone back into her bag and hoisted it onto her shoulder. 'I saw a café in the foyer. It would be a good place to watch proceedings, and to wait for Dawn to put in an appearance. If she's chasing down a story and blows things here for us, then I won't be responsible for my actions.'

'She won't be,' Darren assured her, taking her elbow and steering her towards the door. 'Come on. Despite the extortionate prices this place charges, I think I can just about afford to buy you a coffee.'

Callie knew that Darren was attempting to reassure her, but her concerns for Dawn's safety refused to be pacified. Dawn was a Rottweiler when on the trail of a story, but in this case, it was personal and Callie wasn't sure that Dawn's practical side would have much control over her impulses.

Given that the foyer was busy, the café was surprisingly quiet. The masses hadn't been granted admission yet and so they were easily able to nab a table with a good view of proceedings.

'The symposium opens tomorrow,' Darren reminded her, once they'd given their order to the waitress.

'Then why the queue already?'

Darren shrugged. 'You're asking the wrong person. Getting in the mood, I guess, or sussing out the competition. My understanding is that actual people will take the place of the virtual combatants.'

Callie shook her head. 'A recipe for disaster. The game's violent and so things could easily get out of hand.'

'That's part of the attraction, I expect. The more extreme, the better.'

'I don't understand young people.' Callie probably looked as perplexed as she felt. 'All this makes me feel like I'm about a hundred.'

'Yeah, well…' Darren sat back and smiled at the waitress when she placed his coffee in front of him. 'Thanks.'

'Look, over there.'

Darren turned and let out a low whistle. 'Yeah, that's the guy we saw in the pub the other night, right enough, and he isn't about to let anyone through that door.'

'Which means we need to get in there and see what it's all about,' Callie said, an edge to her voice. 'I wouldn't bet against Dawn having already breached his defences. It's just the sort of irresponsible thing she'd try to do.'

'Talking of irresponsible…' Darren fixed her with a probing frown and allowed his words to trail off.

'I know, but sitting here drinking coffee when Dawn's on the missing list just doesn't feel right. She's keen to build bridges after what she revealed so wouldn't have missed meeting us at that café unless something prevented her from being there.' Callie returned Darren's frown. 'You know it's true.'

'Okay, drink your coffee and take a breath,' Darren said. 'In order to get into that room, we need to distract Ambrose. Something needs to draw him away from the door so that we can nip through it.'

'A disturbance, perhaps?' A fleeting smile touched Callie's lips.

Darren sighed. 'Are you sure?'

'What alternative is there? Sit here until I'm recognised? Chances are that George will put in an appearance at some point, and before he does, I would very much like to know what the hell this is all about.' She sent Darren a defiant look. 'If you don't want to be involved, I'll understand.'

'Okay.' He withdrew his phone from his pocket and conducted a brief conversation. 'Be ready,' he said, ending the call. 'Give it ten minutes.'

'What have you done?'

'Ordered up the disturbance that madam asked for.'

Callie bit her lower lip to prevent a full-on smile from escaping, thinking Darren was a very creative person to have fighting her corner. He was either playing a dangerous game in an effort to disguise his loyalty to Gavin, or he really was with her every step of the way.

Time would tell.

They watched the comings and goings as the stage for the symposium slowly emerged from the chaos.

'Why was this event moved here at such short notice?' Darren asked a guy clutching an iPad and looking stressed.

'Don't ask me, mate. Something about objections to it being held in Birmingham, where it was supposed to have been staged. We were all prepared up there,' he added, frowning at Darren as though the change of location was his fault. 'Probably too tame for that part of the world,' he added, shrugging. 'Brawling on a Saturday night is a ticket-selling regular event up there, I'm told.'

The man hurried off, leaving Callie and Darren staring at one another.

'Do you buy that?' Darren asked.

'Not for a second, but even if that guy knows the real reason, which I doubt, he's never going to tell us.'

Shouting coming from the queue outside drew the attention of everyone in the foyer.

'Game time,' Darren muttered.

Callie watched a scuffle break out as several lads sauntered along, apparently taking the piss out of the costumed queue. Callie already knew that they took the costumes in question seriously. They were in character, for want of a better description, and didn't take kindly to being ridiculed.

'It's getting out of hand,' Callie said anxiously.

'Don't worry. It'll be okay and,' he added, glancing at Chris Ambrose as he strode across the foyer, unable to resist getting involved, 'now's our chance. Come on!'

* * *

'Where are we going?' Dawn asked, trying not to wince as her son grasped her upper arm in a vicelike grip and pulled her along. She might have wished for their first physical contact to be gentler but was realistic enough to know that she was getting off lightly, all things considered. She wanted to tell Jago that he didn't need to force her. She'd go anywhere to have a five-minute conversation with him and try to abate some of the seething anger she sensed radiating from his core. He would have questions, of course he would, and she vowed to answer them with brutal honesty.

She owed him at least that much.

Chris Ambrose saw them approaching, raised one brow and opened the door he was stationed in front of without saying a word.

Dawn found herself in a lobby with a deep cupboard at one side. It led to windowless conference room, dominated by an oval table surrounded by eight mismatched chairs. The carpet was fraying at the edges and there was a smell of musty disuse about the place. A table at one end had an array of computer equipment whirling away. A closed door to an adjacent room had a temperature-control panel on the outside and was, presumably, the hub of the operation.

'Sit!'

Jago barked the word as though speaking to a dog. Dawn wordlessly complied, unable to stop herself from staring at her son and admiring his handsome features. His strong physique and dominating presence which effortlessly filled the dreary room.

'So, we meet at last,' he said scathingly, perching his backside against the edge of the table and looking at her, arms folded across his torso.

'Yes.' Dawn swallowed, awash with a whole raft of emotions that made speaking a challenge. 'We finally meet.'

'I hope you're not expecting me to fall at your feet in adoration and gratitude, or some such shit.'

Dawn felt it was a rather immature statement to make, especially given the fact that her son was so intelligent. Perhaps he too was on emotional overload but somehow, Dawn doubted it. It was more a case of venting pent-up rage, and she was willing to be his whipping boy. It was less than she deserved.

'I had hoped that you'd try to find me,' she said evenly, feeling a need to break the penetrating silence. 'Not that I expect you to believe it. I only recently discovered that you'd been adopted by a local couple and that you're a genius with computers. Once I knew that, I also had to accept that you would have discovered my identity easily enough but didn't want to know me.' Dawn dashed at a tear as she stared at her hands, folded in her lap. 'I can't say as I blame you for that.'

Jago seemed momentarily discomposed by Dawn's calm

acceptance of blame. He stood up and turned his back to her, obviously not wanting her to read his expression. A genius he might be, but she could already tell that he was immature in other ways with anger issues that he'd failed to address. Anger issues created by her when she gave him up for adoption, she accepted with a sinking heart, wondering if the damage ran too deep to be repaired.

'Whatever happened twenty-eight years ago, know one thing,' Dawn said, nervously clearing her throat. 'I never wanted to part with you, but your father left me with no choice.'

'Liar!' The ferocity behind the one word as he swirled on a heel to face her stole Dawn's breath away and suddenly, she was afraid of the man her son had become. 'I just knew you'd blame him, but I know the truth. He's told me you were too focused on your career to have time for a baby. I was an inconvenience you couldn't wait to be rid of.'

Dawn's jaw fell open. 'You're in touch with Gavin?' she asked.

20

'If the door's locked then we're screwed,' Darren said tersely as he hustled Callie across the foyer to the door in question. Everyone's attention appeared to be on the scuffle outside and no one took any notice of them as they pushed in the opposite direction to the surging crowd.

Callie held her breath, sensing that this would be a defining moment. She felt a burning need to discover what was going on and baulked at the idea of being deterred by a locked door. She exhaled when Darren turned the knob and the door opened on silent hinges. They moved quietly into a small lobby and could clearly hear agitated voices coming from an adjoining room.

'That's Dawn's voice. It can only be Jago she's talking to, can't it?' Callie whispered. 'What should we do? It sounds heated. Will he hurt her, do you suppose?' Callie shuffled on the spot, filled with indecision. 'Should we intervene?'

'Stay here and listen for now. There will be a lot of pent-up emotion being spilled. Let them talk it through. We can be in there in seconds if it turns violent.'

Callie hesitated. 'I'm not sure.'

'Don't you want to hear what's said? Jago is Gavin's son too, remember. You must be curious.'

'Like I could forget who his father is!'

'Sorry. That was crass,' Darren whispered.

'Don't be. I'm sorry for snapping. But Jago's parentage is one of the reasons why I'm worried for Dawn's safety. I'm guessing the kid has a lot of anger issues.'

'Shush!' Darren held a finger to his lips and Callie obediently stopped speaking.

'When did you first meet Gavin?' they heard Dawn ask in a commendably calm tone.

Callie gaped at Darren, who simply shrugged. It hadn't occurred to her that Gavin and Jago would be acquainted, but perhaps it should have done given that O'Keefe had already seen the kid's potential. It would explain why Jago had been drawn into something that appeared to be on the dodgy side of legal, given Jago's close association with the dark web. It was typical of Gavin to move with the times, if it was he who had encouraged the kid's potential and shown him how easy money could be made. He'd obviously cottoned on to the fact that cyber criminals were a lot harder to catch and prosecute, and the rewards were arguably more... well, rewarding.

'Why do you care?' came the petulant response. 'At least Gavin gives a shit, which is more than can be said for you.'

'Oh fuck!' Callie muttered, feeling for Dawn, despite all the lies and betrayals.

'I hate to burst your bubble, Jago,' Dawn said, 'but Gavin didn't want to know about fatherhood. Now that you're an adult and useful to him, I dare say things are different, but a word of advice: don't fall for his hype.'

'Don't tell him that he wanted you to have an abortion,' Callie muttered, grasping Darren's hand as her jangling nerves played havoc with her equilibrium.

Darren curled his fingers round her palm and gave it a reassuring squeeze, clearly understanding her anguish. The almost overwhelming desire to burst into that room and tell Jago just what a shit Gavin actually was became harder to resist as the seconds ticked by at a snail's pace. Darren put his free hand on her shoulder in a restraining gesture and Callie knew he was right to hold her back. Her intervention would only make matters worse and anyway, Jago wouldn't believe a word she said. The kid clearly hero worshipped Gavin and had cast Dawn in the role of the bad guy.

'Yeah, that's what *you* would say. He told me you were too focused on your career to have time for a baby. I was nothing more than an inconvenience and you couldn't wait to be shot of me. He wanted to take me though, but his bitch of a wife was having none of it.'

'News to me,' Callie said softly.

'You haven't told me when the two of you first made contact.' Callie listened to Dawn calmly pose the question, wondering how she could remain so impassive at such an emotional point in her life.

'That's what I'd like to know,' Callie whispered, glancing up at Darren, wondering if Gavin had confided in him. He didn't show any reaction and Callie regretted doubting his integrity, even though he'd been keeping stuff from her ever since Gavin went missing. She was torn between wanting to believe that he was firmly on her side and suspecting him of still reporting every little thing to Gavin.

Except he couldn't have done, she reasoned, at least insofar as Gavin wasn't aware that O'Keefe was dead. Now that she knew her waste-of-space husband was still alive himself, there was absolutely no doubt in her mind that he was only laying low because of his dispute with O'Keefe. He would have been back long since if he'd known the coast was clear and that others were about to encroach on his territory. She took a perverse sort of satisfaction of knowing that she had rid the world of Gavin's nemesis without him being aware.

'As if you care!'

'You seem to be carting a lot of anger about with you. I've spoken with your adoptive mother—'

'My *mother*. She's the only one I have.'

'Fair point. I've spoken with her—'

'Leave her alone! I don't want her upset.'

'She isn't upset and was happy to talk about you. You're her pride and joy and she enjoyed the opportunity to bask in reflected glory now that you've made something of yourself. You're her shining star, but then you already know that. I'm so very glad.'

'More like it's eased your conscience, always assuming you have one.'

'Oh, trust me, I'm on first-name terms with my conscience,' Dawn continued, seemingly unmoved by Jago's spite, but Callie knew she would be absolutely feeling it. 'Anyway, it seems to me that you had an ideal childhood. Now you're an adult and father yourself, you'll know that not everything you hear is true. There are two sides to every story, and not everything is black and white. There are degrees of grey that only become apparent when one is mature enough to understand the issue.'

There was a prolonged pause which Dawn, an experienced interviewer, had the good sense not to break.

'My dad worked for Gavin and Mr O'Keefe,' Jago eventually said in a grudging tone. 'That's how our paths crossed, since you insist upon knowing.'

Callie nodded, glad to have her suppositions confirmed.

'Gavin said I look a lot like him in his younger days. I told him I was adopted, and he joined the dots. Said he'd wanted to find me but didn't know where to start looking. Nor did I because you didn't even bother to put his name on my birth certificate,' Jago added venomously.

Callie could hear the accusation in his tone and felt for Dawn. Despite the fact that she'd betrayed Callie so badly, she was starting to understand how hard it must have been for Dawn all these years. She'd plastered on her game face and suppressed the guilt, never knowing what had happened to the baby she'd been forced to abandon.

'And then the woman you loved, the mother of your baby was brutally murdered.' Dawn's voice was now so soft, so full of compassion, that Callie strained to catch the words. 'How do you get past that?'

'Stop pretending that you care!'

Jago yelled the words. Callie, sensing that Jago was close to the edge, glanced at Darren, wondering if the time had come to intervene. Darren shook his head.

'Let it go on a bit more,' he said softly. 'He might know where Gavin is and blurt something out.'

'Stop behaving like a spoiled brat,' Dawn said, her voice now hard. 'I had to give you up for adoption. I don't expect you to believe that it broke my heart, so I won't bother to try and convince you. And the reason I had to give you up is because your beloved father, the man you seem to think walks on water, wanted me to have an abortion.'

'Rubbish! He told me not to get in touch with you because he knew you'd put the blame on him.'

'I have proof. Not with me but I have the cheque that Gavin gave me to pay for the procedure together with a handwritten note giving the details of the clinic he told me to use. But when it came to it, I couldn't go through with it.'

'I... I don't believe you.'

'I didn't suppose that you would but it's the truth for all that. Gavin paid off your mortgage, I assume.'

Callie found herself nodding. She'd assumed the exact same thing. It was just the sort of thing that Gavin would do to make him seem like the good guy.

'He gave me a hand. So what?'

'We can none of us change the past, Jago. If we could then I would act very differently. Anyway, I'm glad that Gavin developed a conscience. Better late than never. But I'm more concerned about what you've got yourself involved with here and why it requires a convicted criminal to guard the door.'

'None of your business,' Jago snapped.

'Nope, it's not, but I am a journalist and if it's all above board, I don't suppose you'll mind giving me the low down. Publicity can only help your cause.'

Jago laughed. 'Enrarvis doesn't need publicity. In fact, our USP is *not* advertising, which makes it more exclusive and creates curiosity. You've seen that queue outside. It's getting longer by the hour. They started queuing two days ago when it was announced online that the venue had been changed from Birmingham to here.'

'Why was that?'

'Dunno. Health and safety issues, I think. Not my problem. I just make sure the technical side of the game runs like clockwork.'

'Did you invent the game?'

'I was part of the development team, but we parted ways a while back. Professional differences.'

'Why are George Markham and Archie Taylor involved? They're bad news, Jago.'

'Look, what is it that you want from me?'

'I should be asking you that question. After all, you're the one who recognised me and dragged me into this room.'

'I just wanted to see for myself what a piece of work you are. If you're thinking along the lines of a soppy reunion though, then think again.'

'You're very close to your own daughter.'

'What the hell...' Callie could hear Jago's sharp intake of breath, even through the solid door. 'What have you been doing? Spying on me? You leave Lisa out of this, do you hear me? You forfeited the right to show any grandmotherly concern when you gave me up.'

'I'm so very sorry about Caroline.' Callie nodded her approval when Dawn had the sense to change tack. No wonder she was such an intuitive interviewer. She had a natural empathy and a sixth sense when it came to steering a conversation away from sensitive areas. She realised almost immediately that Jago didn't want his child brought into the conversation. 'It was a case of mistaken identity is the impression I'm getting from all the press cuttings.'

'Was it?'

Callie and Darren locked gazes. There was something in Jago's taunting tone that implied he knew more about the situation than had ever reached the press.

'Why on earth would anyone want to deliberately kill Caroline, a harmless clerical assistant on maternity leave?'

Callie suspected that the cogs would be turning in Dawn's brain every bit as quickly as they were in her own. Something was off here. Something serious that Jago probably shouldn't be talking about. Callie suspected that he wanted to shock his birth mother by demonstrating just what a hard man he'd turned into, hoping that she would shoulder the blame for his emotional issues.

'I assumed your adoptive father was the target,' Dawn said slowly. 'He worked for Gavin and O'Keefe, I'm told. Perhaps he heard something he shouldn't have and spoke out of turn. Or,' she added when Jago remained silent, 'perhaps Caroline picked up pillow talk when you confided in her about... something or other that was going down in Gavin's world. You were in bed with Gavin at that point, figuratively speaking, and believed every word that spilled from his lips. Oh, don't worry. You wouldn't be the first. He had me under his spell for quite a while too.'

'You're talking bullshit!' But Jago's angry retort lacked some of its former conviction.

'Caroline liked the money and the easy life, but she didn't like you getting pulled into Gavin's criminal enterprise, especially once she'd become a mother. She wanted you to get out but that wouldn't have been possible. Gavin's world doesn't come with an escape clause. So you went to Gavin, asked him what you should do to placate Caroline and effectively signed her death warrant.'

'No! It wasn't like that. She wasn't supposed to get killed.'

Callie's jaw dropped when Jago made the admission. Darren looked equally bemused.

'Fucking hell!' he muttered.

'Caroline and I had a big fight, and she threatened to tell the police everything she knew about Gavin and O'Keefe if I didn't get out from under.'

Jago sounded like a little boy again, admitting his misdemeanours to an understanding mother. He was apparently a genius when it came to computers, but Callie wondered if he was completely sane or if his mind had been affected by his hangups about adoption and abandonment. There was supposed to be a thin dividing line between brilliance and madness. The clever people lived in a different stratosphere.

'Gavin swears he didn't know what would happen. O'Keefe said he'd handle the matter and that Dad was the target. Caroline went to him when she couldn't get me to see things her way. Dad told her stuff that he shouldn't have. O'Keefe wanted to teach him a lesson, but Caroline got in the way.'

'And it was after that when Gavin paid off your mortgage, I imagine. Blood money.'

'He helped me when I needed him the most.' Jago's voice sounded small, hesitant.

'So where is Gavin now? And O'Keefe, for that matter.'

'No idea. I'm not their keepers.'

'You're playing a dangerous game, Jago, no pun intended. I think, and correct me if I'm wrong, that Enrarvis was a joint project between Gavin and O'Keefe. They bankrolled the game, probably told you how extreme they wanted it to be, and you've sat back raking in the cash ever since. But they're both on the missing list and George Markham and his cronies have seen an opportunity.'

'You're out of your tree! George represents Gavin.'

'Ah, so he knows where he's legged it to with the O'Keefe girl then?'

'Probably. Dunno. Not my problem. I do what I'm paid to do. Nothing more. Nothing less.'

'Come on, Jago, you're not stupid. Far from it. O'Keefe is a family man through and through. You imagine his business partner can take off with his precious daughter and there will be no repercussions? Grow up!'

'Yeah well, I did hear there was a bit of a barney but neither of them will let their personal affairs affect their business relationship. They'll both surface eventually, that's what George says, and he's holding the fort until such time as they do. Ask your friend, Gavin's wife, if you doubt me. We're having an executive meeting at her spa next week with some interested buyers after this symposium. If this event goes well then we can name our price.' A note of pride and refreshed confidence had entered his tone. 'Anyway, Mrs Renfrew is in ultimate control until such time as Gavin returns and she has the final say on any offer to purchase.'

'First she's heard of it.'

Dawn and Jago's heads swivelled in the direction of the door when Callie walked through it, flanked by Darren. There was no mistaking the relief that flashed through Dawn's expression. The lies and deceptions fell away, and Callie felt at one with her friend again. None of this was her fault, not really. Callie reckoned now that if their situation had been reversed when they'd been so young, if Dawn had been married to Gavin and he'd come on to Callie, then she probably wouldn't have been able to resist his quite disgusting mercurial charm offensive either.

'What the hell!' Jago stood tall and pushed out his chest. 'Who let you in here? Where's Chris?'

'He's settling a bit of a disagreement in the queue outside,' Darren replied.

'You'd best tell us what this is all about, Jago,' Callie said, feeling every year of her age suddenly and cursing Gavin for having landed her in this position. 'Rest assured, it's all news to me.'

'I think you need to get the hell out of here!'

'And I don't think you're in any position to make threats.' Darren spoke quietly as he stepped forward but there was obviously something in his stance that gave Jago pause and he took an instinctive step backwards. A computer nerd who invented bloodthirsty games but disliked physical violence.

'Tell us why that lot outside are so keen to get in here but look like they've been invited to a funeral,' Callie said.

'There's nothing illegal,' Jago replied, sounding defensive.

'Then explain as quick as you like.' Callie folded her arms and tapped her toe. 'I don't have all day.'

The kid looked so much like Gavin in his younger days that Callie felt disorientated. Having met his son, she could see why fatherhood would have appealed to Gavin now that the child in question was an adult and could be useful to him. He would have enjoyed moulding him in his own image. Someone to pass the baton to when the time came.

But even at a glance, she could see that Jago had too much of his mother in him for that ever to be possible. He wasn't ruthless enough and far too wrapped up in self-pity to become the sorcerer's apprentice. He had his father's ambition. Being brought up in a modest bungalow by people who cared about him and put his interests first hadn't been enough for him. He wanted what the proceeds of criminal activity combined with his computer brain could bring him, but he didn't want to leave his computer cave and live in the real world in order to achieve that ambition.

'Look, it's just a game that's taken off. The latest "big" thing.' Jago waved his arms in a vague gesture. 'But it will only stay in vogue until something better comes along. Gavin and Mr O'Keefe know that and want to cash in.'

'So why isn't Gavin—'

Darren held up a hand to cut off Callie's words. He was right to do so, she realised. Jago was about to talk, probably wanted to boast about how clever he was, and didn't need side-tracking.

'The game goes up in levels,' Darren said musingly. 'And the people outside are going to take the places of the virtual characters, I get that much.'

'But what happens at the highest level?' Callie asked, catching Darren's drift.

'Nothing much. No one gets hurt.'

'Is that what you really believe?' Dawn asked, apparently catching on too. 'The top level is pay-to-view, isn't it?' Jago shrugged and remained silent. 'And that's where the real money comes in. The subscribers go to the dark web for their enjoyment and expect value for money.'

'I think there's more to it than that,' Callie said. 'I assume there's a lot of heavy betting. That's where the money's made.'

Darren glowered at Jago. 'What happens?' he asked. 'Is it an actual fight to the death for audience gratification?'

21

Dawn gaped at her son. 'Please tell me they've got it wrong,' she said softly.

Jago failed to look at her. 'Of course. They're pissing in the wind.' He windmilled his arms, not quite managing to pull off the indifferent look he'd probably been aiming for. 'It's all just make-believe. Escapism.'

'What happened to escaping in a good book?' Callie muttered.

'The weapons that lot have in the queue outside looked pretty genuine to me,' Darren said.

'That's kinda the point.' Jago spoke with exaggerated patience, enunciating each word. 'They just give a very mild electrical charge, nothing worse, but it means reactions are more genuine. It's pure illusion, and everyone involved knows it.'

'People who pay a small fortune to watch this stuff on the dark web are aware that it's "illusion"?' Callie glowered at Jago, making her scepticism clear as she moved to stand beside Dawn. 'Get real! Someone's going to get badly hurt, which I guess is kinda the point, and probably why Gavin left you to take the flack.'

'You're asking the wrong person.' Jago held up a hand. 'Stop bullying me, Mrs Renfrew. I'm in charge of the online stuff, making sure it all works as it should and doesn't get overloaded. I don't get involved with anything else and frankly, I don't much care what goes on. Nor will your disapproval cause me any sleepless nights. We're supplying a need here and if we don't, there are dozens of others waiting to fill the gap. It's the way of the world nowadays. Ask your husband if you don't believe me.' Jago flashed a cynical smile. 'Oh, sorry, you can't because he's taking a break from your daily dose of moral indignation.'

'Watch it!' Darren growled.

'Ignorance is no defence in the eyes of the law,' Callie told him, indifferent to his lashing out. 'If someone dies or gets badly hurt then your neck will be on the line. You sure it's worth it?'

'You just don't get it.' Jago let out an exaggerated sigh. 'Gaming is the new clubbing and gamers are pacifists. Sad creatures for the most part. Solitary. They don't know how to interact in the real world and so don't understand what you'd refer to as the social niceties. But cyberspace *is* real to them. We're just making it more accessible and encouraging them to mingle at events like this one.'

'You sound like you're reading from a script,' Dawn said, shaking her head in obvious disappointment.

'Like I give a shit what *you* think of me.'

The door flew open, and Chris stood there with blood dripping from a cut on his forehead. 'What's going on?' he asked, looking at Jago for clarification. 'Who are these people?'

'Pacifists?' Darren asked, glancing at the blood Chris only just appeared to notice and which he attempted to stem with a handkerchief. 'You'd better see a medic, mate. That cut looks deep.'

'Mock weapons?' Dawn remarked at the same time.

'This was done by one of the troublemakers, not one of our lot,' Chris said quickly. 'He took me by surprise.'

'Of course he did.' Callie sent him a condescending look.

'You need to leave,' Chris said, belatedly recalling his duties and pocketing his handkerchief even though the cut was still oozing blood. 'This is a restricted area for authorised personnel only. I have instructions to ensure that no one gets in.'

'How's that working out for you?' Darren asked, not budging an inch.

'I'm Callie Renfrew and in my husband's absence, I guess that makes me the boss, so technically speaking, you work for me. Not that you'd stay in my employ for long. You don't seem to be very good at what you do.'

'Oh, Mrs Renfrew. No one told me to expect you,' Chris replied, his bravado evaporating. He seemed nervy on and edge, causing Callie to wonder if he was on drugs.

'I need a word with George,' she said. 'Is he here?'

Jago shrugged. 'What do I look like? His keeper?'

'What you look like is a petulant child who needs to learn some manners.' Darren stood close to Jago, invading his personal space. 'Apologise to the lady.'

'What lady? I don't see one.'

When Chris made no move to protect him, Jago dropped his gaze and backed away, mumbling an apology.

'I think we're done here,' Callie said. 'You had enough, Dawn?'

Dawn gazed at her son with a combination of longing and regret etched into her expression. She nodded just once, touched Jago's arm and turned away from him.

The three of them left the room without a backward glance, with Dawn lingering behind Callie, who instinctively turned to grasp her hand. She'd hesitated in the hope that Jago would call her back, Callie suspected, but she knew it wouldn't happen.

'Let's get back to the spa and talk this through,' Callie said, releasing Dawn's hand once they reached the foyer. 'My head's spinning. You okay?' she added, turning to Dawn. 'That couldn't have been much fun.'

'Yeah, I will be. Jago caught me slinking about and dragged me into that room, which is why I couldn't meet you or even warn you.'

'You could have sent a text,' Darren pointed out. 'Callie was worried.'

'I should have, I know, but my mind was all over the place. Sorry. It was an emotional moment. One I've imagined a million times, and which worked out pretty much the way I'd always expected it to.' Dawn waggled a hand in a considering fashion as they pushed through the crowd. 'Well, at least insofar as Jago's resentment towards me is concerned. I hadn't reckoned on Gavin having got his grimy claws into him, though.' She rolled eyes that were suspiciously moist. 'Talk about a hypocrite!'

'Nothing less than I'd expect.' Callie sensed Dawn's overloaded emotions, could see that she was hanging in there by a thread, and her resentment fell completely away. Jago being Gavin's son was absolutely not going to break up their friendship, she decided. 'See you at the spa and we'll talk it through there.'

'Yeah, I'll be right behind you. I'm in the multi-storey.'

'You okay?' Darren asked Callie, once they were back in his car.

'I'm fighting mad with Gavin for turning that boy's head, if that's what you're asking. And I feel for Dawn. The kid is clearly full of anger, and she doesn't deserve to have it directed at her. She especially doesn't need to hear her son to be singing Gavin's praises. Grrrr!' Callie thumped her fisted hands on her thighs. 'It's *so* typical of him to cultivate the services of a kid he didn't want in the first place and make himself seem like an avenging angel in a disturbed child's eyes.'

'Because he could be useful to him. Yeah, no one can accuse Gavin of being stuck in a time warp. He realises just how influential social media can be and all the new crazes that have sprung up around it. Gaming in particular. Once he understood Jago's skill set, I reckon he saw an opportunity to make a killing.' Darren flashed a sideways smile at Callie. 'No pun intended.'

'Exactly. And we now know why the use of my rooms is so vital to George's plans. His would-be investors are probably people Gavin had lined up before he did a runner and George saw an opportunity to step into his shoes. Gavin probably told George to mind the shop until he returned, and Gavin intends to be at that meeting.' Callie shrugged. 'Who knows, but it would explain why he told you to get me to accede to George's demands. Anyway, if I'm right and that's the way it happened, then in his own head, George morphed from custodian to top man when Gavin remained out of sight but still has to convince his investors that he's a safe pair of hands. Gavin and O'Keefe, if they were in this together, both disappearing at the same time will have given the investors the jitters and George knows he has to steady the ship with a show of strength.'

'All well and good,' Darren replied, frowning, 'but unless Gavin or you show your faces at the meeting, George has no real clout. This is a dangerous business and I expect a lot of money is involved, so the investors will want to deal with Gavin and O'Keefe, who are the men with the reputations.'

'You think George was planning to trot me out?' Callie gave a little laugh. 'How would that work? I'm nobody's poodle.'

'Well, that's his problem. He thought you'd be a pushover and if he'd spun you some line about caretaking for Gavin, he must have been confident that you'd step up. I mean, you've never shown resistance to Gavin in front of anyone before now, have you? Not even when he's gone on the missing list in the past.'

Callie chewed her lower lip. 'True, I suppose. Which means that I can expect a visit from George sometime soon. Especially now that we've shown our hand.'

They arrived at the spa and didn't continue with their conversation until they were in Callie's office, where Dawn arrived hot on their heels.

'Phew!' Dawn threw herself into a chair and fanned her face with the side of her hand. 'That went well.'

'I'm sorry,' Callie replied, wondering why she felt the need to apologise, or why Dawn needed to put a brave face on things. They all knew that her reconciliation with her son had been nothing short of a car wreck. 'Gavin's a shit!'

Darren handed round coffees and joined them on the sofas. 'We think Gavin's stoked Jago's feelings of injustice and then exploited his talent, letting him know just how comfortable his life can be if he utilises said skills,' Darren explained.

'Hmm.' Dawn rubbed the side of her nose. 'I'm more concerned about his lack of obvious emotion when he implied that his fiancée had brought her fate upon herself. He clearly doesn't do empathy, which is worrying, and seems to think that getting murdered was her own fault.'

'Yeah, I got that too,' Callie said, nodding.

'I don't think he loved Caroline. In fact, I don't think he's capable of genuine love, and I have to shoulder some of the blame in that regard.'

'Don't beat yourself up,' Darren said. 'You did what was best at the time.'

'There's a recognised disorder known as empathy deficit,' Dawn said. 'I did a feature on it once and if memory serves, some of the symptoms include being extremely critical of other people *and* blaming the victim.'

'He's transferred the guilt for grassing Caroline up by making it her fault.' Darren rolled his eyes. 'Geez!'

'He needs help,' Dawn said. 'But I don't suppose he'd ever agree to speak to anyone, even if I ever get the chance to suggest it.'

'I doubt it too. He thinks he's intellectually superior to us mere mortals and totally in control of himself,' Callie replied.

'How are we going to stop that horrible game going ahead?' Dawn asked. 'I think we all know that the top levels being fought out on the dark web won't be done with fake weapons.' She shook her head, clearly fighting to hold back tears. 'I can't bear to think of Jago's casual indifference when we pointed out what must be obvious to him, but he chose to ignore. That's what's upset me most of all, I think. He really doesn't think any of this is his fault.'

'He's compartmentalised,' Callie replied. 'You heard him. He only does the technical stuff online and has convinced himself that he isn't responsible for what happens in the real world.'

'Yeah, I guess.' Dawn sighed. 'I wish I could help him, but he can barely stand to look at me.'

'You did the right thing, I think,' Callie said. 'I'm not a mother so in no position to give advice, but from what we overheard, he expected you to trot out all the reasons why you were forced to give him up and to beg his forgiveness. You'd have been wasting your breath with someone so emotionally dead.'

'If you'd seen him with his little girl then you wouldn't say he was emotionless.'

'Perhaps not, but like I say, he's an expert at compartmentalisation.'

'He has a point to prove by being an exemplary parent, I take it you mean.' Dawn shook her head. 'Yeah, I get that part.'

'If you *had* tried to explain all the reasons why you couldn't keep him and how you did what you thought would be best for him, he'd simply have thrown that confession back in your face and made you feel guiltier than ever.'

'Sorry to interrupt, ladies,' Darren said, holding up a hand. 'But we have more pressing matters to discuss.'

'Yeah, like what to do about George,' Callie replied. 'Obviously, I've been thinking about that a lot, but I don't see what he can do to force my hand. I won't let him use my rooms, and I sure as hell won't put on a show in front of his investors, allowing them to think that I'm party to their vile moneymaking scheme.'

Darren frowned. 'Think this through, Callie. If George is acting as Gavin and O'Keefe's right hand in this gaming thing, you think word won't have spread amongst the criminal fraternity that the two big guns are on the missing list.'

'He can hold off those that want a word or two with Gavin if I go along with him, or he can let them loose on me. Is that what you're suggesting?' Callie shook her head. 'Even if what you say is true, if I buckle then that game will go ahead and someone will get killed. I can't let that happen. There has to be another way.'

'George will hear about your visit to the hotel today,' Dawn said, 'so he'll know that you're onto him. I suspect you'll be seeing him sometime soon.'

'And I'll tell him to take a hike. Don't forget that Fallow is Gavin's tame copper and if I ask him to intercede with that game, well...'

'Point taken.' Darren nodded. 'Gavin won't want to lose out, both financially and credibility wise. He knows you won't have your hand forced so he'll have to move fast to rescue the situation. I'm guessing that his wannabe investors are already in the country. The symposium opens tomorrow, and they are here to witness proceedings.'

'So, George will have to have an initial meet and greet with them at the hotel. And we just happen to have a suite there,' Callie said, smiling at her PA. 'So, we need to invite the investors for a little drink, don't you think?'

'What will that achieve?' Dawn asked, sharing a frown with Darren. 'Other than to put you in the firing line. Besides, how will you know who they are?'

'Good point.' Callie felt that her frustration was in danger of boiling over. 'We can't just have Fallow's men raid the place without just cause. It would create havoc.' She paused as an idea occurred to her. 'Have you considered calling Gavin and letting him know what's going on?' she asked, turning her attention to Darren.

'I could do that, but my bet is that he already knows,' Darren replied. 'He's running scared of O'Keefe but reckons he can handle George, which is why he's letting him take all the risks. He won't break cover until he's absolutely sure that no one from O'Keefe's organisation is out for his blood. Or until he knows for sure that O'Keefe is dead.'

'Perhaps you should let me talk to my beloved,' Callie remarked sweetly, well aware that Darren wouldn't do it. Part of her understood why. Darren was protecting his mother by doing as Gavin asked of him and if he proved to be disloyal then it wasn't Darren who would be the recipient of Gavin's ire.

'Sorry.' Darren shook his head decisively. 'No can do.'

'I could have my cyber guy have a little look-see at the hotel's register,' Dawn suggested. 'I'm betting that the overseas investors will have booked suites there.'

'Now that,' Callie said, brightening, 'is inspired.'

'Okay, I'll do it now,' Dawn said, extracting her phone from her bag, having a short conversation with someone and then hanging up. 'He says it'll be a doddle.'

'If the hotel's records are *that* easy to hack into, it makes you wonder about all this cyber security organisations are supposed to have,' Callie remarked, 'but on this occasion, it'll work to our advantage.'

'I have to love you and leave you, children.' Dawn glanced at her watch, stood up and blew them a kiss. 'I have an interview to do. I'll touch base later. Let me know how it goes.'

'She's forgiven, I take it,' Darren said into the silence that ensued once the whirlwind that was Dawn had departed.

'I can't say I'm happy about what happened between her and Gavin, and especially not about Jago, but I don't hold her responsible. Well, only partially. Anyway, let's try and figure out how to neutralise George. Then we run Gavin to ground. After that will be the time to think about friendships, loyalties and the future.'

'Not much to do then.' Darren's smile faded. 'I'm going to increase security around here and you are not to go anywhere alone until this business is sorted.'

'Hang on a minute!'

Darren held up a hand. 'Not negotiable, I'm afraid. We've boxed George into a corner, and we know how dangerous cornered animals can be. If you scupper his one big opportunity to take control, then he will be out for revenge. Think of O'Keefe and how he came after you if you doubt me.'

'Yeah, okay point taken. Do what you have to do.'

'I'll be your personal bodyguard,' he replied, winking at her. 'We know it won't be for long. The symposium opens tomorrow. Let's see if we can end this thing using our brains, without any violence being employed or blood being spilled.'

22

Darren left Callie's office, intent upon increasing the security around the spa in general and on Callie in particular. The strain of juggling so many balls was starting to show and Darren knew she was reaching the end of her tether. He had grown to admire her strength and determination enormously, especially during these past few months when she'd had to deal with all the upheaval that Gavin's disappearance had caused. The fact that he'd been in contact with Gavin all along had really been playing on his conscience.

Callie's reaction to Dawn's catastrophic revelations had only served to increase his respect for her. She hid it well, but from one or two off-the-cuff remarks she had made, Darren suspected that she regretted her childless state. To find out about Jago must have hit her hard. But still, now that things were out in the open, he could shoulder some of the weight, keep her safe and prove to her that he really was on her side.

And sides did have to be taken, he realised. His days of sitting on the fence and claiming ignorance were behind him. He'd taken the easy way out, he could see that now, using the protection of his mother as an excuse to make amends for his brother's misdeeds. Misdeeds that had resulted in a murder that he hadn't wanted to know anything about, as though that could distance him from what he had been told was a case of mistaken identity.

He knew now that his brother had followed instructions to the letter and cold-bloodedly murdered an innocent young woman. A woman who'd been pushing a baby's buggy at the time, for fuck's sake! Darren's own blood froze in his veins as he absorbed that unpalatable truth. How was it even possible for him to be related to someone so ruthless? Would he still have protected his mother and ultimately his brother too had he known the truth? More to the point, who had given the order? Jago believed it had been O'Keefe, but he only had Gavin's word for that, so Darren remained to be convinced. Gavin could be at least as ruthless as O'Keefe when it came to protecting his own hide.

Part of the blame rested on Jago's own shoulders. He was the one who'd warned his paymasters that Caroline was uneasy about Jago's activities. What the hell had he imagined that would achieve? Was he so blinded by the prospect of easy money that he was prepared to sacrifice the life of the mother of his child on the altar of his ambition? If that was the case then there had to be a well of his natural father's ruthlessness in him and that possibility caused Darren to shudder.

With a sigh, he picked up his phone and put arrangements in hand for the added security. Callie would be safe enough for the next couple of hours. She had back-to-back meetings arranged in her office. Her departmental managers had just gone in, he knew, and the first one was already under way.

Darren tried to concentrate on his work and ignore the fact

that his burner had already rung twice that day. He had declined the calls on both occasions but when it rang for a third time, he reluctantly picked up.

'Yes,' he said.

'Why the hell haven't you taken my calls?'

'I was with your wife. And you've told me not to ring you.' Darren's voice was curt, as evidenced by the sharp intake of breath from Gavin's end.

'Don't get clever with me, son. Meet me in half an hour in the Royal Oak.'

'You're in Brighton?' Darren blurted out, shocked. He and Gavin hadn't met face to face since he'd taken off. Darren had convinced himself that his boss must be sunning himself abroad somewhere but even if he had been, he was obviously now back on home soil. Darren couldn't help wondering what had brought him rushing back. But then again, if Enrarvis was such a big money-spinner for him and if negotiations were coming to a head regarding the franchise, Gavin wouldn't leave those negotiations to George.

'No, I'm in fucking Timbuctoo,' Gavin snarled. 'Just be there! You have some explaining to do.'

The line went dead.

What the hell was that all about? Darren wondered, leaning back in his chair and thinking it through. Gavin must be aware of the confrontation in the Majestic earlier, but how? Presumably, he and Jago were in contact, in which case, Gavin would want to know why Darren hadn't kept him up to speed *and* kept Callie away from his son. Ha! It would take a stronger man than he'd ever be to stop Callie and Dawn when they joined forces and set their minds on a particular course of action.

He'd realise, Darren assumed, that knowledge of his affair

with Dawn would have been one blow too many for Callie to absorb. Gavin assumed that Callie would stick by him no matter what. She always had, but even he couldn't be so cocksure of his hold over her as to assume this particular betrayal could be explained away.

Could he?

'Couldn't have happened to a nicer bloke,' Darren muttered as he sent a text to Callie telling her he'd be out for an hour.

He then gathered up his phone and keys and headed for the door. He gave his security man further instructions as he left, emphasising that no one whose name wasn't on the list he handed to him be given access to Callie's office. No exceptions. The man looked surprised but nodded and Darren knew his instructions would be adhered to.

Satisfied that Callie would be safe, Darren headed for his car and drove swiftly to the meeting at a pub on the cliffside overlooking the grey sea crashing against the rocks below. It was popular with locals and tourists alike at all times of the year and Darren knew Gavin would have chosen it for that reason. It was easier to be anonymous in a crowded place.

The car park was almost full. Darren squeezed his BMW into almost the last spot, locked it and walked towards the pub, glancing at the array of parked vehicles, wondering what form of transportation Gavin was currently using. Nothing stood out as being expensive or pretentious, but then it wouldn't. Gavin knew how to blend in.

Darren walked into the pub and saw his boss at once, occupying a quiet table for two in an alcove. Darren bought himself a soft drink, took a deep breath and walked across the crowded room to join Gavin.

'Afternoon, boss,' he said, hand outstretched.

'You're late,' Gavin replied, shaking Darren's hand in a perfunctory manner and dropping it quickly. 'Sit down before you draw attention to us.'

Darren complied, holding back his shocked reaction when he looked properly at Gavin. He *was* suntanned, supporting Darren's view that he'd been hiding out abroad, but he also looked... old. Gavin prided himself on his appearance and never let himself go, but today, he was dressed in clothes that Darren wouldn't give houseroom to. He sported a thick beard and wore glasses with tinted lenses on a day when the sun wasn't shining. *So much for knowing how to blend in,* Darren thought with a wry smile when he noticed a few curious glances being shot their way.

Darren sipped at his drink, saying nothing and waiting for Gavin to open the conversation: a contrivance disguised as a sign of respect. Gavin clearly had a lot to say, otherwise he wouldn't be here looking like something the cat had thought twice about dragging in. For the first time, Darren felt as though he had the upper hand in his dealings with Gavin, who looked uncomfortable and disgruntled, but wasn't sufficiently naïve to assume that situation would endure.

'What the fuck's going on?' Gavin eventually demanded to know in a low growl. 'Why didn't you let me know that things were running out of control? What the fuck do I pay you for?'

'I did point out that George was getting heavy with Callie,' Darren replied, his low, conversational tone clearly further irritating Gavin. 'But the rest was out of my control, given that things moved so quickly and I'm under orders not to contact you.' Darren held up a hand when Gavin opened his mouth. 'It would have helped if I'd known the full picture, then I might have steered Callie clear of the car wreck that ensued,' he added, his voice now firm.

'You ungrateful little shit!' Gavin's voice rose, drawing the attention of nearby diners, some of whom tutted in disapproval.

'Do you really want to have this conversation here?'

'Your motor,' Gavin replied, abandoning his half-consumed beer and standing up so abruptly that he knocked the table and slopped beer all over it.

'You didn't drive here?' Darren asked as they left the building.

'Cab.'

'Ah, right.' He unlocked his car and Gavin climbed into the passenger seat. 'I'll drop you wherever you need to go.'

'What I need is to know what the fuck is going on!' Gavin was shouting now, his voice bouncing off the car's roof.

'You tell me, boss.' Darren shrugged, forcing himself to remain calm when all he wanted to do was to throttle the bastard for what he'd put Callie through. 'All I know is that in the past twenty-four hours, Dawn has discovered that the son you asked her to abort is now working for you and, more to the point, Callie knows it too.'

Gavin's face turned bright purple. 'Now you look here—'

'Don't tell me I should have kept it from her because there was no way on this earth I could have done so. Not without advance warning and perhaps not even then. It was you who chose to keep from me the not insignificant fact that you'd been casually fucking your wife's best friend all those years ago.'

'None of your damned business.'

'Correct. But it became my business when you brought Jago into the picture.' Darren glowered at Gavin, who couldn't hold his gaze and looked away. 'Did you really think it would never come to light?'

Gavin shrugged one shoulder. 'How did Callie take it?'

Darren shook his head. 'Well, she didn't throw a party if that's what you're thinking.'

'What I think doesn't matter. I pay you to tell me what's going on.'

'You've underestimated the strength of two women scorned, boss, if you really want to know. Jago is convinced that Dawn didn't want him but that you did. That probably wasn't clever.' He held up a hand. 'You asked me what's going on. Dawn's devastated.'

'Never mind her.' Gavin dismissed thoughts of Dawn with a casual flap of one wrist.

'Callie is spitting tacks. She's hurt, deeply hurt by what she described to me as the ultimate betrayal.'

'Fuck! I guess she's gone all moody. She can get that way.'

Darren hid his surprise with difficulty. Gavin had more neck than a giraffe but surely even he must realise that he'd pushed his wife too far and that there would be no way back for him this time.

'She's also quite determined to shut down the game that George is trying to flog off on your behalf,' he said.

'Shit!' Gavin thumped the dashboard with considerable force. 'I leave for five minutes and everything goes to hell in a handcart.'

'Then call George off.'

'It ain't that simple, son. Things are running out of control, which always happens when I take my eye off the ball. The first symposium was supposed to be in Birmingham, to whet the appetites of potential investors. Then it was coming down here and I'd have come out of retirement and taken control. Pushing the price up, like. These people only want to talk to the organ grinder.'

'My suggestion, for what it's worth, is that you come back now and put an end to it. Because if you don't then Callie will, and I can't say as I blame her. Someone's gonna die, all for the sake of sickos' viewing pleasure, and Callie won't let that happen.'

'I knew she'd get all emotional and not see the bigger picture.' Gavin harrumphed. 'Women have no stomach for business when it gets tough. That's why I've never involved her.'

'So, you'll come back?' Darren metaphorically crossed his fingers, hoping the answer would be in the negative.

'Nah, I can't right now. I have issues to fix. The fucking Birmingham mob have queered my pitch.'

'Birmingham? That's where the first symposium was supposed to be held?'

'Yeah, but there's a crew up there flexing their muscles and getting too big for their boots. There's been a bit of aggro. They're looking to move in down here and so—'

'So they found legitimate reasons to cancel the symposium up there, hoping to make you delay the launch.' Darren glowered at Gavin. 'Why?'

'Use your sense!' Gavin made it sound as though it ought to be obvious. It was to a degree, but Darren wanted him to spell it out. 'They want to drive us out and take over. They know how lucrative that game will be. It'll see me set up for life, which is kinda the point. There ain't room for O'Keefe, me and the Birmingham boys in this part of the world, so I'll withdraw and let the others fight it out. I'm getting too old for all the drama.'

'I see.' Darren wanted to ask if he planned to ride off into the sunset with O'Keefe's daughter but thought better of it. Best not to show his hand. 'Sorry, I still don't get it. What's stopping you?'

'O'Keefe, you dumbbell!' Gavin looked away. 'He and I had a falling out.'

'You're scared of him? Blimey, I never thought to see the day when you'd back down from anyone.'

'I ain't scared precisely, but I know to pick my battles.' He shuffled in his seat, clearly disliking having his actions questioned. 'It's complicated.'

In other words, until such time as Gavin was absolutely sure that O'Keefe wasn't coming back, he didn't have the balls to face him and explain why he'd swanned off with his favourite daughter in tow. It really must be love, otherwise Gavin would have dumped Jackie long since. Except, he couldn't do that if Jackie wanted to hang in there, and the women did seem to cling tenaciously to Gavin. There would only be one thing worse than seducing her and breaking up her marriage, at least in O'Keefe's eyes, and that would be seducing her and then kicking her into touch.

Darren had trouble withholding a satisfied chuckle, thinking it couldn't have happened to a nicer chap.

'Okay,' Darren said. 'So what do you want me to do about George? Presumably, if you're not able or willing to call him direct then you want me to do it for you. But if you do that then George will likely tell Callie that you and I are in touch. Sorry, boss, but I think you're gonna have to pick up the phone. You're the only one he'll listen to.'

'That's just the point.' Gavin threw up his hands in obvious frustration. 'O'Keefe and I jointly decided to make him the front man and he won't back off unless we both tell him to. He also knows that I'll be back for the negotiations.'

'Even though the venue was changed at the last minute?'

'Yeah, that shouldn't have happened. George had to think on his feet.'

'It didn't occur to you that George would use the opportunity to cut you and O'Keefe out?'

Gavin growled. 'He ain't got the balls!'

'If you say so, but with you and O'Keefe both on the missing list...'

'Any word on him?'

'Nope, but his wife is making extensive enquiries.'

'Yeah, she would be, the silly bitch!'

'As to George, he probably saw an opportunity, what with you not giving him any means of getting in touch.' Darren glanced at his boss. 'Wasn't that a mistake, what with so much being at stake?'

'I had my reasons. George is a safe pair of hands.' Gavin grunted. 'Or so I thought.'

'Well, the sharks are gathering, boss, and George will have sensed which way the wind blows. I didn't know about the guys from Birmingham, but presumably George did. The way I see it, if you or O'Keefe don't surface soon then you'll have lost your patch, and George wanted to get in while the getting was good.'

'I wouldn't have been gone so long if I was worried about that, you moron! Like I say, it's time to retire. I just need the funds from the sale of that game and I'll be minted, what with the funds I already have stashed away.'

'What will you do then?' Darren glanced at his watch. He hadn't expected to be away from his desk for so long, leaving Callie without his personal protection. She'd be quite safe, just so long as she remained at the spa, but if she felt the need to go somewhere then none of his security men would be able to prevent her.

'Better you don't know. Just keep Callie under control for another couple of days, then it'll all be over. Okay, you can drop me at the station.'

* * *

Callie struggled to keep her mind on the subjects under discussion during her meetings. Fortunately, her managers knew what they were doing, and she doubted whether her inattention would result in any disasters.

'Where's Darren?' she asked, opening the door that led to his office and finding only a security guard in occupation.

'He had to go out about an hour ago. Said he wouldn't be long.'

'Oh okay, thanks.'

Callie checked her phone, worried by his sudden disappearance, but was reassured when she saw a text confirming what the guard had just told her. It had been sent two hours previously though and Callie suddenly felt vulnerable. Alone. She gave herself a mental shake, recalling that she didn't need Darren's shoulder to lean on.

Even if she did.

About to return to her office, the door burst open and Dawn swanned through it.

'Excuse me.' The guard stood in front of her, stopping Dawn in her tracks. 'Your name, please.'

Dawn sent Callie a what-the-hell look as she told the man who she was. He consulted his list and shook his head.

'Sorry. Your name's not on the list so I can't let you in.'

'Don't be so ridiculous!' Callie said, irritated. 'What list?'

The guard looked flustered as he explained.

'Not to worry,' she said, ushering Dawn into her room ahead of her. 'Darren's getting above himself is all.'

'He's going all caveman on you,' Dawn said, laughing. 'I'm glad that he's taking care of you, though. Someone needs to.'

'Not sure I agree with you there. One controlling man in my life has taught me how to take care of myself.'

'Well, there is that.' Dawn glanced at Callie as they sat on the sofas, looking hesitant. 'Are we okay?' she asked.

'Sure. Well, I guess. Can't say I'm thrilled about what you've told me, but we can't change the past. The here and now is more important.'

'That's what I came to see you about. My friend at the paper has come through with names of two businessmen from Malaysia booked into the Majestic.'

'That was quick work.'

'Yeah well, I think he had a point to prove.'

'He wants to impress the hell out of you.' Callie smiled. 'Makes sense. I mean most men would revert to flowers and romantic dinners, but he obviously understands the way to your heart is through a little creative hacking.'

Dawn grinned. 'Whatever it takes.'

'It sounds as though the guys he's identified must be our mystery buyers,' Callie said. 'The Malaysians are big on gambling and, presumably, gaming too. All well and good but what do we do about them? Presumably, they're aware of the violent nature of the game. I'm pretty sure that fights to the death, if that's what this is all about, are illegal anywhere in the world. I know it's cyberspace but if the symposiums take place in England then our laws apply.'

'But not necessarily if the Malaysians stage it elsewhere…'

'The plan was to find the identities of the potential buyers and dissuade them.' Callie pursed her lips. 'But we didn't really think it through, did we? It was a knee-jerk reaction.'

'Yes, but for the fact that they think Gavin and O'Keefe are the sellers, and presumably, they have some sort of reciprocal trust going. If you were to make them aware of the facts insofar as Gavin's missing and O'Keefe is believed to be dead, implying that he was killed over ownership of the game, it might give them pause.'

'Yeah, but if they've come all this way, if negotiations are so far advanced, will they really back off now?'

'They will if the real-life version of the game doesn't live up to its online counterpart,' Dawn pointed out. 'But to make that happen, we need to persuade Jago to screw up, and I really don't think he'll listen to me. As far as he's concerned, Gavin is God and his passport to financial freedom.'

Callie puffed out her cheeks. 'Then the only other option is for me to call Fallow and let him know what's going down. He does still look upon himself as a law-enforcing officer, hypocritical though that stance might appear to those of us who know him better, and he'd have to go in there and take a look-see.' Callie frowned. 'Wouldn't he?'

'What's keeping Darren?' Dawn tapped her toe impatiently. 'We need to ask his advice.'

'We really don't,' Callie replied, but her tone lacked conviction.

Before Dawn could respond, her phone rang. Callie knew she never ignored her calls. It could be a heads-up on some breaking news story.

'Not a number I recognise,' she said, taking the call. 'Hello.'

'Jago?' She glanced up at Callie, frowning. 'Jago, is that you? I can't understand you. You're not making any sense. Slow down. What do you need?' She listened some more. 'Okay. Stay where you are. We'll be right there.'

'What?' Callie asked.

'I don't know. Couldn't get much sense out of him. He sounded in a right old panic. Just said he needed help and didn't know who else to call. And it must be serious, otherwise he wouldn't have called me. We need to get over to the hotel now. Immediately.'

Dawn seemed concerned and yet pleased that Jago had chosen to call her.

Callie collected up her bag. 'Let's go then,' she said.

'Go where?' Darren breezed through the door. 'Sorry to be gone for so long. Had to drop someone at the station and the traffic was brutal. There was an accident on the way back here, and it took me ages to get past it. Why are you two looking so stressed?'

Darren frowned when Dawn explained. 'Fucking hell!' he breathed. 'Not already, surely?'

'Not already what?' Callie asked, sending him a suspicious look. 'Where is it that you've been precisely?'

'Never mind all that. We need to get to the hotel!' Dawn hopped from foot to foot. 'Jago needs me. Us.'

The drive was made in terse silence. Whatever had happened at the Majestic, Darren appeared to know more about it than he was telling but Dawn was right; now wasn't the time to test his loyalty.

They arrived and miraculously found a parking spot on the street, eliminating the need to traipse from the multi-storey. Dawn opened the door as soon as Darren cut the engine. Callie jumped out too and had to restrain her friend from running inside. Not that she would have been able to. The queue of weirdly dressed would-be Enrarvis now cluttered the pavement three abreast and wound its way around the block. Darren left the car too and walked between them as they headed for the foyer. Not being dressed like aliens ensured that their progress wasn't hampered and the guy on the door nodded them through with a grunt.

'Blimey!' Callie glanced around at a foyer now lit up like a planet, so authentic that she felt as though she could reach up and touch the stars.

'Come on!' Dawn bustled ahead. 'Jago said he'd be in the room where we saw him before.'

Chris, looking pale and concerned, let them in, followed them inside and locked the door behind them.

'What the fuck!' Darren demanded.

'There you are.'

Jago emerged from the temperature-controlled room, looking green.

'What's happened?' Dawn asked, rushing up to him and taking his arm. He didn't shake her hold off and appeared to have lost the resentful attitude, which is when Callie knew that something serious must have gone down.

'It's... it's George. He's dead.'

'Dead?' Callie glanced at Darren, who seemed shocked but not that surprised, which made no sense at all. 'What do you mean, dead? How can he be? Sit down before you fall down and tell us what happened.'

'I don't know what happened,' Jago wailed. 'There are... were, some Malaysian guys here. They were interested in franchising the game. George told me to show them around and give them any help they needed. Anyway, one of them burst in here just before I called you—'

'About half an hour ago then,' Darren said.

Callie wondered why the precise timing was so important but refrained from comment. There would be time enough for questions, for explanations, later.

'Yeah, I guess. The guy was in a right old state. He'd returned to his suite and found George sprawled across his bed with a bullet hole through his head.'

'Christ!' Dawn inhaled sharply. 'Did you call the police?'

'No. The guy told me not to. They wanted a chance to get on a flight. They didn't want to get caught up in the investigation.'

'I'd best call Fallow,' Callie said, reaching for her phone. 'We can't just leave a dead body lying about for the maid to trip over.'

'Before you do, there's more.'

'Go on, Jago,' Dawn said, squeezing her traumatised son's hand when he hesitated. 'What is it that we need to know?'

'I found this on the floor in that room. I didn't know what to do with it. I... I couldn't leave it there and incriminate Gavin.'

He opened his hand and revealed a cufflink with Gavin's initials picked out in tiny sapphires. Callie gasped. She'd had them made for him as a present in the early days of their marriage, when men still customarily wore cufflinks. Gavin, she knew, still did.

'Fuck!' she muttered, clutching a hand over her mouth.

'It's okay,' Darren replied, touching her shoulder. 'Gavin didn't do this, not personally.'

'How can you be so sure?'

'Because I dropped him at the station at about the time the killing took place.'

'You did what?' Callie gaped at him.

'No time to explain now,' Darren replied. 'Let's make sure there's nothing else that's incriminating up in that room. But this is the clumsiest fit-up in the history of fit-ups. Did you see anyone you recognised loitering?' Darren addressed the question to Chris.

'Actually, I think I saw O'Keefe's son-in-law sneaking out the back way.'

'Sean?' Darren asked. 'Sean Barlow?'

Jago nodded. 'I know him because... well, because I've worked for the family before now. He's been inside but was released last week. He looked furtive and in a hurry. He had a hood up and I don't think he saw me.'

'Gavin's shacked up with his wife, so it makes sense that he'd want revenge as soon as he was released, I guess,' Callie said as dispassionately as though she was discussing the weather despite the dizzying raft of conflicting emotions roiling through her bloodstream. 'But why screw up the deal that was intended to make both families a small fortune?'

'It's not only women who thirst for revenge when they've been crossed,' Dawn replied.

'Stay here, ladies,' Darren said. 'We've got this.'

'Not a chance!' Callie replied. 'You stay with Jago, Dawn. Chris, do you have a keycard to the room?'

'Yeah, as it happens.'

'Okay.' Callie touched Dawn's shoulder. 'We won't be long.'

23

Three days later, Darren and Callie sat together in her conservatory, drinking wine. Callie was still vaguely in shock but wasn't about to be fobbed off any longer, which she sensed was what Darren had been doing. He seemed to think she needed protecting from the truth but it was a bit late for that.

'Okay, run it past me properly this time,' she said. 'Why did you meet Gavin? Was it the first time? What did you talk about? Why do you think he arranged George's murder?' She counted off the points on her fingers as she spoke.

Darren held up a hand to ward off the barrage of questions.

'He called me a couple of times on the day that George died, but I was otherwise engaged and didn't take his calls. When he rang the third time and I picked up, he insisted upon meeting up in a pub on the cliffs. I haven't seen him in person since he legged it and that's the God's honest truth.' He offered her a crooked boy scout's salute. Callie smiled in spite of herself. A more unlikely boy scout it would be hard for her to imagine. 'Anyway, I went and frankly, he looked a wreck.'

'Where's he been living? Not that I really give a shit.'

'Didn't ask but he was tanned so somewhere warm is my guess. Anyway, he and O'Keefe promoted the development of the game and financed it up front. I think it was Gavin's original idea, when he realised what capabilities his son had in that regard, but it was too big, too rich for him to handle alone. It was his swansong, apparently, and he was counting on it giving him enough to retire comfortably for the rest of his life. He said he'd had enough ducking and diving, or words to that effect.'

'So George was fronting it for him and O'Keefe?'

'Right, but when they both went missing and showed no immediate signs of returning, George saw an opportunity.'

'Didn't Gavin keep in touch with George, tell him what to do?'

Darren shrugged. 'Seemingly not, which would explain why he was on my case, insisting that I let him know what George was up to every step of the way.'

'He was too scared to show his face because he couldn't depend upon O'Keefe being dead, is my guess,' Callie said, nodding. 'And didn't trust anyone other than you with his number because phones are traceable. Even burners, I've heard. Anyway, I still don't get why he stayed away at such a critical time. It makes no sense.' She inhaled sharply. 'Assuming that he did arrange for George to be killed and for you to be with him when the murder went down so that he was alibied, why did he do that and give up on the swansong he'd gone to great lengths to arrange so easily?'

'That's your fault.'

'Me?' Callie pointed to her own chest for emphasis and widened her eyes. 'What did I do?'

Darren laughed. 'I might have mentioned to him that you knew what was happening and wasn't about to let anyone get killed. That added to the fact that you knew about him and Dawn, and about Jago, brought him to the realisation that he could no longer depend on you and that you would shaft him in order to save anyone getting killed.' Darren flashed a grim smile. 'Not to mention getting your revenge.'

'Hmm.' Callie felt into momentary reflection. 'He would have contacted someone in O'Keefe's organisation. His son, who's taken temporary control, would be my guess. Spun him some line about George being out of order and the police being involved and that would have been enough to seal George's fate.'

'And Sean Barlow just happened to be out on licence, champing for revenge.'

'How did he get hold of Gavin's cufflink?' Callie frowned. 'He used to wear them everywhere, but I checked in his dressing room yesterday and there's only one there. I assume that he brought Jackie here and she took one as a talisman. Then Sean found it, so...'

'Yeah, a hastily contrived means of revenge.'

'Why didn't Gavin simply pitch up at the hotel and take control? Even if I called the police, he could have had Fallow hold them off.'

'Who knows?' Darren shrugged. 'I'm thinking he perhaps does have some pride in his son and belatedly didn't want to get him mixed up in it all.'

'A conscience, you mean? Ha! That would be a first but yeah, that could be it, I suppose.'

'There's another possibility that reached my ears. The Birmingham connection.'

Callie blinked. 'What about it?'

'It was the Malaysians who were interested in purchasing because they are big on gambling. I've heard there is a large Asian community in Birmingham, which is why Gavin wanted to trial the game there, but the local heavies heard about it and demanded a cut. That much I do know. The rest is speculation.

Not sure how or why but negotiations got out of hand I do happen to know that the leader of the Birmingham crew turned up face down in a canal. It made the inside pages of the local paper. I checked.'

'Oh hell!'

'Right, and I suspect that they now have Gavin in their sights.'

'And because Gavin has broken up O'Keefe's happy family, he can't turn to him for protection because he knew that once the game was flogged off, O'Keefe would turn his attentions to him.' Callie rubbed the back of her neck. 'Blimey! No wonder Gavin kept his head down.'

'Right, but you need to be careful now. I do think Gavin was depending upon the proceeds from the game to allow him to ride off into the sunset, set for life. You'd better make sure all those funds offshore are moved because Gavin will want them for his retirement fund. I'm surprised he hasn't taken them already.'

'Already done,' Callie replied, grinning. 'I moved them last week, when I sensed things were coming to a head. Oh, I left a few thousand in each. I mean, I wouldn't want Gavin to starve now, would I?'

Darren smiled. 'Be careful, Callie,' he repeated. 'He won't take kindly to what he will look upon as a rip-off. Don't count on his ethics insofar as he doesn't harm women and children either. Look what happened to Jago's fiancée, probably on his orders.'

'I hear you, but Gavin can't hurt me. Not if he wants his money back.'

'He will resurface soon, Callie; don't underestimate the lengths that a desperate man will go to.'

Callie smiled. 'Gavin's not the only person who knows how to watch his back.' She paused. 'It's illegal to remove something from a crime scene, isn't it?'

Darren frowned. 'What have you done?'

'Well, Gavin's cufflink just might have slipped from my hand and finished up under the bed where George died.'

'Bloody hell!'

'It won't be enough to convict Gavin, especially if he was at the station at the vital time, but it will slow him down.'

Darren nodded his admiration, lost for words.

'Well anyway, at least Dawn and Jago are speaking now,' Callie said into the ensuing silence. 'I'm guessing that he'll soon realise that Gavin sold him a pup and the blinkers will come off, so something good has come out of this.' Callie stretched her arms above her head and yawned. 'She tells me there's talk of Jago actually introducing Dawn to his daughter, and I am glad about that.'

'Yeah.' Darren smiled. 'Me too.'

'Dawn being Dawn, she's up and running with an insightful piece about the perils in the fostering system that have got her editors wetting themselves, so her career has a reprieve, it seems.'

'That's good.' Darren drained his glass. 'So, what now?'

'Now we run Gavin to ground. I'm fed up with waiting for him to make a move and so we become proactive. I can sell up but will never feel safe if I know he's looking for me, and he will be. So...' She grinned at Darren. 'We find him whilst he's still looking over his shoulder, worrying about the Birmingham crew who he knows are chasing his tail and negotiate. The ball's in my court and I fully intend to turn the tables on him.'

'Fair enough. Go to bed now. You look bushed. Get some sleep and tomorrow, we'll start figuring out how to play this so that we get him out of your hair once and for all.'

'Good plan,' Callie replied, feeling that for the first time in over thirty years, she had the upper hand in her relationship with Gavin. Even so, there was no time for complacency. Gavin would have gone to ground again to lick his wounds whilst he waited for the dust to settle. Callie would never have a better opportunity to get him out of her life once and for all.

It was simply a matter of deciding how best to go about it.

***

MORE FROM EVIE HUNTER

Another book from Evie Hunter, *Dirty Secrets*, is available to order now here:

https://mybook.to/DirtySecretsBackAd

ACKNOWLEDGEMENTS

My grateful thanks as always to the superb Boldwood team and in particular to my talented editor, Emily Ruston.

ABOUT THE AUTHOR

Evie Hunter is a British author, who's spent the last twenty years roaming the world and finding inspiration from the places she's visited. She has written a great many successful regency romances as Wendy Soliman but has since redirected her talents to produce dark gritty thrillers.

Sign up to Evie Hunter's mailing list here for news, competitions and updates on future books.

Follow Evie Hunter on social media:

- x.com/wendyswriter
- facebook.com/wendy.soliman.author
- bookbub.com/authors/wendy-soliman

ALSO BY EVIE HUNTER

Revenge Thrillers

The Sting

The Trap

The Chase

The Scam

The Kill

The Alibi

The Takedown

Dirty Business

Dirty Games

Dirty Secrets

The Hopgood Hall Murder Mysteries

A Date To Die For

A Contest To Kill For

A Marriage To Murder For

A Story to Strangle For

PEAKY READERS

GANG LOYALTIES. DARK SECRETS. BLOODY REVENGE.

A READER COMMUNITY FOR GANGLAND CRIME THRILLER FANS!

DISCOVER PAGE-TURNING NOVELS FROM YOUR FAVOURITE AUTHORS AND MEET NEW FRIENDS.

JOIN OUR BOOK CLUB FACEBOOK GROUP

BIT.LY/PEAKYREADERSFB

SIGN UP TO OUR NEWSLETTER

BIT.LY/PEAKYREADERSNEWS

Boldwood

Boldwood Books is an award-winning fiction publishing company seeking out the best stories from around the world.

Find out more at www.boldwoodbooks.com

Join our reader community for brilliant books, competitions and offers!

Follow us

@BoldwoodBooks

@TheBoldBookClub

Sign up to our weekly deals newsletter

https://bit.ly/BoldwoodBNewsletter

Printed in Dunstable, United Kingdom